To Bella M., Adri, Sophia, Evelyn, and every other teenager who has surprised me by falling in love with these books. And to Micah and Savannah, my teenagers, who won't read these books because they don't want to read anything romantic their mom has written but are infinitely supportive and excited for every book I publish.

CHAPTER ONE

"I don't think this is a good idea," I said, standing on the sidewalk outside Lucille's Clip and Curl with a very pregnant Penny.

"You need to trust me," she said insistently. "I read online that this is going to be the hot new hairstyle next year. You could be on the cutting edge of this trend."

"But a perm?" I asked incredulously.

"The eighties are back, baby," she said. "I'd do it myself, but I'm not sure the chemicals would be good for the baby." She put her hand protectively over her belly.

The leaves on the trees lining the street were brilliant shades of yellow, orange, and red. Halloween was a week away. Penny wanting me to get a perm was perhaps the scariest part of the season. "Any chemical that's not good for a baby won't be good for me either," I pointed out.

Penny looped her arm through mine and tugged me toward the door. "Eh," she hedged. "Wine isn't good for a baby, but it's just fine for you. This is the same thing."

"I'm not sure a perm is good for my love life," I argued as we got closer to the bright-red door.

"Or it could be very good. A real test to see who likes you for you," Penny said with more enthusiasm than the situation warranted.

"Wait a minute." I managed to pull Penny to a stop. Miraculously, she'd only gotten stronger in her pregnancy. "You can't tell me I'll look amazing with a perm one minute and then tell me that it'll be a test to see if Finn and Chris like me for who I am the next. Those two ideas completely contradict each other."

Penny hesitated. It took a lot to make Penny hesitate. I grabbed the opportunity, dislodged myself from her grasp, and walked through the door saying, "Hey, Lucille, just the trim I originally scheduled for today."

Lucille's platinum-blonde hair was in its signature beehive hairdo. You wouldn't want to get too close to her with an open flame. I could only guess at the amount of hairspray it took to keep her in the style she'd been rocking since before I was born. She gave me a sideways look, like I was being weird—which, in her defense, I kind of was.

Penny followed me in. "Spoilsport," she muttered under her breath.

"I'll be ready for your trim in a few minutes," Lucille said with a smile, recovering from my bizarre entrance. "Can I interest you in adding acupuncture to your appointment today? It's a wonderful way to de-stress."

Penny leaned in close and whispered, "It's a wonderful way to hit a nerve and end up with half of your face paralyzed."

I gave Lucille a big smile. "Just the haircut today," I said. I hooked my thumb in Penny's direction. "Penny's going to hang out if that's okay. We're going to lunch after this."

Lucille's eyes lit with interest. "Can I talk you into some acupuncture?" she asked Penny. "I have a few minutes before Gwen's appointment."

"I don't think it would be good for the—" Penny started.

"It's a known remedy for heartburn," Lucille interrupted.

Penny went silent. I'd known her my whole life. I could see she was considering it. I needed to save her from herself. It wasn't that I was against acupuncture. It was that I was against Lucille, who'd only taken a weekend class at a strip mall in Rose Lake, doing acupuncture.

"Penny's doctor told her not to," I said, which was sort of a fib but sort of the truth. While I'd never been to one of Penny's doctor appointments, I couldn't imagine her doctor would be okay with this setup.

"But the heartburn's been really bad," Penny murmured to me.

"Just the haircut today," I said confidently.

"That's just as well," Lucille said. "I haven't had much time to practice." She got a far-off look in her eyes. "Burt had a strange reaction yesterday when we were unblocking his chi," she said quietly, as if she were talking to herself. After a few more seconds of awkward silence, she shook herself, her gaze snapped back to us, and she gave us a wide smile. "I'll just get my station ready. One minute."

Lucille bustled away, and I turned to Penny. "You're welcome for saving your life from Lucille's needles," I said.

Penny rubbed her chest. "But the heartburn," she said with dismay.

"I'll buy you a Costco-sized bottle of Tums," I replied. I shuddered at Lucille's strange behavior. "I wonder what happened to poor Burt."

"That would make a good horror movie," Penny said. "The mild-mannered salon owner murders people with her acupuncture needles. Like a female version of Sweeney Todd."

I snorted out a laugh.

"I'm ready for you, Gwen," Lucille called out from the other side of the room. "Penny, you can sit in this empty chair."

The spot next to Lucille's station was unoccupied. Besides Penny and me, there were two other women getting their hair done. Penny followed me to Lucille's station.

Lucille fluffed my honey-brown hair that now reached my waist. "What are we thinking today?"

"Just a trim," I said. "Including the bangs." Penny had talked me into cutting a long fringe of curtain bangs last year that actually suited my face. Some of her ideas were amazing. Just not the perm-related ones.

"Maybe a few layers?" Lucille asked.

"No, just a trim," I said again.

"Lucille, what do you think of perms?" Penny asked.

"Just a trim," I said through clenched teeth, trying to keep my voice cheery while shooting Penny a look of pure death. She wanted to see a horror movie? She should keep bringing up the perm.

"For you, dear?" Lucille said to Penny. "I think you'd end up looking like a poodle."

Penny's shoulder-length, jet black hair would be quite the sight with a perm. I chuckled as Penny shot me a sour look.

"Let's get you shampooed, and then we'll give you that trim," Lucille said.

Ten minutes later, I was back in the chair wearing a leopard-print cape with my hair up in a bright-red towel. Lucille released my hair from the towel and combed it.

"You've got to be kidding me," the woman sitting across from Lucille's station said. "He did it again?" The woman's head was half-covered in silver foils.

"I'm not kidding. Right in the middle of the produce section of the Piggly Wiggly," Michelle said as she added more foils to the woman's hair. Michelle had been working for Lucille for years. I didn't know her well, but she'd cut my hair a few times.

"This has gotten completely out of hand," said the woman in the chair.

"What's gotten completely out of hand?" Lucille asked. She spun my chair around so I was facing the other women and continued to comb through my wet hair. "Gwen," she continued, "I'm not sure if you know Michelle and Christine."

"I know Michelle," I said. "Hi."

Michelle gave me a tight smile, but it was clear she was still upset about whatever they were talking about. Christine nodded the best she could as Michelle continued to work on her highlights. "Nice to meet you," Christine said.

Lucille introduced Penny quickly before asking, "What's the gossip?"

I shot Penny a wide-eyed look. Gossip could be interesting, but you also risked learning something about someone that you wished you didn't know.

Michelle put her fist on her hip and said, "Trevor Baker is a nasty man who treats his wife Sandra horribly. Yesterday, Ruth Ann and everyone else who was grocery shopping overheard Trevor berating Sandra because she'd accidentally gotten the organic apples instead of the regular. The price difference wasn't even that much, but he shouted at her for forever about how stupid she was."

"You're kidding," Penny said. "That's awful."

"Trevor and Sandra are my neighbors," I said. "They live across the street from me."

Michelle looked at me thoughtfully. "Do you live in the cute white house with the blue shutters or the brick ranch?"

"The white house," I said, loving that she'd called my little house cute.

Michelle nodded, looking thoughtful. "Then you must know what Trevor is like," she said.

I grimaced and said, "He argues with Chip, who lives next door to him, all the time. It doesn't matter what the season is. They argue about the property line in the summer when they're mowing their lawns. They argue about the property line in the winter when they're shoveling the sidewalk." I leaned in. "One time I saw Chip blowing his leaves into Trevor's yard. That one was a huge fight."

I didn't see Sandra, Trevor's wife, often, but they had two little boys who played in the front yard on weekends.

"He's rude to everyone," Christine said. "And he treats Sandra like his own personal, verbal punching bag. Plus, I'm sure he's cheated on her. Multiple times."

"And it's been getting worse," Michelle said.

"The cheating?" I asked, not sure how cheating could get worse. I guess doing it more would be worse. If you asked me, once was "worse" enough.

"All of it," Christine said bitterly. "He's a sorry excuse for a husband."

"He's a sorry excuse for a human being," Michelle added.

"Christine and Michelle are close friends with Sandra," Lucille explained to Penny and me.

Michelle went back to applying whatever was in the little bowl at her station to Christine's hair. "And her poor kids," Michelle said.

Christine shook her head. "If he talks to Sandra that way, imagine how he talks to those boys."

"How old are their kids?" I asked. "I've seen them getting on the bus, but I'm really bad at guessing ages."

Lucille had started cutting. I desperately hoped the conversation wasn't going to be too much of a distraction to her. The last thing I needed was a crooked haircut.

"Seven and nine," Michelle said. She applied the last foil to Christine's head. "Those boys do everything right, but Trevor is just as nasty to them as he is to Sandra."

"That's because he's a jerk," Christine said with conviction.

"Someone needs to teach him a lesson," Michelle said.

Christine and Lucille murmured their agreement.

"You know that Dixie Chick's song, 'Goodbye Earl'?" Michelle said. "We need to 'Goodbye Earl' Trevor's butt."

I was familiar with the song. It was about a woman and her friend killing the woman's abusive husband and getting away with it because no one in the town was sad that he was dead. I shot Penny a grimace.

"Don't you worry," Lucille said to me. "Michelle's just blowing off steam. She plans Trevor's murder every time he steps out of line."

"So, pretty often," Michelle said. At least her smile was mischievous instead of murderous.

"What's the plan this week?" Lucille asked.

Christine chuckled. She'd clearly heard of Michelle's murder plans.

Michelle tapped a comb to her chin as she stared at the ceiling in thought. "I think I'd go with stabbing him in the kidney and then shoving an organic apple in his mouth." She paused before saying, "Nah, I did *stab in the kidney* a few weeks ago. I'd definitely do the apple though," she added.

"She always makes sure the revenge fits the crime," Christine explained to Penny and me.

Suddenly, the organic apple made a lot more sense.

"I'll have to think about it," Michelle said. "I've already murdered him so many ways."

"What we really need to do is convince Sandra to leave him," Christine said. "It's getting worse. I'd hate to see how much worse it could get."

"Besides, I don't think you want to plot someone's murder in front of Gwen," Penny said. "She's practically dating the new police detective."

All three women looked at me like sharks sensing blood in the water. Actually, I couldn't see Lucille, but she'd stopped snipping, which I took as a sign that she was as riveted as Michelle and Christine.

"Practically dating seems like a stretch," I said with a nervous chuckle. "And when does Finn stop being the 'new' police detective? He's been here for almost a year."

"She has a point," Lucille said as she resumed cutting my hair.

"Thank you," I said, giving Penny a pointed look. "Finn's not new to town."

"I meant that Penny's right about you practically dating," Lucille said. "I heard from Margie that the new police detective is smitten with you."

My cheeks flared with heat. I was going to kill Penny. "Back to Trevor," I said.

I felt bad for steering the conversation back to a fake murder plot, but desperate times called for desperate measures.

Christine shook her head, the silver foils bouncing around her face. "Sandra's not going to leave Trevor, because she doesn't want the kids to have to be with him half the time without her there as a buffer."

Michelle snorted. "Like he'd want the kids half the time. He doesn't lift a finger to actually care for them now."

"He might file for full custody just to spite Sandra," Lucille said. "I've seen it happen before."

We all sat in silence for a moment. I wasn't sure what the other ladies were feeling, but I was sad for Sandra. She probably felt trapped.

"Well, who gets the kids won't matter if Trevor winds up dead," Michelle said. She turned to me and added, "Figuratively of course." She turned back to Christine. "We'll rinse you out in thirty."

"How do you kill someone figuratively," Penny asked quietly as Michelle left to wash out the bowl she'd been using.

"I think she meant fictionally," I said.

"All done," Lucille said. "Do you want me to dry it?"

"Yes, please," I said. It was really the only way to make sure the cut was straight. I felt bad for doubting Lucille. She was good at her job, despite her own outdated hairstyle. She'd never given me a bad haircut. Maybe it was all the talk of perms and murder that was making me unnecessarily jumpy.

CHAPTER TWO

I saw the fence before I heard the yelling. How in the world had Chip managed to put up a fence in the hours I'd been gone with Penny? I'd left my house that Saturday morning with Trevor's and Chip's lawns semi-happily co-existing. I'd come home to a white picket fence. Normally used as a symbol of small-town Americana, this one seemed to have instigated a war.

I climbed out of the car and stared at the scene before me. Trevor stood on one side of the picket fence, a chainsaw in hand. Chip stood on the other side, plastered up against the fence. If Trevor wanted to use that chainsaw, he was going to have to go through Chip to do it.

"You don't have a permit for this," Trevor yelled. Trevor was tall, and it seemed like he was trying to use every inch he had on Chip to intimidate him. His jet-black hair was slicked back like he was heading into the office, despite it being the weekend.

Trevor was the kind of guy who appeared charming on the surface, but enough of his cruelty leaked through that most people kept their distance. He had a perpetual five o'clock shadow to go with his perfect head of dark hair. If he wasn't such a jerk and you squinted a little, he could pass for Clark Kent, or Superman, although I knew Trevor was no superhero.

"The fence is coming down," Trevor growled at Chip.

"I do have a permit, and if you'll put your chainsaw away, I'll go get it," Chip shouted back. He leaned in, dangerously close to the chainsaw. At least it wasn't on. "I don't have to inform you of what I do on my own property."

"It's not your property," Trevor snapped. "You built it over the line."

The curtains in the front window of Chip's house fluttered, and I thought I saw his wife, Rose, peering through them before they fell back into place. Smart woman. I'd stay far away from this mess too.

"What are you looking at?" Trevor shouted with distain.

I turned to see who he was talking to, but there was no one else on the street. His wife Sandra was nowhere to be found, and the curtains were back in place at Chip's house. I looked back at the men to see them watching me.

My heart gave a little skip before breaking into a full-on gallop. I pointed at myself. "Me?" I asked, still looking around for someone else to have drawn Trevor's ire.

"Yeah, you," he said like I was stupid. "This doesn't have anything to do with you."

"Oh, yeah, I was just, you know, coming home, and Penny wanted me to get a perm, but I put my foot down, which isn't easy to do with her, but I did, and then we went to lunch and have you noticed how red that maple on the corner is this year? It's insane," I said.

I laughed. Then I coughed on my own spit.

Both men looked at me like I'd suddenly grown two heads. They weren't wrong in their assessment of my behavior. The problem was Trevor with that chainsaw. Throw a hockey goalie mask on him, and I'd walked smack dab into the middle of a horror movie.

"Don't mind him," Chip said. "He's just angry that he doesn't get to control every human on the planet like he does his poor family."

My stomach dropped, and not in the fun-rollercoaster way. More like the that's-it-we're-all-about-to-die way. "I was just going to get my mail," I said, pointing to the mailbox five feet in front of me. It was also five feet closer to Trevor and Chip.

Chip gave me a wide smile. "Don't let us stop you," he said as if we were chatting like good neighbors on a beautiful fall day.

I gestured weakly toward Trevor and said, "I didn't want to spook anyone and create a situation that might require the police, the ambulance—" I paused before adding "—or the coroner."

Chip turned his smile to Trevor, although I could see the strain in his expression. "No one is going to call the coroner because Trevor is going to back up, and we're going to settle this like good neighbors."

Trevor scoffed, but he did back up and lower the chainsaw. "I'll expect to see a copy of the permit. Today," he added with a snap. Then he turned and glared at me before stalking back toward his house.

"What did I do?" I murmured to myself as I unglued my feet from the ground and approached my mailbox.

"Sorry you had to see that," Chip said as he jogged across the street toward me. Despite the chilly fall day, he was dressed in his signature super-short running shorts and a T-shirt from the Star Junction Labor Day 10k he'd run a couple of months ago.

"I didn't know you were putting in a fence," I said as I pulled the pile of junk mail from my mailbox. "And you did it so fast."

Chip turned and stood shoulder to shoulder with me, both of us facing his house. "I got sick of the fights over the property line. Now it's settled."

"Until Trevor chops it up in the middle of the night," I said, half joking, half deadly serious.

Chip regarded me, all serious. "I'd like to see him try," he said with a dark chuckle.

"Because you booby-trapped it?" I asked, once again only half joking. I'd seen Trevor and Chip bicker often, but I'd never seen a standoff like the one today.

Chip ran a hand over his graying hair that he'd recently buzzed short. "Nah, I'm not smart enough to do that, but I do have a permit for the fence. I filed all the appropriate paperwork at city hall, and I know exactly where the property line is. I did everything by the book."

Chip clapped his hands together. "Trevor will be in a world of legal trouble if he touches my fence." He turned and looked at me with a mischievous smile. "It'll give that boyfriend of yours something to do. Destruction of property is a crime."

"He's not…" I trailed off, sensing that it would do no good to argue that Finn wasn't my boyfriend. At least not yet. You'd think that two single people would have more time to hang out, but it was proving harder than it should've been to spend time together.

My gaze drifted over to Trevor and Sandra's house. It was very similar to Chip's. Both houses were two stories, with wide front porches. Chip's house was a beautiful forest green that, honestly, looked really good with the new white fence. Trevor's was a deep-maroon color. They both took meticulous care of their yards, hence the constant squabbles.

"Is that a for sale sign?" I asked, just now noticing the small, white *For Sale by Owner* sign in Trevor and Sandra's front yard.

"Yeah," Chip said, sounding understandably excited. "Trevor put it out last night. I was going to ask Sandra about it, but I haven't seen her since it went up. She doesn't leave the house much when Trevor is home, unless he's with her."

I nodded, thinking about Sandra moving away from her friends, who obviously cared a lot about her a lot. "Are they staying in Star Junction?" I asked.

"Beats me," Chip said. "Any-whoo, I better go dig up that permit before Trevor works himself into a frenzy and comes back outside." He looked at his fence fondly.

It was a nice fence, but it looked a little weird that it was only on one side of his yard. It made a very specific statement.

"I better get going too," I said. "Lots to do." What I needed to do was call Penny and serve up some interesting Star Junction gossip about Trevor.

Chip and I said our goodbyes, and I let myself into my house. Dropping the mail onto the kitchen counter, I called Penny, putting the call on speaker.

"Are you regretting not getting the perm?" she asked as a form of hello. "I don't think it's too late. I'm sure Lucille could squeeze you in before Halloween."

I snorted out a laugh. "Am I going with an eighties theme this year?" I asked as I sorted through the mail.

"What is your costume?" she asked, thankfully dropping the perm talk, although I had a feeling I'd hear about it again.

"What do you think?" I asked.

Delilah, my kitten that was no longer the size of a kitten, came around the corner meowing her greeting. "Hey, girl," I said as she rubbed up against my legs. "Miss me? Are you glad I didn't come home with a perm?"

Penny chuckled but answered my question. "Let me guess. You're dressing up as Queen Guinevere."

"I have to stay on theme," I said good-naturedly.

Not only were we decorating Camelot Flowers, our family flower shop, for Halloween, but we were also participating in Star Junction's first annual Halloween Festival. It was being held on the grounds of city hall. There would be bounce houses, face painters, booths set up by local businesses and churches handing out candy, and a kid-friendly haunted hay maze. I would be handing out candy at our booth that afternoon. Kids loved a good princess. Probably more than an eighties-themed Barbie or some other costume that would rock a perm.

"I didn't call about perms," I said. "You'll never guess what I discovered when I got home."

"That you no longer have any feelings for Chris and you're going all in with Finn?" she teased.

"First the perm. Then my love life," I said. "Fine, I guess I won't tell you my news," I added archly.

Penny bit. "I'm sorry. I'll stop teasing you. What's the big news?"

I paused dramatically before saying, "There's a for sale sign in front of Trevor and Sandra's house."

Penny gasped. "Do you think her friends know?" she asked.

"I have no idea," I said. "I would think they don't or they would've said something."

"Do you think they're leaving Star Junction?" she said.

"I don't know that either," I said. "I'll try to catch Sandra alone and ask her."

"Oh," Penny said with delight. "An investigation. I'm in."

I laughed and scooped up Delilah, who had not stopped begging for attention. "It's not an investigation. It's a neighbor asking another neighbor details about her impending move."

"Investigation sounds more fun," Penny said in a tone that had me picturing her curling her lip at the boring nature of my logic.

"Fine," I said with a chuckle. "I'll investigate the mystery of the for sale sign. At least that will be an easy, safe investigation."

"Nothing like murder," Penny said.

"Thank God," I added.

It was the weekend, which meant Trevor would be around, but Monday morning, once I knew Trevor had left for work, I'd head over and talk to Sandra about their plans. Sandra was a good neighbor and her two boys were cuties, but I would be lying if I said I'd be sad to see Trevor go.

CHAPTER THREE

My mom stood back from the display we'd been working on for over an hour. Monday morning had started earlier than I would've liked, but my mom was too excited to decorate the store for Halloween to wait any longer.

"What do you think?" she asked me.

The front window of Camelot Flowers had been transformed. A life-sized knight in a suit of armor stood next to a large gray rock. Out of the rock, a sword jutted into the air, but not just any sword. The hilt was covered in yellow sunflowers. The knight even had a flower tucked into his helmet like it was tucked behind his ear. The knight was posed as if trying to pull the sword from the stone. The background was a wall of fall flowers. More yellow sunflowers, pink mums, goldenrod, purple aster, and orange marigolds.

"It's perfect," I said. "It gets better every year."

My mom beamed at me and clapped her hands together in excitement. "I can't wait for your dad to see it," she said. "He's going to love it. I told him I wanted it to be a surprise this year. His Knights of the Round Table display last year was so clever, with the table covered completely in yellow roses. I wanted to top it this year."

"It's going to be a close one," I said. They better not ask me to vote. No way was I choosing between my parents. I glanced at the clock on the wall. "I'm going to drop off the last form for our booth at city hall." I shook my head as I moved to grab my coat from behind the counter. "I don't understand why the city doesn't create an online form for this event."

My mom fiddled with one of the sunflowers. "Maybe no one over there knows how to do it?" she suggested, always prepared to give people the benefit of the doubt.

Someone working in that building had to know how to work the internet. I picked up the paper form that would officially complete our registration for our booth at the Halloween Festival. It was the third paper form we'd had to turn in in the last two months for this event. Thankfully, it was also the last.

Shrugging into my caramel-colored wool coat, I said, "I'm happy to open the store tomorrow morning."

My mom gave me a bright smile. "Thanks, dear. I'll take you up on that. There's a new breakfast place in Rose Lake I've been wanting to try out."

"That's a great idea," I said. "Let me know how it is. Penny and I are always looking for new places to try."

"Or you could go with Griffin," my mom said in a sing-song tone.

"You can just call him Finn, Mom. It's what everyone else does," I said, feeling myself blush from her teasing tone.

"But Griffin and Guinevere," she said. "They sound so good together."

I wrinkled my nose. "That's a lot of G's," I said doubtfully. Even though discovering that Finn was short for Griffin had been a fun little game between us when we first met, I never thought of him as Griffin. Maybe that's why I'd never considered how our full names sounded together.

"Well, I like it," she said resolutely, like the matter was finished.

"Okay, Mom," I said as I dropped a kiss on her cheek. "I'll be back soon."

"Bye, dear," she said absently as she went back to work adjusting the knight's arm.

I decided to walk to city hall. It was just a few blocks away, and the weather was perfect. The sunshine was warm on my face, while the breeze was cool but not yet cold. I felt the urgency to spend as much time outside as possible before winter set in.

"Looking good today, Gwen," a voice said from behind me.

It was funny how much the meaning behind a statement could change based on the tone. Coming from Derek Thompson, that statement had skittered over my skin like a thousand spiders.

I debated continuing forward without acknowledging Derek, but he wasn't big on social cues. At least not where I was concerned. "I'm busy, Derek," I said over my shoulder, not bothering to slow my steps. "See you around."

He caught up to me then slowed to match my pace. "Halloween's coming up," he said. "What's your costume? Sexy nurse? Sexy witch? Sexy pirate?"

I didn't even bother to hide my groan of frustration. The last thing I needed was Derek following me all the way to city hall. Better to send him on his way now. I stopped walking and turned to face him. He was dressed like he'd been on his way to the gym. Or coming from the gym. Considering my eyes were watering from an overdose of cologne and not the pungent smell of cologne mixed with sweat, I'd guess he was getting ready to work out.

"I'm dressing up as a princess, and I'm busy," I said pointedly.

Derek crossed his formidable arms over his chest. It was his notice-my-muscles move. I hated that I knew him well enough to know that. "A sexy princess," he said with approval. "Nice."

"No," I said, shaking my head. "No, no, no. A nice, normal princess. A kid-friendly princess."

Derek scowled. "Where's the fun in that?" he asked.

"I know this is hard for you to believe," I said with more patience than he deserved. "But I didn't choose my costume based on your preferences."

"Whatever," he said, rolling his eyes.

This was good. Moving Derek from skeevy flirting to frustration usually meant his departure was imminent. I decided to push him along. "I've got to get to city hall to turn in our form for the festival. See you later," I said. *Unfortunately.*

"We've got a booth at that thing too," he said. Since businesses and churches were the ones running the booths, he must have been referring to his family insurance business. "I'll go through the haunted maze with you," he said suggestively. "Keep you safe from monsters."

I looked up at him, blinking like a damsel in distress. "Then who would keep me safe from you?" I asked, pouring an overdose of innocence into my tone.

Derek's lips pressed into a thin line, and he stalked away without comment. Overall, it had been a successful battle with my only real enemy in this town. He clearly didn't see us as enemies, but his perception of things was not to be trusted, as evidenced by his relentless pursuit of dating me.

Continuing on to city hall, I took a moment to admire the other business's storefronts. Everyone had been busy decorating. Just Beans had a classic display of a few haybales with pots of flowers sitting in front of dried-out stalks of corn. Fairytale Sweets took a more Halloween-themed approach with a window display of a mad scientist's lab. All the beakers were filled with chocolates. Frankly, it looked delicious.

Burt at Cozy Cuts Pet Care had outdone himself once again. His front window had been transformed into a pet cemetery with tombstones containing witty puns. The one in front read *Gone But Not Fur-Gotten.* The kicker was the smoke machine and realistic-looking backdrop of an old, crumbling cathedral with lights flickering in the windows. Somehow, he'd managed creepy and cute all at the same time.

City hall sat at the edge of a large lawn that measured a full city block long and wide. The garden club was responsible for the beautiful garden beds in front, as well as the ones along the perimeter. In the center of the lawn, a crew was constructing a haunted maze out of haybales. Between the haunted maze and the steps to city hall was a large fall display with more haybales, groupings of sunflowers, and two scarecrows.

My mom wasn't going to love that the garden club had also used sunflowers. I was surprised that she and Margie, president of the garden club and my mom's best friend, hadn't collaborated to ensure their designs weren't similar.

The two scarecrows sat side by side on a strawbale, one of them leaning against the other one. The whole display was striking, but it looked like one of the scarecrows had had too much to drink and was sleeping it off, which was not very kid friendly.

I thought about stepping into the display and straightening it up. I didn't want to bother anyone else, but that would mean stepping over three lines of haybales. One set served as a fence of sorts, as the other two separated a ring of red, gold, and orange mums in wooden pots that looked like barrels cut in half. Finally, the central display sat in the middle with the scarecrows, sunflowers, and dried-out stalks of corn.

Sunflowers, Scarecrows, and Scandal | 23

I'd just tell someone inside. They could either have the groundskeeper fix it up or call Margie and have the garden club do it.

Climbing the seventeen steps, a number I knew from when I was a little kid and had had great fun counting them, I walked into the stone fortress of city hall. It looked like a cross between a castle and a gothic mansion. Constructed in the late eighteen hundreds, it had been the pride of the town for hundreds of years.

A woman at the reception desk looked up and gave me a tight smile, like smiling was a requirement of her job but she wasn't happy to do it. A nameplate on the desk read *Reception*, but the woman was wearing a name badge that said her name was Debra. Her red hair was cut in a short bob. With her glasses and classic cardigan, she looked like the stereotype of a librarian. I half expected her to shush me.

"How may I help you?" she asked briskly.

I approached the desk and pulled the form from my purse. "I'm turning in the last form for Camelot Flowers' booth at the festival," I said. "Do I turn it in to you?" My mom had dropped off all the previous forms.

"I'll take it. Thank you." She looked over the one page and sniffed. "You missed an initial here."

"I'm sorry," I said. "I thought I'd double checked it." I took the form from her and put my initials where she'd indicated.

"Most people miss at least one thing," Debra said. "No one pays as much attention as they should."

Debra was obviously a rule follower and wanted everyone else to be as well.

"Is there anything else I missed?" I asked.

She scanned the form again before saying, "This will do," in a tone that indicated I'd been dismissed.

"I love the display out front," I said. "It's so cute. The kids are going to love it."

"The garden club really outdid themselves this year," she agreed with the first genuine smile I'd seen from her.

"And I love that there are two scarecrows sitting side by side like buddies," I said. "We were going to have a scarecrow in the window of Camelot Flowers, but my mom insisted on buying a full suit of armor. The knight is trying to pull the sword from the stone. You know, *Camelot* Flowers?"

Her face pinched in what looked like concentration. "There's just one scarecrow in the display out front. I was there when they set it up. It's wearing a burlap jumpsuit and has a red scarf around its neck."

"No," I said slowly, mentally picturing what I'd just walked past. "There are two. The one you described and one wearing brown pants with colorful patches, a green shirt with straw sticking out of the end of the sleeves, and a brown pointed hat." I tapped my chin. "Now that I think about it, it looks like the scarecrow from the *Wizard of Oz*. Maybe the garden club wasn't done and added it later when you weren't there? Did you walk past it this morning?" I remembered why I'd brought up the display in the first place. "And the one in the hat is leaning weird. I didn't want to try to fix it myself and mess it up," I added.

Debra shook her head and said, "The employees park in the back and come in through a rear entrance. I haven't walked past the display since they put it up this past weekend."

A man walked by in dress pants and a shirt and tie.

"Herb?" Debra said. "Are there supposed to be two scarecrows in the display out front?"

"Just one that I know of," Herb said as he walked past, not even slowing down.

"I need to see this," Debra said, standing and putting a little sign on her desk that read *Be back soon*. She smoothed down the front of her cardigan.

"I'm sure it's no big deal," I said, following her to the door. If Debra had decided to see the display because she was excited about seeing two cute scarecrows, I'd be excited right along with her, but instead she radiated tension that had me hurrying to keep pace with her. "The display looks good."

"The garden club had to file a plan with the mayor's office, and that plan was approved for one scarecrow," she said as she took the stairs at a brisk pace. Her heels clacked on the stone steps. Further confirmation that Debra was a stickler for the rules.

"I wasn't trying to be a bother," I said. "I could have just straightened it up myself."

We'd made it to the display, where Debra stood with her hands on her hips, regarding the offending scarecrow that was still tipped toward the other one and apparently wasn't supposed to be there.

"This was not in the plans," she said again. "The mayor is not going to like this."

I wanted to make a comment about how maybe the mayor had better things to do than worry about a Halloween display, but the look on Debra's face told me she wouldn't find the joke funny. "What should we do?" I asked instead.

"What do you mean?" she said, finally turning her attention to me.

"I mean, should we straighten it up so it looks better?" I said, pointing at the display.

"I think we should remove it," she said resolutely.

"And do what with it?" I asked in shock. This was getting out of hand. "Let's just straighten it up, and then you can let Margie or the mayor or whoever you want to know that the scarecrow that's supposed to be here has a friend."

Debra shot me a look like I was being ridiculous. She was the one being ridiculous.

"See, it's not even going to be that big of a deal," I said as I stepped over the first row of haybales.

"You're not supposed to go in there," Debra objected. "It's city employees only."

I shot her a sheepish smile as I continued toward the center of the display. "Almost there, and then you can write a report for the mayor."

Debra did not look amused. At least once I was done, it wouldn't look like one of the scarecrows was drunk. Debra continued to object, but it was more of the same, so I tuned her out.

Reaching out, I gripped the scarecrow's shoulders to move it. Instead of sinking into bunched-up straw, my hands closed around something solid. Something that felt suspiciously human.

"Hey, Debra," I called out, my voice tight and my hands still gripping the scarecrow's shoulders, "are these scarecrows supposed to be super realistic?"

"I don't know what you're talking about," she said in a snippy tone. "They're scarecrows."

My heart slammed into my ribs, and my breath grew shallow. Sunshine beat warm against my back, but a chill skated down my spine. With a growing sense of dread, I pulled the scarecrow into a sitting position. Its head flopped back.

I gasped and dropped my hold, causing the scarecrow to drop back to lean against the other one.

"What are you doing?" Debra scolded. "You're going to break them. Here, let me do it. You obviously can't be trusted to handle this."

The sound of her heels clacking against the cement as she stepped over haybales blended with the telltale pounding of my heart. She shouldered me out of the way. "You have to prop it up with something, or it will never stay," she snapped.

"Debra, wait," I started, but she was already grabbing the scarecrow.

She screamed and jumped back. As she let go of the scarecrow, it flopped the other direction, leaning against a wooden post that was holding one end of a string of twinkle lights.

"What is that?" she screeched.

The scarecrow's face was tilted up in this position, the eyes closed, the mouth turned down in a frown. Even dressed like a scarecrow, I knew exactly what that was.

"It's my neighbor, Trevor," I said. "We need to call the police."

CHAPTER FOUR

Debra's screaming turned to frantic muttering, which was better in a way. We didn't need to draw a crowd over to what was clearly a crime scene. She was wringing her hands, her gaze never leaving Trevor. It was going to be up to me to call the police.

I could call 9-1-1, but I couldn't think of a better time to use my personal connection than right now. I dialed Finn's number.

He answered with: "Hey, beautiful. I was just thinking about you. Are you free for dinner tonight? I thought we could try that new place in Rose Lake."

"Finn?" I said weakly, hearing the threads of anxiety lacing my tone.

"If tonight doesn't work, I can do later in the week," he said, completely misreading my tone.

I cleared my throat and tried again. "Finn," I said, sounding slightly stronger. I sat on the haybale behind me, my gaze also laser-locked on to Trevor. It was like Debra and I were working together through sheer force of will to make sure he didn't come back to life like some kind of zombie.

"Or we can stay in town," Finn said. "I know you've been working hard on decorating the store."

"Griffin Butler," I said, using his full name. "I need you down at city hall."

"City hall?" Finn asked, sounding confused. "What's going on?"

I didn't know it was possible to feel nothing and everything all at once. Numb, scared, horrified, maybe a little hysterical. "There's a problem with the Halloween display out front," I said. Somehow, I couldn't make myself say that I'd found another dead body. Saying it out loud would make it true, and I didn't want it to be true.

"I'd love to help, but I'm buried in paperwork right now. That's really more of a garden club thing anyway. Do you want me to get Margie?" he asked.

I was going to have to say it. There was no way around it. I took a bracing breath and blurted out, "Margie can't help unless she knows what to do with a dead body."

Margie had been working at the front desk of the police station for years. She might actually know what to do with a dead body.

The call went silent. I looked at my phone to ensure the call hadn't disconnected. It hadn't.

"Finn?" I asked.

"Did you say you found another dead body?" he asked, his voice low and rough. It was a tone I usually found incredibly sexy. Right now, it just felt like I was in trouble.

"Here's the thing," I said. "I was here to drop off the last form for Camelot Flowers' booth at the Halloween Festival, and I stopped to admire the display the garden club made. It's really impressive this year because it's huge with all these haybales and sunflowers and mums and two scarecrows, but then I talked to Debra, and she said there weren't two scarecrows, and I said yes there are, and she said no there isn't, and I came outside to show her, and one of them was tipped over so I tried to fix it, and it's not filled with straw, it's filled with human, and I'm kind of freaking out but also kind of calm, and that worries me, and I thought maybe you'd want to come down and see it, but also it's my neighbor, Trevor."

"Wait, what? Your neighbor is there too?" Finn asked, sounding confused.

"Yes, my neighbor is here," I said impatiently. I didn't understand what was so difficult about this. "He's the dead one."

"Don't go anywhere," Finn said. It sounded like he was moving now. "Stan?" I heard him say. "We've got a body at city hall."

I couldn't make out Stan's reply. Full-time police chief and part-time surrogate uncle to me due to his status as my dad's best friend, Stan was not going to be happy to find out that I was messed up in this. But was I really messed up in this? Maybe I didn't need to be involved in this one. "Finn?" I said into the phone. "I think I'm just going to go home and forget I was here."

"Gwen, no, stay where you are," Finn said. "Don't leave. I'll be there in five."

"Gwen is there?" Stan said loudly enough for me to hear through the phone.

I grimaced, but I didn't run to my car, drive home, lock my doors, and pretend I'd never gotten out of bed this morning. I stayed put as instructed.

"Gwen, I'm going to stay on the line with you," Finn said. "I'm on my way."

I heard a car engine start.

The longer I sat staring at dead-Trevor, the less numb I felt. Numbness had been keeping the panic at bay. Time to focus on something else before I had an all-out panic attack sitting on a haybale in front of two scarecrows who weren't even best friends because one was made of straw and the other was made of dead body.

I dropped my head into my hand and massaged my forehead. "Still want to go out to dinner tonight?" I asked Finn, my voice tight.

"Uh…" he said hesitantly. "I don't know if tonight will work."

I kept my focus on the ant walking toward my shoe. "If you're worried that you'll be busy with a new investigation, I think we can wrap this up right now. Trevor got drunk, dressed up like a scarecrow, wandered to city hall, sat down in the Halloween display to rest, and passed away from natural causes."

"I'm two blocks away," Finn said, sounding worried.

He didn't need to worry about me. I was fine now that I had my friend, the ant, to focus on. "So, you won't be busy tonight because there's nothing to investigate," I said, making complete and total sense.

"Gwen, I didn't know your neighbor, but your scenario seems unlikely," Finn said patiently, like he was talking to a small child.

"I know," I said softly. "But can we pretend it's true?"

"Sure, we can pretend for one more minute," he said. I heard a car door slam through the phone. "I'm almost there."

Sirens sounded in the distance. Finn wasn't coming alone.

In the time I'd been talking to Finn, Debra had tentatively approached and then retreated from Trevor's body multiple times. I understood the morbid fascination. I also understood the visceral disgust that warned a person away.

"There's something in his front pocket," Debra said over her shoulder on one of her approaches.

"I'll see you soon," I said to Finn. "Debra found something."

Right before I disconnected the call, I heard, "Who's Debra?"

"What'd you find?" I asked Debra as I moved to her side. "A dead body?"

"Is this a joke to you?" Debra asked harshly.

"No, I, uh, I just," I stammered as I shrugged. "Find it easier to make jokes than face the reality of the situation, I guess."

Debra sniffed her disapproval before pointing at poor Trevor and saying, "There's something tucked into the front pocket of his overalls."

Debra was right. There was a folded piece of white paper in Trevor's pocket. "Do you think these are his overalls? Because I've never seen him wear anything like this before. He's more the business suit during the day, trendy workout clothes at night kind of guy, like he has a lot of money and wants you to know it." I cocked my head to the side in thought. "Although nothing else in his life screams money. Normal house. Normal cars. It's not like he lives out on Star Lake. Now those people have money."

Debra looked at me like I'd grown two heads. "The paper?" she said, clearly not appreciating my musings.

"Oh yeah," I said, refusing to feel bad for being curious, even though it felt like Debra was trying to use every bit of her effort to shame me into focusing. "The paper." I reached forward.

"Don't touch it," she shrieked.

I jerked my hand away. "Geez, you're going to give me a heart attack," I said with my hand now protecting my pounding heart. "Then there would be two dead bodies. Finn wouldn't like that."

"What wouldn't Finn like?" a deep voice I'd know anywhere said from behind me.

Debra and I turned together. She stiffened. I melted. As usual, Finn was dressed in a dark, swoon-worthy suit. Today, he'd paired it with a green tie. I knew from experience that he wore a holster that strapped around his back, keeping his gun easily accessible inside his suit coat. Believe me, going in for an enthusiastic hug only to be jabbed with hard metal will burn that fact into anyone's memory.

"Detective Butler," Debra said formally. "I assure you that I did my best to keep her from contaminating the crime scene, although she did touch the body."

"So did you," I said defensively.

"Not once I knew it was a crime scene," Debra said imperiously.

"Me neither," I protested.

"But you were going to," Debra said. She turned her attention to Finn. "She was going to," she said, as if he wouldn't have heard her the first time.

Finn looked bewildered and rightly so. He held up his hands. "Let's start over," he said. Turning to me, his whiskey-brown eyes softened. "Are you okay?" he asked softly.

Forget melting. I was bypassing the liquid stage and turning right into steam. "I'm fine," I said sweetly. "Thanks for asking," I added in a snarky tone aimed right at Debra.

"I am also fine," she said, although no one had asked. "This poor gentleman is not."

The sounds of the sirens grew louder. "Tommy will be here soon," Finn said. He shook his head. "I told him he didn't need sirens. He was out at Star Lake looking into vandalism to someone's boathouse. Let's see what we've got here."

He stepped between us toward Trevor, who was still looking up at the sky, although with his eyes closed, he wasn't seeing anything. Actually, being dead, he wasn't seeing much either.

"I already told you how we discovered him," I said to Finn. "Debra noticed he has something in his pocket. How do you think he died?"

"It's too soon to say." Finn shot me a sideways look. "Although I doubt he put himself in this position," he said in a tone that was somehow professional and teasing at the same time.

I gave him a ha-ha-very-funny look.

"Gwen was going to remove the paper before you arrived," Debra tattled.

I couldn't deny it was true. "Carefully," I said in my defense.

"Touching evidence as little as possible is ideal," Finn said absently as he leaned forward to look at Trevor more closely.

Debra shot me a triumphant look over the top of Finn's back. He definitely wasn't winning any potential boyfriend points with me right now. I understood he had a job to do, but he didn't need to give Debra the satisfaction of agreeing with her.

"What d'ya got, boss?" Tommy said as he approached.

"Do you have any evidence bags on you?" Finn asked without shifting his gaze from Trevor.

"I've got the whole kit," Tommy replied. He looked at me. "Hey, Gwen. We should hire you full time with how often you're at crime scenes," he said with a cheeky grin.

"Ha-ha," I deadpanned. "Nice to see you, Tommy."

Tommy and I had graduated from high school together. He'd been the responding officer when I stumbled onto my first dead body, a fact he liked to remind me of often.

Tommy handed Finn a pair of gloves, which Finn put on with a snap. "Take some pictures of the scene before I remove whatever's in his pocket," Finn said to Tommy.

I grimaced. I'd been prepared to remove the paper out of a dire overdose of curiosity, trusting in Finn's feelings for me to smooth over any issues it would've caused. I hadn't thought about needing to document where the paper had been before removing it. I hated to admit it, but Debra had been right.

Tommy pulled a camera from his bag and snapped pictures at a variety of angles. Debra, Finn, and I stood shoulder to shoulder, watching.

"Done," Tommy said, taking a step back.

Finn looked down at me. "Let's see what all the fuss is about," he said. He stepped over to Trevor and removed the paper from his pocket. It looked like normal printer paper. Finn unfolded it. Tommy, Debra, and I crowded in on Finn to look over his shoulder.

Printed on the paper were the words—*I'm a liar, a cheat, a jerk, and I've finally paid for my crimes.*

Tommy let out a low whistle. I gasped. Debra sniffed disapprovingly. Nice to know she didn't reserve all her judgment for me. Finn looked between the note and Trevor before turning his attention to me. "What made you gasp?"

I thought of Sandra's friends at the beauty salon, convinced that Trevor had cheated on Sandra, convinced that he was a jerk, and the most troubling part, convinced that he deserved to die.

CHAPTER FIVE

Finn, Tommy, and Debra looked at me expectantly. I should've held that gasp inside. I didn't condone murder, but I also didn't condone throwing suspicion on two women whose only crime was caring about their friend.

I adopted what I hoped was an innocent expression and said, "It's nothing. I just remembered that I left a load of towels in the washing machine this morning." I shook my head dramatically. "Now I'm going to have to rewash them or they'll stink."

Debra and Tommy turned their attention back to the note, but Finn studied me. He wasn't buying it. I shot him a sunny smile. He narrowed his eyes. I cleared my throat and said, "I can't believe there's been another murder."

"And right around Halloween," Tommy piped up. "Spooky."

We all looked at Trevor, and I wrinkled my nose. "I was too distracted by the fact that my neighbor was dead. I didn't even think about the spooky factor. You're right. It's weird that he's dressed up."

"It's weird that he's in front of city hall in a display meant for children," Debra said.

It was the first time we'd agreed all day.

"The killer wanted to make a statement," Finn said thoughtfully. "This was about putting Trevor on display. Humiliating him. This was personal."

Once again, I thought of Sandra's friends. Or Sandra. I worked to keep my expression neutral. I wasn't going to accuse anyone until there was a stronger motive than gossip and harmless murder plotting to blow off a little steam. We'd all done it. Heck, if my imagination had any power, Derek Thompson would've died years ago.

Finn turned to Tommy. "Is the medical examiner on her way?" he asked.

Tommy checked the time and replied, "Should be here sometime in the next thirty minutes."

Finn nodded. "Let's get the rest of the pictures we need before she arrives." He turned to Debra and me. "And I'll need your statements."

We both nodded. Unfortunately, I knew the drill.

Finn looked at the body. "We've got pictures of him as we found him," Finn said. "Is this what he looked like when you walked by?" he asked me.

I shook my head. "He was flopped the other direction, leaning up against the other scarecrow. His head was down, so I couldn't tell it wasn't just another prop."

Finn nodded slowly as if in thought. "I don't see any apparent cause of death," he said as if talking to himself. "Tommy? Another pair of gloves?"

Tommy handed Finn the gloves, which he handed to me.

"What are these for?" I asked suspiciously.

"I'm going to shift the body so Tommy can take pictures from some other angles. I don't want him falling over onto the ground and contaminating evidence. I'd like you to stand on the other side of him. If he starts to fall backward, catch him."

I stared at Finn blankly.

"You can handle that, right?" Finn asked. He looked confident in my abilities to be helpful. Midwest rule number twenty-two—if you can be helpful, do it.

I stepped over haybales until I was standing on the other side of Trevor. It took a minute. The garden club had arranged the display in a way that it took some work to get to the center. Yet, when I'd walked by earlier, I hadn't noticed anything out of place. No haybales had been knocked out of alignment. No sunflowers were bent at the stalks. Whoever had left Trevor in the middle of the display had either done an amazing job cleaning up after themselves or been very careful to begin with.

I opened my mouth to tell Finn what I'd noticed, but Debra caught my eye. She was still glowering at me like somehow this whole mess was my fault. Better to tell Finn later in private. Besides, he was amazing at his job. He'd likely noticed the same thing.

I crouched down a little like I was getting ready to guard a basketball player. "I'm ready," I said, although I couldn't be held responsible if my natural instinct was to jerk away if Trevor tipped toward me. Hopefully, we wouldn't have to find out.

Finn took Trevor by the shoulders and eased him into an upright seated position. "Take pictures of his torso like this," Finn said. "As soon as the medical examiner gets here, we'll move him to the ground."

Tommy took a bunch of pictures before saying, "Done."

Finn shifted Trevor again. This time, Trevor's head jerked back and his straw hat fell off, landing at my feet. Finn had a grip on him, which prevented me from having to touch Trevor again, but it didn't save me from seeing the deep gash on the side of Trevor's head.

"Nope," I said, backing up until I bumped into a haybale. I scrambled over it. "Nope, nope, nope, nope. I don't do blood. I'm done. It was nice seeing you, Finn. Have a good life. I'm moving to a town where there is no crime."

"Got him?" I heard Finn say.

Tommy replied with, "Got him."

I had no idea what they were talking about because I'd stripped off my gloves and walked with purpose toward Camelot Flowers, where I could get in my car and drive far away from here. I refused to focus on the details of Trevor's injury because losing my breakfast of a blueberry muffin, eggs, and coffee was not something I was interested in.

Even as I kept the visual image locked up tight in my mind, I had no doubt that we'd just discovered the cause of death. Someone had hit Trevor over the head with something sharp.

"Gwen," Finn called out. A moment later, he caught up with me. He slowed down to match my stride. "Are you okay?"

Many responses cycled through my mind from *Do you really think I'm okay?* all the way to *Are you serious?* What I settled on was, "Yup, just fine."

"Gwen," Finn said, the compassion in his tone threatening to break me wide open. I didn't want to revisit breakfast. I also didn't want to cry at a crime scene. He grabbed my hand and pulled me to a stop. "I'm sorry. I shouldn't have asked you to help. I should have just waited for the medical examiner."

I stared toward the businesses of Main Street, still several blocks away. If I kept my gaze locked in this position, there'd be no chance I'd accidentally see Trevor and his split-open skull.

"Look at me," Finn said gently.

"I am," I replied. Lie number one. "And I'm fine." Lie number two. "I just have to go move that laundry to my dryer." Lie number three.

Finn cupped the side of my face and turned my head until I was forced to meet his gaze. Tears burned the backs of my eyes, and my throat closed up. Finn must have been able to see the emotion I was working so hard to keep inside, because he pulled me into a hug. I was sure Debra wouldn't approve.

Finn's hand ran up and down my back in soothing strokes that equally calmed my nerves and made the tears harder to hold in. "Do you want me to call Penny?" Finn asked.

"No," I said, melting into his embrace. "She's still at school."

"I know you want to leave," Finn said slowly.

I tensed in his arms, but he just tightened his hug as if he was afraid that I was about to bolt.

"But I need to take your statement," he finished.

"Can we do it far away from Trevor?" I asked.

"How about we sit on the steps over there," he said.

I followed his gaze to the set of steps that led to the front doors of city hall.

"Sure," I agreed. "But I'm not going back over there."

"Deal," Finn said. He released me from the hug and took my hand, walking us to the steps. He went up to the tenth step and sat down.

"You'll get your suit dirty," I said as I stood before him.

He patted the step next to him. "I'm not worried about my suit," he said, the look on his face making it clear that what he was worried about was me.

I sat as requested.

Finn took a small recorder from his pocket and clicked it on. After stating the date, time, location, and who he was with, he said, "Tell me what happened."

I started with arriving at city hall and ended with sitting on the steps, making sure to emphasize that I'd only touched Trevor when I thought he was just a simple scarecrow. I didn't mention that I would've taken that note out and read it, no gloves, no pictures to show how it had been placed on the body, if Debra hadn't put up such a stink. No harm, no foul.

Finn clicked off the recorder and looked off into the distance at the crime scene. A van pulled up to the side of the road, and a woman with her blonde hair pulled back into a ponytail stepped out. She disappeared around the back of the van and then reappeared carrying a black duffel bag. She joined Tommy, who was standing with Debra and Trevor's body.

"That's the medical examiner," Finn said. "I need to be there while she does her preliminary inspection."

"I get it," I said. "Can I head out?"

Finn rubbed my back, and I leaned into his touch. "You can leave," he said. "If I have any more questions, I know where to find you," he added with a small smile.

"Can I ask you a question?" I asked.

Finn stood and extended his hand to help me up. "Of course."

"When do you plan to tell Trevor's wife?" I asked. "I don't know her well, but she lives across the street from me. I feel like I should check in on her once she knows."

"I'll go over there later today," Finn said somberly. I had to imagine that this wasn't a pleasant part of his job. His eyes narrowed slightly. "Any chance that you'll also be going over there to ask her questions about who might have wanted to kill Trevor?"

The thought had crossed my mind. I didn't know why it was a problem. Checking on Sandra to see if she needed anything was the neighborly thing to do. Finding out who took her husband away from her and their father away from her boys was also a neighborly thing to do. Unless she'd finally snapped from all the abuse over the years and killed him herself. Then she probably wouldn't find my poking around very helpful. I had a sudden itch to get home and make a list of who wanted Trevor dead.

"I mean, if it comes up…" I finally said to Finn.

"Mm-hmm," he said noncommittally, which I took as a victory. He hadn't said no.

"Good luck with everything," I said, gesturing toward the crime scene.

Crime scene was an interesting word for what I was looking at. Leaving a dead body in a public place was probably a crime, but it was clear that Trevor hadn't been killed at the garden club's display. As much as I'd like to forget, I'd seen the head wound. That thing would have bled all over the place. The "crime scene" was pristine.

"What are you thinking?" Finn asked, pulling me back from my theorizing.

"That Trevor wasn't killed here," I said. "There's no blood. No sign of a struggle."

"That's good," Finn said proudly. "You're thinking like a detective. I'd noticed the same thing."

"You probably noticed it sooner than I did," I said in disappointment.

"Maybe," Finn said kindly. He held up a finger toward where Tommy, Debra, and the medical examiner stood watching us. "I'll check in on you later," he said to me.

"You're always checking on me," I said. "How about I check in on you later? You're the one with the stress of solving yet another murder in this idyllic, sleepy small town."

We started down the stairs. "You're more than welcome to check in on me. Anytime," he added with a sexy grin and a tone that was saturated with all sorts of innuendo.

My body responded to Finn's sexy grin in every cliché way possible—weak in the knees, butterflies in my stomach, lightheaded, racing heart. Either I was completely smitten with Detective Finn Butler, or I was coming down with dengue fever.

CHAPTER SIX

I walked away from city hall filled with indecision. I'd planned on going back to Camelot Flowers and spending the afternoon scheduling our social media posts for the next week. If I did that, my mom would ask how it went, and I'd have to tell her about finding Trevor. Although, Stan would be sure to tell my dad that I'd found another dead body. My dad would tell my mom. There was no way around it. I was going back to the shop.

Arriving with coffee for my parents from Just Beans, or chocolate from Fairytale Sweets, would buy me some good favor, but I'd still have to have the conversation eventually. Better to rip off the Band-Aid.

I stopped in front of the door to Camelot Flowers and took a bracing breath. It wasn't that I was going to be in trouble. That wasn't how my parents operated. It was more the worrying, the handwringing, and the general questioning of the universe about why their only daughter kept ending up at crime scenes that I was worried about.

The little bell over the door gave a cheerful jingle when I walked in.

My mom glanced briefly in my direction. She was at the workbench, surrounded by flowers, "Hi, honey. How'd it go?" She focused on trimming the sunflowers in her hand.

"Dropping off the form? That went fine," I said, trying to figure out how to bring up the fact that I'd found another dead body without freaking her out. "Where's Dad?"

My mom looked up, setting the clippers and sunflowers down. "Guinevere? What happened? And your father is having lunch with Stan."

This was why I could never get away with anything as a teenager. Still couldn't as an adult. My mom could read between the lines like no one else.

"Don't get upset," I said.

My mom crossed her arms and leaned her hip against the workbench. "I'm listening," she said, her tone no-nonsense.

"I dropped off the form, and I mentioned to Debra at the front desk that the garden club put together a great display this year," I said.

My mom waved her hand through the air and said, "Get to the important part."

I pulled in a deep breath and let it out with a sigh before saying, "There were two scarecrows in the display. There was only supposed to be one. Turns out the other one was my neighbor, Trevor. He was murdered."

I wasn't sure what I was expecting, but my mom staring at me blankly wasn't it.

"Mom?" I said.

She'd become like a statue. It was more upsetting than if she'd been ranting. Turning slowly, she picked up the sunflowers and looked at them in a way that made it clear she wasn't really seeing them. Finally, she said, "It's like you have some kind of magnet inside you that attracts dead bodies. I told your dad naming you Guinevere carried this potential. Her brothers were killed. Arthur was killed. Death followed that woman around. Now it follows you around too."

Oh boy. I hadn't expected her to go all Dark Ages on me. Maybe it was the Halloween season that had her seeing ill omens around every corner. "My name isn't cursed, Mom," I said. "The thing is, I'm all over town delivering flowers, running errands, seeing friends. It's a small town. I just happen to be in the wrong places at the wrong times."

My mom nodded, still staring at those sunflowers. "Maybe you're right," she murmured. "I supposed you're going to investigate?"

I picked up a pen and clicked it over and over. "I wasn't really planning on it. Finn can handle this one."

At this, my mom looked at me. She clearly didn't believe what I was saying. "Trevor wasn't very nice to his family," she said.

"Yeah, I overheard some of Sandra's friends talking about it at Lucille's the other day," I replied. "And he fights with our neighbor, Chip, all the time about their yards."

"I bet Sandra killed him," my mom said with conviction.

What was happening right now? First, she accused my name of being a magnet for death. Then she accused sweet Sandra of murder. The last time I'd discussed suspects with her in an investigation, she'd gone out of her way to irrationally explain how no one had committed the murder because she didn't like to believe that anyone was capable of murder. At least she seemed to have moved on from her anguish over my namesake.

"What's makes you say that?" I asked.

My mom's eyes sparked with interest. "Your dad and I were watching a movie last weekend. I don't know if you've heard of it. Jennifer Lopez is married to a horrible man, and in the end, she—" my mom smacked her hands together hard, making me jump "—takes care of him."

I knew exactly what movie my mom was talking about. "You mean *Enough*?" I asked.

"That's it," my mom said, pointing at me. All the quiet horror of the moment when she'd learned I'd been at the scene of another dead body was gone, replaced with an excitement that I hadn't expected. "I bet Sandra had had *enough*," she emphasized the play on words, "and took Trevor out."

"I can't really picture sweet, quiet Sandra killing anyone," I said slowly. "And besides, I thought you didn't want me investigating this."

"We're not investigating," my mom said. "We're just talking. Plus, I didn't tell you not to. I just asked if you were going to."

"In a disapproving tone," I pointed out.

"In a concerned tone," she corrected with a smile.

I leaned against the workbench as she went back to trimming the sunflowers. "So, you think Sandra killed Trevor."

"Yep," she said, nodding.

"Because of an old Jennifer Lopez movie," I said.

"It's not that old," she protested. "We just watched it last weekend."

My mom always thought that things started when she discovered them. It was why she also thought that Spotify was the newest thing in the music streaming world.

"If Trevor was mean to Sandra and his kids, maybe he was mean to a lot of people. He fought with Chip all the time about where the property line was between their yards," I reasoned.

"That's true," my mom said. She set the sunflowers in the vase and added white roses and mini hydrangeas. "But I still think it was Sandra. Anyway, Finn will figure it out. I know I was teasing you before, but how are things going with you two?"

I picked up a discarded rose and twirled it between my fingers. "Things are…" I tried to figure out the right way to describe what I was experiencing with Finn. "Slow," I finally finished. "When we're together, things are great, but it feels like something's always getting in the way."

"How's his mom doing?" she asked with concern as she moved flowers around in the vase.

Over the summer, Finn's mom had fallen and had to have surgery on her knee. Finn had traveled back to the Chicago suburb of Lombard, where he was born and raised, multiple weekends to visit and help out. I was glad he'd had the chance to be with his family. It just hadn't given us much time to spend together.

Throw in how busy the summer was for me at Camelot Flowers as we set up booths at farmers' markets and festivals around the county. Finn and I had managed to sneak in a few dates, but nothing had progressed passed that initial stage. We hadn't even kissed yet.

"And Chris?" my mom asked, interrupting my thoughts.

I hadn't kissed Chris either. Not for lack of trying on his part. Always respectful, unlike Derek Thompson, he'd been disappointed when I found reasons to deflect but kept saying he understood.

"Timing hasn't been our friend," I said.

A year ago, I would have jumped all over the chance to have a relationship with Chris. Finn moving to town had changed everything.

"Just have fun," my mom said. "Enjoy this time. You'll never get it back."

"I thought you wanted me married and having babies so you can spoil your grandchildren," I teased.

"There's plenty of time for that," my mom said, which was a very different message than what she preached to me five years ago.

Before I could ask her what had changed, she stepped back from the arrangement and said, "What do you think?"

It was beautiful. My mom had a real gift with flowers. The yellow of the sunflowers with their chocolate brown centers looked gorgeous next to the white roses and white mini hydrangeas.

"It's perfect," I said. "Does it need to be delivered?"

My mom checked the order slip. "No, the customer is picking it up later today."

My mind swirled with thoughts of Trevor's murder, including my mom's belief that Sandra had finally had enough and killed her husband. I wondered what Finn was doing right now. Was he still at the crime scene? Had he told Sandra yet? Was he already crafting theories of who could have done it? And where had it happened? Somewhere, there was a crime scene waiting to be discovered.

Finn was going to be busy the next few days. Finding that crime scene was going to be important but probably difficult, like searching for a needle in a haystack. Finn would have to cover the town and surrounding areas. Finding suspects would likely help narrow the search.

The bell above the door jingled, bringing me back from thoughts of death and violence. My mom greeted the two women who walked in, asking if they needed any help. While she was busy with them, I put the bouquet she'd finished in the cooler and headed toward the break room.

We kept a list of weekly tasks that needed to be completed pinned on a corkboard near the sink. It had a mix of business and cleaning tasks that kept Camelot Flowers running. I'd check in with Finn later today and find out how Sandra had taken the news of her husband's death, but in the meantime, I needed to keep busy or I was going to do something reckless, like run out and try to figure out who had killed my neighbor.

CHAPTER SEVEN

I'd only gotten a few short texts from Finn the night before, and none of them had given me the information I'd wanted—how did Sandra react to finding out that Trevor was dead, and did Finn have any suspects?

I had a plan to remedy that problem. It involved waiting until mid-morning and stopping by the station to bring Finn his favorite coffee from Just Beans. Don't ask me why the man's favorite coffee was black with a splash of heavy cream when things like caramel macchiatos existed, but in all the months I'd known him, I hadn't been able to change his mind.

I stood in front of the large picture window in my living room, a s'mores Pop-Tart in one hand, a mug of home-brewed, and therefore less tasty, coffee than what I could get at Just Beans in the other. Trevor's house looked like it had every other day I'd lived across the street from them, but I knew nothing would ever be the same for his family. I also knew that losing someone was hard, even if that person wasn't nice.

I'd hoped to catch Sandra outside, maybe walking the boys to the bus stop on the corner, but the curtains were drawn and no one had left since I'd been watching. My gaze landed on the *For Sale by Owner* sign in their front yard. Had Trevor been trying to run from something? I needed to find out why they were moving.

"You can't just stand around all day like a stalker," I said to myself, although that was exactly what I wanted to do. Most of my motivation was out of concern. The rest, curiosity.

Forcing myself away from the window, I got ready for work, cleaned up my dishes from breakfast, and wandered around my house, trying to kill time. I wasn't in the mood to clean, although in all fairness, I never was. It was a beautiful fall day for late October. The high would be in the sixties, and it was sunny with a bright-blue sky.

One of the benefits of a small town was how walkable it was. I was going crazy sitting around the house, and it was too early for my plan to drop in on Finn. However, if I walked to the coffee shop and then walked to the station, I'd arrive right around the time I'd planned.

I put on my coat, slung my purse over my shoulder, and headed toward downtown. What I'd failed to anticipate was all the people I ran into who'd already heard about Trevor's murder.

Amanda, the owner of Just Beans, wanted to know if the expression on Trevor's face had looked surprised, because she'd seen that happen on true crime documentaries. A customer, who'd overheard my conversation with Amanda, had wondered if there was a serial killer in town and this was just the beginning.

On my way to the police station, I'd run into Burt, the owner of Cozy Cuts Pet Care, who was sweeping the stoop in front of his store. He'd stopped me and told me that he'd heard a rumor that Trevor had been shot twenty times at close range. I'd shut that rumor down, but I could tell that Burt hadn't wanted to believe me.

By the time I turned the corner on Sycamore Street and the station came into view, I'd heard more rumors about Trevor's death than I knew what to do with. Good thing I was about to see the detective in charge of the case. Finn would sort through everything to separate the truth from fiction.

I shouldered open the glass door of the police station with a coffee in each hand. Margie looked up from her desk, her expression brightening. "Guinevere, wonderful to see you. And you brought me coffee." She bustled around her desk toward me.

Her shoulder-length graying hair curled around her head in what looked like a fresh perm. I said a silent thank-you to the universe that I hadn't let Penny talk me into getting one.

I held the coffee Margie was reaching for out of the way. "That's for Finn," I said.

She looked hopefully at the other one.

"And this one is for me," I said matter-of-factly. It was best to be blunt with Margie, or she'd find a way of talking you out of your own good intentions.

"That's probably for the best," she said, returning to her desk. "My doctor told me to cut down on the caffeine, which means my three cups in the morning are now down to two, and I've already drunk them both."

Three cups of morning coffee? No wonder Margie was bouncing off the walls most of the time, even in her early sixties.

"Is Finn in?" I asked, trying to see if his door was open at the end of the hall.

Margie sobered. "I'm not sure he left last night. He was writing up warrants, going over the statements he took from you, Debra, and Sandra. I tried to tell him to let the officers handle the paperwork, but he wanted to do it himself." She shook her head as she glanced over her shoulder toward his office. "You stopping by is exactly what that boy needs."

"He didn't leave last night?" I asked with concern. I'd known he'd been too busy to talk and his texts had been short and to the point, but I hadn't considered that he'd worked all night.

"If he did go home, it wasn't for long," Margie replied. "Go on back there and force him to take a little break."

I wasn't going to argue with her. Not only did I want to find out what happened with Sandra yesterday, but now I wanted to see with my own eyes how Finn was doing. I headed down the hall.

Stan, or Uncle Stan as I'd called him since the moment I could talk, looked up from his desk as I passed by. "Guinevere," he said, smiling beneath his bushy mustache. "Come on in."

"Oh, I'm here to see…" I gestured toward Finn's door with one of the cups of coffee.

"I know," he said. "But I haven't seen you in weeks. Sit a minute, and let me worry about how you're doing after finding the victim yesterday."

I immediately felt bad for not checking in with him more often. As my dad's best friend, he was family to me growing up in a town where I didn't have anyone but my parents. I sat in the chair across from his desk and set the coffees down.

"Finn filled me in on the scene yesterday," Uncle Stan said as he ran his hand over his chin and shook his head. "I sure hired that boy at the right time. He comes with experience we've needed these last months."

I had no doubt that most of this stress would have fallen to Stan if he hadn't hired Finn. "My dad was telling me that you're all set up with a new ice fishing rig for the winter," I said, steering the conversation away from murder.

Uncle Stan beamed. "A brand-new heater. Wi-Fi capable. It even has a composting toilet. Maybe I'll even get you out sometime."

"The heater goes a long way toward me agreeing to that," I said with a chuckle. I was happy to check in with Stan, but my heart kept tugging me to the office next door. I must not have been very good at hiding it.

"Go on and check on Finn," Stan said with a genuine smile. "I know he's fallen into the murder investigation wormhole. It's the worst in the beginning. Not a lot of evidence, but a lot of pressure to close the case."

"Does he have any suspects?" I asked.

Stan regarded me before saying, "I'll let Finn decide what he wants to tell you about the investigation."

I couldn't tell if his statement was meant as disapproval over Finn involving me in past investigations or showed respect for Finn's decisions as a detective. I decided to leave just in case it was the first one and a lecture was imminent. "It was nice to see you," I said sincerely. "I'll tell my dad you say hi."

"No need," Stan said. "We're bowling tonight."

"That's fun," I said. "My mom didn't mention it."

Stan grimaced. "I hope she knows."

I laughed. "Well, if she doesn't, that's my dad's problem to work out."

"True enough," Stan said. I turned to leave, but Stan stopped me by saying, "Stay safe, Gwen."

He didn't call me Gwen often. Because of that, it had the same effect as someone who normally called me Gwen calling me Guinevere. I turned back and said, "I will, Uncle Stan."

He looked worried, but I left before he could get himself worked up about something that wasn't even going to be a problem.

Finn's office door was closed. I tucked one of the coffees into the crook of my elbow and transferred the other coffee to my now-free hand. The situation was precarious. I needed to get that door open if I didn't want to end up wearing Finn's black coffee with a splash of heavy cream.

As my hand closed around the doorknob, Tommy came around the corner in uniform. "Let me help you with that," he said. He rushed forward and took the coffee from my hand, allowing me to hold the cup I'd been balancing. "How're you holding up?" he asked.

At this rate, I was never going to see Finn.

I shot Tommy a smile. "I'm fine. Not my first rodeo," I said. Before he could respond, I opened the door, took the coffee back from him, and scooted into Finn's office. Closing the door, I leaned back against it dramatically.

Finn looked up from a stack of paperwork. His expression shifted from confused to delighted. "This is a nice surprise," he said warmly.

I glanced over my shoulder at the closed door like it was about to swing open with one more person who wanted to ask how I was doing or tell me some crazy theory about Trevor's murder.

"Everything okay?" Finn asked with a bemused smile. Clearly, he was getting used to my eccentricities.

When no one came bursting in, I relaxed and gave Finn a wide smile. "Everything's great," I said. "I just had to go through Margie, Uncle Stan, and Tommy to make it in here."

"It can be like a gauntlet for me to get to my office in the morning," he said, commiserating.

"Not to mention Amanda at Just Beans, Burt at the pet groomers, and a variety of other people who stopped me on my way here to ask me about Trevor's murder," I continued.

Finn grimaced. I wasn't sure if the frown was out of sympathy or concern that people around Star Junction were already talking about the murder.

I held out one of the cups. "Coffee?" I asked.

Finn huffed out a breath. "I would love coffee," he said.

I handed him his cup. Now that I wasn't worried about someone interrupting us, I had a chance to really look at Finn. Dark circles ringed the bottoms of his eyes. He took a long drink of the coffee I handed him before giving me a weary-looking smile. Those observations would have indicated that Margie was right about the lack of sleep he'd gotten, but what really gave it away was what he was wearing.

"Are you wearing jeans?" I asked in shock.

Finn looked down at his forest-green sweater and jeans. "Yeah," he said slowly, as if trying to make sense of my question.

I leaned against his desk, studying him closely for signs that he'd finally succumbed to the pressures of the job and cracked. "I've never seen you in anything but a suit at work," I said.

"To be fair, you don't see me at work every day," he said with a small smile.

I quirked an eyebrow, challenging the validity of his statement with one look.

Finn chuckled. "Okay, you're right. This is my first time wearing jeans during normal business hours. I went home to grab some sleep around four and came back at six. This is what was clean."

"You only got two hours of sleep?" I asked in horror.

"I'll be fine," Finn said. He lifted the coffee I'd brought like he was toasting me. "This helps."

Worrying about Finn wasn't going to make him less tired, and I'd learned from experience that telling him he should get more sleep was about as effective as him telling me to stay out of a murder investigation. I sat in the chair across from his desk. "How's it going?"

"Personally?" he asked, a mischievous twinkle in his eye.

"I think we both know I'm asking one professional to another," I teased.

Finn gave me a wry smile. "It's early," he said vaguely.

"Margie mentioned you talked to Sandra?" I said.

Finn's gaze turned haunted. "I'll never get used to having to tell someone their loved one is dead," he said.

"I can't even imagine," I said in sympathy. "How did she seem?"

"Devastated," Finn said. "In shock. The usual."

"Anything else?" I asked. I wanted to know if she'd seemed guilty or like she was hiding something. I didn't want to come out and say it. I was fishing, but Finn wasn't biting.

"Like what?" he asked.

There was no way around it. I was going to have to spell it out. "Like did she seem guilty about anything?" I muttered. If I didn't say it clearly, maybe it wouldn't count as picking on a woman who had just lost her husband.

I peeled the edge of the label on my coffee cup. When Finn didn't respond, I looked up to find him looking at me with a stern expression on his face. Why did I suddenly feel like I'd been called to the principal's office?

"What?" I said defensively. "You had to have considered that she killed her husband. My mom certainly did," I added as an afterthought.

"Your mom…" Finn started before trailing off. "Your mom thinks that Sandra killed Trevor?"

I bobbed my head back and forth. "Sort of. She watched a movie where a woman kills her abusive ex, and now she's convinced she's an expert."

"That doesn't seem like your mom," Finn said in surprise.

"She also thinks she cursed me into finding dead bodies by naming me Guinevere," I said. "She's in a weird headspace."

Finn looked baffled. I didn't blame him. It was a lot to take in. He rubbed his hand across his forehead. If it was possible, he looked even more exhausted. "I'm considering anyone who might have had a motive to kill Trevor, but no, his wife is not my prime suspect."

I sat forward with interest. "So, you have a prime suspect?" I asked.

"It's early," Finn repeated, once again being infuriatingly vague.

I sat back in my seat. I was hitting a brick wall. I might be too curious for my own good, but even I knew when to back off. "I really did come to see how you're doing," I said sincerely.

"Mostly," Finn said with a smile that let me know he wasn't upset.

"Mostly," I admitted.

"I'll be fine," he said. "It's part of the job."

I opened my mouth to ask if Finn wanted to come over for dinner. I'd discovered, over the summer, that spending time with me was motivation enough for Finn to leave work on days he would've stayed too late. I had no doubt that he often left my house and went home to work more, but at least he was taking a break.

Before I could ask, the intercom on Finn's desk crackled and Margie's voice said, "Finn, someone is here to talk to you about the investigation."

As far as I knew, there was only one current investigation. It had to be about the murder.

"I'll be right out," Finn said to Margie.

He finished the coffee and threw the cup in the trash next to his desk. "Thanks for the coffee and stopping by." Despite his exhaustion, the look he gave me managed to arrow right through my body with a heat that could have rewarmed my cooling coffee.

"Anytime," I said, sounding a little breathless.

"I'll walk you out," Finn said.

Finn met me on the other side of the desk. He reached out and cupped my cheek, his thumb tracing my bottom lip. I held my breath. This was the moment. He was going to kiss me. No starlit night. No ending to a perfect date. Finn Butler was going to kiss me standing in the middle of his office with coffee breath and an open murder investigation. I couldn't have been happier.

The intercom crackled. "Finn?" Margie's voice said.

"I'll be right there," Finn barked.

That tone was so unlike him that silence weighed heavy on the other side of the intercom. His hand slid around the back of my neck.

"I'll forgive your tone because I know you're under a lot of pressure," Margie said, never sounding more like a disapproving mother. "There are now two people waiting to see you, and they're not exactly getting along." Her voice had dropped at the end like she was trying to prevent whoever was waiting for Finn from overhearing her.

Finn let out a long sigh and gave me a tight smile. "Let me walk you out," he said, his tone filled with regret.

I felt that regret deep in my bones.

Finn opened the door and placed his hand on the small of my back as I passed in front of him. The sound of arguing voices floated down the hall.

"Go home before you say something you'll regret," a woman said.

"*You* go home before *you* say something that *you'll* regret," another woman snapped back. "I know what I'm doing."

We reached the waiting room. Michelle, the hair stylist who worked at Lucille's, and Christine, the customer she'd been working on when Penny and I had first learned how awful Trevor was to his wife, were arguing next to Margie's desk.

"Oh good. Here's Finn," Margie said loudly, drawing the attention of both women.

They turned on Finn and me with determination, and both started talking at once.

Finn held up his hands and said, "Slow down. One at a time."

Michelle angled herself in front of Christine. "I'm here to confess to Trevor's murder. I killed him, and I need to pay for my crime."

My mouth dropped open, and my gaze cut to Margie, who looked as shocked as I felt.

Christine elbowed Michelle out of the way and said, "She's lying. I killed Trevor."

Finn's lips pressed into a thin line. If he was feeling shocked, he was doing a good job of hiding it. "You're confessing to killing Trevor?" he asked the two of them, his voice even.

"Yes," they both said at the same time before shooting each other dirty looks.

The door opened, and another woman walked in, looking timid. She clutched the strap of her brown leather purse. Glancing briefly at Michelle and Christine, she moved in on Finn. She cleared her throat and said, "Excuse me, but I need to confess to a crime?" The statement came out more like a question.

"No way," Michelle barked.

The new woman straightened her spine and apparently her resolve, because her voice rose as she said, "I killed Trevor Baker."

"What is happening?" I said to Finn out of the corner of my mouth.

He ignored me, focusing on the scene in front of us. "You all killed Trevor?" he asked. "Together?"

"No," Christine said, grabbing the new woman by the shoulder and pulling her back until she was in line with Christine and Michelle. "I did it. They're just trying to cover for me."

Michelle snorted her disbelief at Christine's statement.

The door opened again. This time two women walked in. One of them hesitated, almost stumbling, at the sight of the small gathering in the lobby, but she recovered. "I'm here to confess to the murder of Trevor Baker," she said confidently.

"Me too," the other woman said.

At this, Finn finally cracked. He rubbed his hand across his eyes before echoing my statement from earlier. "What is happening?" he asked no one in particular.

I looked at the five women, all watching Finn expectantly between shooting one another hostile, confused, or determined looks.

"It looks to me like you've solved the case," I said, knowing in my gut that this investigation just got a lot more complicated.

CHAPTER EIGHT

"Gwen," Finn said, staring at the women gathered in the lobby of the police station, each one of them saying they'd killed Trevor, "I'm going to have to call you later."

I completely understood. I was also a little disappointed. I was dying to know what Finn was going to do with all of this. The way I saw it, there were a few possibilities—none of them had done it and they were trying to cover up for someone else, one of them had done it and the others were covering up for her, or all of them had done it like some kind of weird murder pact.

Instead of explaining all of that, since Finn was likely thinking along the same lines anyway, I said, "I understand."

I wasn't sure how to exit. We'd been a breath away from kissing in Finn's office. If we were in a relationship, I'd probably give him a chaste peck on the cheek or a quick side hug. If we were just friends, I'd simply leave. We were somewhere in between, so in true Guinevere Nimue Stevens fashion, I waved awkwardly then left my hand up for a high five.

I regretted the move immediately, as evidenced by the way my face felt like the sun was sitting on it, but at this point, I'd committed. The only way out of this was for Finn to high five me back.

Everyone in the lobby watched as Finn looked at me in confusion, then finally raised his hand and blessed me with a high five. I needed to leave before my body spontaneously combusted from the embarrassment of it all.

"See you later, Margie," I said.

I wasn't sure whether or not to say goodbye to the murder suspects, who were staring at me like I was the weird one, when they were the ones who'd just allegedly killed a man and dressed him up like a scarecrow. I chose to give the group of a women a tight smile and said, "Good luck," as I walked by.

"I'll walk you out," Margie said, scrambling after me.

A moment later, we were outside. I took a deep breath of the chill fall air and fought the urge to glance over my shoulder to see if anyone was watching me.

"What was that all about?" Margie asked in wonder.

I groaned. "I know. I wasn't sure how to say goodbye to Finn, and then it was like my body had a mind of its own. I've never been more embarrassed."

"Not that," Margie said. "Although, that's the most embarrassing thing you've done? I've known you your whole life, Guinevere. That's not even remotely the most embarrassing thing you've ever done."

"Gee, thanks," I muttered.

"No, I was talking about every single one of Sandra Baker's friends coming in to confess to the murder of her husband," Margie said.

She glanced over her shoulder at the glass doors. I followed her gaze. Some of the women were seated. Finn was nowhere to be seen. He must have already taken at least one of the women back to be interviewed.

"I know a confession is a good thing in an investigation, but in this case, it just makes it more complicated. Especially since they didn't march in and agree that they'd done it together. It seems like this would just create a lot of reasonable doubt if it ever went to trial," I said.

"You're not wrong," Margie said ruefully. "And it's going to busy Finn up, making it hard to follow up on other leads. If every single one of those women in there is innocent, it will mean the real killer is walking around with no one looking at them until Finn can sort this out." She shook her head. "That boy needs help, and you're the one to do it."

I wanted to argue that if Finn wanted professional help, he could ask Tommy, Stan, or one of the other officers to run down leads while he sorted out the best-friend-murder-pact in there, but only because it felt like the right thing to say. Instead, I decided to be honest. "I was thinking the exact same thing."

Margie nodded, her expression grim. "Finn will be grateful for the help, even if he won't want to admit it," she said.

My mind was already putting together a plan to talk to Sandra. "Can you send me the recipe for that casserole you brought to the church potluck last month?" I asked.

"The one with the cornflakes on top?"

"That's the one," I confirmed.

"Of course I can send it to you," she said. "What're you thinking? Because I know you didn't suddenly get a hankering for a creamy potato and ham casserole…"

"I was thinking that taking a casserole to someone who just lost her husband is a really good way to be neighborly and have a chance at a conversation all at the same time," I said innocently.

Margie nodded enthusiastically. "I like the way you think."

At exactly five o'clock, I rang the doorbell at Sandra's house with my elbow while holding a hot casserole dish with my oven mitts that looked like ice cream cones. I had a canvas tote bag over my shoulder with a bagged salad and a package of cookies for the boys. I wasn't sure if Sandra was a drinker, but I'd included a bottle of wine in case she was.

Several moments later, I was still standing there, the heat from the casserole dish slowly making its way through my oven mitts. I wasn't going to be able to hold this forever. I knew I should have let it cool for a few minutes before I came over. I pressed the doorbell with my elbow again. I hadn't considered what I would do if Sandra wasn't home.

Just when I was considering going back home and digging into the casserole myself, the door opened. Sandra peered out before opening the door the rest of the way. Her dark-blonde hair hung limply around her face. Eyes bloodshot and puffy, it was clear she'd been crying. "Can I help you?" she asked.

"Hi, it's me, Gwen, from across the street?" I said as I jerked my head in the direction of my house, my only way of pointing with my hands full. Introducing myself might not have been necessary. Sandra knew who I was, even if we'd never done much more than wave at each other from across the street, but she seemed so vacant, I figured it couldn't hurt. "I wanted to bring you dinner, because of, you know, everything. Can I come in?"

Sandra's gaze flicked to the casserole in my hands before stepping back. "Sorry about the mess," she said.

I took that as my invitation inside. She turned and headed toward the back of the house. I followed, not seeing the mess she was referencing. The living room was cozy. A blue couch with two green velvet throw pillows sat on a colorful rug. Family pictures in gold frames covered the wall behind the couch. Two backpacks leaned against the side of the couch, and a pair of shoes that looked like they'd belonged to Trevor were under the coffee table.

The kitchen was similar in that tidy but lived-in way that I found comforting. I was a big believer that a house that was too clean ended up looking sterile, like it existed solely for social media content. If Sandra thought this was messy, she'd likely think my house was a disaster.

"I'm sorry for your loss," I said as I set the glass baking dish on the counter, where she'd moved a mug and dishtowel out of the way. I opened the canvas bag and took out the salad and tray of cookies. "I wasn't sure if you drank wine," I added as I took out the wine and set it next to everything else.

Sandra tucked her shoulder-length hair behind her ears. "Actually," she said, sounding a little more with-it, "I'd love some right now." She opened a cabinet next to her and took two juice glasses down. "Have a drink with me?"

"Are you sure?" I asked, even though this was the opportunity I'd been hoping for. "I don't want to impose." My compassion for what Sandra was going through warred with my desire to find out what happened to Trevor.

"It wouldn't be an imposition. The boys are at a Cub Scout party. It was already planned, and I want to try to keep their lives as normal as possible," she said as she went to work opening the wine. Her voice hitched on the last word, and she took in a shuddering breath before giving me a tight smile.

"How are the boys doing?" I asked in a hushed tone.

Sandra filled the small juice glasses and handed me one. She sat at the white farmhouse table, and I followed suit. "I'm not sure how they are," she said. "I'm not even sure it feels real to them. It doesn't to me, and I'm an adult."

Sandra didn't seem like a woman faking grief in order to cover up a murder, but I didn't know her well. It was best to not jump to conclusions out of sympathy for her situation.

"I know you were the one who found him," she said quietly as she stared into her wine like it held the answers for how her life had gotten so turned upside down.

"I'm so sorry," I said, not knowing what else to say.

"People didn't understand him," she continued. She looked up at me. "Trevor was always under a lot of stress. He worked so hard for us." She smiled, the action touched by sadness. "He would bring me flowers sometimes." She gestured at a bouquet on a sideboard under the window across the room. "He got me those the day before he died."

I recognized the bouquet as grocery store flowers. Camelot Flowers definitely hadn't made it. I didn't have anything against grocery store bouquets. I was a firm believer that it was the thought that counted with flowers, although with what I'd learned about Trevor in the past few days, I wondered how much thought he'd put into the gesture. Were the flowers an apology for yelling at her in the Piggly Wiggly? If so, was it done with sincerity or in an attempt to gloss over his bad behavior?

"Who didn't understand Trevor?" I asked. I had a feeling I knew the answer to that question, but I wanted to see where Sandra was going with this.

Sandra let out a deep sigh. "My friends," she said sadly. "They thought I should leave him."

"Had you ever considered it?" I asked carefully. I was treading on thin ice with a question this personal, but Sandra seemed willing to talk. I might not get a chance like this again.

"I dreamt about it," she said. "But that would have carried its own challenges. I couldn't imagine a life where I only got to see my boys half the time."

Trevor's death had solved that problem. I watched Sandra swirl the wine in her glass before taking another sip, wondering if she'd done the math and realized that murder was less risky than divorcing someone like Trevor. I had no doubt that he would have made her life difficult if she'd dared to leave him. I wondered if she knew her friends had confessed to killing her husband. Only one way to find out.

"You mentioned your friends didn't understand Trevor," I started. "Have you talked to them since Trevor died?"

Sandra sniffed and wiped her nose on her sleeve. "They came over last night, brought dinner for me and the boys. It was nice to have someone here after Detective Butler left. My parents live in Connecticut. They're coming but won't get here until tomorrow."

I nodded. She didn't seem to know about the mass confession. "Did they say anything about Trevor's death?" I asked, once again dancing around the real question in hopes that she'd fill in the blanks for me.

"No," she said wistfully. "I half expected them to come over and be happy that he was dead." She met my gaze. "As I mentioned, they weren't his biggest fans, but they were just really supportive last night."

The more she talked, the more convinced I became that she had no idea her friends had confessed to killing her husband.

"I saw your friends at the police station today," I said. I really should just come out with it, like ripping off a Band-Aid, but I found myself having a hard time being that blunt. She looked so fragile.

"What were they doing there?" she asked in confusion.

"Uh..." I hesitated until an awkward silence filled the kitchen. "They were confessing to killing Trevor," I finally said.

"What?" she yelped. It was the most animated I'd seen her since I'd walked in. "There's no way." She pushed back from the table and paced the room. Running her fingers through her hair, she turned to me and added, "None of my friends killed Trevor. They wouldn't. They didn't like him, but they wouldn't do this to me."

I wanted to suggest that they might if they thought it was going to eventually be easier for her to live without the abuse, but she was already so upset. I didn't want to make it worse. "Why would they confess if they didn't do it?" I asked.

"I have no idea," Sandra said, still sounding upset. She put her hand up to her neck as she stared out the window. "It doesn't make any sense," she murmured.

This led me back to my theories from before. Either Sandra's friends thought Sandra killed Trevor and were trying to create reasonable doubt by muddying the suspect pool, or they thought one of them had finally done it and were confessing to cover for that person.

"Is there someone else who would have wanted Trevor dead?" I asked.

Sandra turned, her eyes flashing with anger. "I know exactly who did it."

My heartrate kicked up a notch, and I sat up a little straighter. Was it really going to be this easy? "Who did it?" I asked.

"Trevor's business partner, Cole. He accused Trevor of embezzling two hundred thousand dollars from their company," Sandra said, her tone shrill. "Look around." She spread her arms out and gestured around the room. "Does it look like we're living with an extra two hundred thousand dollars?"

She picked up a jar of generic peanut butter and showed it to me like it was proof of her point. "It's why Trevor wanted to move. He couldn't work with Cole anymore. Not after he'd accused Trevor of such a horrible thing."

Maybe Trevor wanted to move because he *had* stolen the money and wanted to get far away from Star Junction before spending it. I'd have to find a way to talk to Cole. Asking someone that I knew personally about a murder was complicated, because it meant suggesting they'd killed someone, but I realized now that talking to someone I didn't know at all held its own complications.

"Did you tell Finn, I mean Detective Butler, about your theory?" I asked.

Sandra nodded as she sat back at the table. "I told him. He said he'd look into it."

"How would killing Trevor help Cole get his money back?" I asked.

"Trevor didn't steal any money," Sandra said defiantly.

Defiant seemed better than the vacant look she'd had when I arrived. "We know that Trevor didn't steal any money," I said placatingly.

Trevor was a world-class jerk. I wouldn't put it past him to steal from his business partner. It was exactly the kind of thing an entitled person would do. "But if we work under the assumption that his partner believes Trevor did it, then how would killing Trevor benefit anyone?" I asked.

Sandra looked like she was considering my question instead of dismissing it as irrelevant. "Revenge?" she finally suggested.

Revenge could be a powerful motivation. For argument's sake, Trevor's partner might not have had any solid proof that

Trevor was the reason money was missing. Without proof, there would be no way to get the police involved or get his money back. Killing Trevor out of revenge seemed to fit the violent nature of the crime. Not to mention leaving Trevor's body in the fall display with that note.

"Where was Trevor the night he was killed?" I asked. "Was he home that night? If he didn't come home, was that strange? Did you call the police and report him missing?" Finn would have mentioned if finding Trevor's body had solved a missing person situation.

Sandra's eyes narrowed. "What are you implying?" she asked suspiciously.

I was taken aback by her tone. "I'm not implying anything," I said. "I'm just trying to make sense of the timeline."

Sandra stood stiffly. "Thank you for the casserole. It will be nice to have something to feed the boys tonight. I'm getting tired," she said pointedly.

I was clearly being dismissed. I stood too. "I'm sorry for upsetting you. I was just trying to figure out if Trevor's partner would have seen him the night he died."

Sandra herded me toward the door. "The police will figure that out," she said.

We reached the front door, and she opened it, shooing me forward. I wasn't just being dismissed. I was being kicked out.

"Reheat the casserole at 350 for twenty minutes," I said as she closed the door in my face.

I stood there for a moment like I was having a staring contest with the peephole. Finally, I turned and headed back to my house. Sandra had been all over the place—sad, numb, angry, in disbelief. I knew that grief was a tricky road, but could her emotional swings be due to her own guilt?

If my imaginary husband hadn't come home, I would've been calling the hospital, my friends, and then the police. If Sandra did none of those things, did it mean Trevor was home and she'd killed him in their own backyard?

I stepped inside my house, realizing that I'd left my oven mitts at Sandra's. There was no way I going back over there to ask for them back. Not after she'd just kicked me out. Better to give her some time to cool off. Besides, it would give me an excuse to talk to her again.

I grabbed a journal from a basket of books and magazines I kept by my couch and sat. Pulling the pen from the spiral binding on the journal, I opened to a blank page and started yet another mini murder board.

Trevor's name went in the middle with a circle around it. I drew a line off the circle and added *Sandra, motive=abuse*. Then I wrote *Sandra's friends* and *Trevor's business partner*. Under all of that, I wrote *Find out where Trevor was the night he was killed. Talk to Trevor's partner. Find out what happened with Finn's interviews with the friends.*

I pulled in a deep breath and looked over my to-do list. I wasn't sure how to find out where Trevor had been that night without help from Sandra. What I could do was talk to Trevor's partner. I just needed to figure out how.

CHAPTER NINE

"I know exactly how you can do it," Penny said later that evening in answer to my question about what excuse I could use to talk to Trevor's business partner. She took a chocolate chip cookie off of the small white plate balancing on her pregnant belly.

I'd texted her after my interaction with Sandra. I'd thrown in the promise of treats as an incentive since she was often so tired after a long school day that she went to bed before I'd even eaten dinner.

"Am I going to like this plan?" I asked skeptically.

"Who asked whom for help here?" Penny said before demolishing the cookie in her hand.

"Fair enough," I admitted. "What's your plan?"

"Trevor and his partner own a financial planning business, right?" Penny asked.

I nodded and tried to take a cookie off her plate, but she swatted my hand away.

"Just make an appointment to meet with him about retirement planning," Penny said, as if it was the most obvious idea in the world.

The more I thought about it, the more I realized it should've occurred to me. "I probably should start saving for retirement," I said. "I won't have a pension or a 401(k) to rely on."

"See?" Penny said, gesturing with another cookie. "It's a win-win. Start saving for your future while catching a killer."

I wrinkled my nose in doubt. "Do I really want a murderer setting up my retirement account? How's he going to manage that from prison?"

"That's assuming he's guilty," Penny said. "I still think it was the friends."

I'd told her about Sandra's friends arriving at the police station to confess to Trevor's murder. "But they're all saying they did it alone," I said. "They looked upset when the others were confessing."

"It's a genius plan," Penny said with something that sounded like awe, although we were talking about potential killers. "Everyone confesses to killing Trevor alone. No one backs down. There's too much reasonable doubt, and they all go free."

If Penny was onto something, it was a diabolical plan either hatched in the heat of the moment after they'd accidentally killed Trevor or planned in advance, which made it even more sinister.

A loud cackle filled the air, and I flinched. Penny almost dropped the last cookie on her plate.

"What was that?" she shrieked.

I put my hand over my racing heart. "That was my neighbor's newest Halloween decoration. It's a motion-activated witch that cackles every time someone walks by," I said in disgust.

"How did we hear it all the way in your house?" Penny asked in horror. "It sounded like it was coming from right behind me."

I pointed to the window I'd cracked open before Penny's arrival. It was next to the fireplace and faced my neighbor's house. "I'm trying to get as much fresh air as possible before winter sets in."

Penny shook her head, her eyes as wide as saucers. "You might have to keep that window closed until after Halloween. Can you imagine that thing going off in the middle of the night?"

I pictured myself getting up in the middle of the night, unable to sleep. I'd walk down the stairs to get a nice cup of tea, only to die of a heart attack when a squirrel set off the evil witch next door.

"I'm definitely going to have to keep that window closed," I said with dismay.

"Or find a way to get rid of the witch," Penny said.

"Sounds like you're suggesting I steal the witch," I said.

"I'm just saying that Finn and the other officers are busy solving a murder," Penny said mischievously. "I'm guessing a missing Halloween decoration isn't going to be high on their list of priorities."

I snorted out a laugh. "Thanks for the advice. I think I'll stick with closing this window. Halloween will be over before we know it."

"It's creepy though, right?" Penny said.

My shoulders were tense, waiting for a passing bird or pedestrian to set off the witch's cackle again. "That witch is definitely creepy."

"No," Penny said dramatically. "The way the murderer dressed Trevor up like a scarecrow." She shuddered. "That means that whoever killed him had to stuff his dead body into that costume."

I should have been ready for Penny's abrupt change of subject. "Definitely creepy. I'm trying not to think about that part," I said.

Penny gasped and said, "What if it's meant to be creepy? What if there's a serial killer in town?"

"Stop," I said, laughing uncomfortably. "There's not a serial killer."

"Halloween is coming," Penny said ominously.

"What's that supposed to mean?"

"It means people doing creepy, evil things," she said just as the witch let out another cackle.

"That's it," I said as I stood and closed the window. I locked it and gave it a little tug for good measure. It wasn't like the witch was going to come to life and climb through my window in the middle of the night, but Penny's talk of serial killers was getting to me. "There is no serial killer. Trevor was a jerk, and someone with a motive besides being a sociopath killed him."

Penny brushed crumbs off her belly before standing with an *oof*. She rubbed her back and said, "Fine, I'll stop talking about serial killers if you make an appointment with Trevor's business partner."

I was going to do that anyway, so it was an easy request to fulfill. Checking online, I discovered that I could make an appointment on their website. There was an opening at three the next day, and I took it.

"Happy?" I asked Penny.

"I can't wait to hear what he has to say about Trevor. If Trevor really did steal from the business and then was planning on skipping town, it would be a solid motive for murder," she said.

"Plus, it fits with the note that accused Trevor of being a cheat," I added.

"I'm going to head home," Penny said after yawning. "Keep me posted about what you find out."

"I will," I said. "Thanks for coming over."

"Thanks for the cookies," Penny said with a comical eyebrow wiggle.

"I'll walk you out." I set the plate Penny had handed me on the side table next to the couch.

"Do we need to worry about the witch?" Penny asked as we put on our coats.

"Thankfully, it seems to take something passing directly in front of it to go off," I said.

I'd been right to open my window earlier. It was one of those perfect fall days. The air was crisp, and a faint smell of smoke drifted through the air. The sun had nearly set. Stars twinkled in the purple, twilight sky.

I waved to Rose, Chip's wife, who was raking leaves in their front yard, as Penny got into her car, made me promise one more time to let her know how my meeting with Trevor went, and drove away.

Despite the setting sun, it was too nice to go back inside. I was very cognizant of the fact that at any moment, winter might decide to show up and trap me indoors unless I wanted to bundle up and look like the abominable snowman. I crossed the street to say hello to Rose.

"Beautiful evening, isn't it?" Rose asked as she leaned on the handle of the rake. Rose's hair was a red that could only be achieved through a bottle or an appointment at Lucille's Clip and Curl, but it suited her pale complexion, complete with freckles. I could imagine she'd been a natural redhead but decided to take it up a notch to the deep-maroon color it was now.

"It really is," I said.

Midwest rule number thirty-two: the weather changed so often, sometimes multiple times a day, that it was almost rude to not talk about it.

"How're you holding up?" she asked me.

I gave her a quizzical look.

"I heard you found Trevor's body," she explained.

Word traveled fast in a small town. "I did," I said. "I'm doing okay." I wanted to add that this wasn't the first time, but I didn't think I needed to remind people how many dead bodies I'd seen.

Rose looked over at Trevor and Sandra's house and said, "I can't believe she finally snapped. I didn't think she had it in her."

"You really think Sandra killed Trevor?" I asked skeptically, although I'd wondered the same thing.

"Her decision to dress him up and put him in front of city hall for the whole town to see was a piece of poetic justice," she said as if I hadn't just expressed my doubts about Sandra's guilt. "Trevor deserved it for all the times he humiliated her in public. I would've done the same thing."

I'd dealt with people like Rose before. Sometimes you had to fight fire with fire, which in this case meant fighting a case of the gossips with more gossip. "You really think Sandra killed Trevor?" I asked again, but this time I dropped my voice to a hushed whisper.

It was like chumming the water for sharks. Rose's gaze snapped away from Sandra's house to meet mine, her eyes twinkling. "Chip and I would hear them fight," she said, matching my tone. "He wasn't just awful to her in public. I don't care how sweet and mild someone seems. You can only be pushed so far until you snap."

"Here's a question," I said excitedly to keep Rose feeding me her theories. "Would Sandra have been strong enough to kill him, dress him up as a scarecrow, and then set up his body at city hall?"

"Hmmm," Rose said thoughtfully as she stared into the distance. "She must have had help."

"Help?" I asked, keeping my question simple in hopes she'd keep talking.

"Her friends come over for a girls' night once a month, usually when Trevor was out for some reason or another. A month ago, they were having drinks in their backyard, and I heard them telling Sandra that she should leave Trevor, that she deserved better." Rose snapped her fingers. "That must be it.

Sandra had had enough and killed Trevor. In a panic, she called her friends to help her hide the body. Instead, they decide to humiliate him." Rose looked rather pleased with her theory.

"Seems like it would be easier to get away with it if no one ever found him," I said.

Rose's eyes narrowed and her hands tightened around the rake handle like she was strangling the life out of it. "Some people don't deserve to go quietly," she said with venom in her tone.

I took a small step back, reminding myself to never get on Rose's bad side.

She seemed to snap out of it, because she gave me a sunny smile. "I'm sure that nice detective of yours will figure out that Sandra did it," she said cheerfully.

The witch across the street cackled, and I jumped. "I hate that thing," I said passionately. I couldn't even see what had set it off. Probably a leaf falling off the tree in the front yard of the house.

Rose curled her upper lip before starting to rake again. "Kevin put it up yesterday. He was so excited about it. Said he got it at Henry's Hardware." She raked red maple leaves into a pile.

"I wonder if I can convince him to turn off the motion activation," I said.

"Good luck with that," Rose said with a chuckle.

I said goodbye to Rose and headed back inside. Pulling out my journal, I reluctantly added Penny's theory about a serial killer, although we couldn't know if that was true unless more bodies showed up. I was going to look at the Halloween displays in town a little differently from now on. If there really was some kind of demented serial killer, any one of the cute displays could end up with a real body displayed in it.

I also added Rose's theory that Sandra's friends had helped her stage the body. It was the only way I could wrap my mind around Sandra being guilty. If she was guilty, she'd had help. Her friends were the obvious choice, but really, anyone who hated Trevor or felt sorry for Sandra could've been an accomplice.

I'd need to find out what Finn was willing to share with me about his interviews with Sandra's friends. Based on that, I could decide if I needed to talk to any of them. If they were innocent, getting Sandra's friends to admit that they had nothing to do with Trevor's death would at least get them out of the suspect pool.

The problem with a jerk like Trevor was that there were too many people who wanted him dead. Sandra, her friends, Trevor's business partner, Cole. Heck, even Chip had an ongoing feud with Trevor. I added Chip's name to the list. I couldn't imagine someone committing murder over a yard dispute, but one of the things I'd learned over the last year was that you could never predict what might make someone snap.

CHAPTER TEN

The next afternoon, I parked in front of the strip mall at the edge of town. This wasn't the charming downtown of Star Junction, with buildings from the eighteen hundreds boasting their false fronts and brick facades. The strip mall had been built in the eighties to house a Blockbuster, which was obviously no longer there, a dry cleaners, a tax accountant, and apparently Baker and Johnson Investments.

No one was seated at the receptionist desk when I walked in. "Hello?" I called out.

"I'll be right with you," a man called from the office to my left. "Go ahead and have a seat."

I did as instructed, picking up a copy of *Money* magazine and leafing through it. I landed on an article entitled *Did You Miss the Boat? Starting Retirement Savings in Your Thirties*. I snapped the magazine closed. I was going to turn thirty in two months. I didn't need an article shaming me for my lack of a robust portfolio.

I sat up a little straighter in my chair, feigning a confidence I wasn't feeling. I'd come to find out if Cole Johnson was a murderer, but there was no harm in finding out how to save for retirement at the same time. It was called multitasking.

A man walked out of the office in a dark suit with a blue tie. I'd put his age somewhere in his fifties. He had a full head of graying hair that looked like it was once jet black. His face was covered in acne scars, giving it a pockmarked look. He looked somewhat familiar to me, but I couldn't place him. Maybe he attended the Methodist church. Maybe we did our grocery shopping around the same time every week. It was hard to say in a small town. He smiled and said, "Ms. Stevens?"

"That's me," I said, standing.

"I'm Cole Johnson," he said, extending his hand.

My dad always said you could tell a lot about a man by his handshake. Cole's was firm without being aggressive. My dad would have liked him.

"Call me Gwen," I said as I shook his hand.

"Come on in, Gwen." Cole gestured that I should lead the way into his office. "I know your father from the LARPing circuit."

Live Action Role Playing, or LARPing as the participants called it, was my father's fourth love after my mom, me, and Camelot Flowers, although sometimes I wondered if it was in a constant battle for the third place slot. I studied Cole more closely. That's where I knew him from. "Are you usually a court jester?" I asked.

Although he was seated, Cole put his arms up to the side and did a little head wiggle dance move. "I've been the court jester of various local ren faires for twenty years running," he said proudly.

I gave him a wide smile, immediately feeling more at ease. My dad had been taking me to Renaissance faires and other medieval reenactment events since before I could walk. My memories of those events were filled with joy and excitement. Who didn't love being surrounded by princesses, knights in shining armor, and funnel cake? We'd gone to one when I was ten that had a mermaid show. I'd been in seventh heaven.

"It's nice to officially meet you," I said sincerely.

"What can I help you with today?" he asked.

Knowing that Cole knew my dad and was a fellow LARPer made this much less awkward than approaching a total stranger. "I need help with two things," I said confidently.

Cole picked up a pen and waited for me to continue.

"With being a small business owner, I don't have the help of a larger company or state job to save for retirement, and I'm embarrassed to say I've done nothing to start that process," I said.

Cole gave me a fatherly smile. "It's never too late to start. How old are you, if you don't mind me asking?"

"I'll turn thirty a few days before Christmas," I said. "On the twenty-second."

Cole jotted down something on the legal pad in front of him. "I know a lot of people who don't start thinking about retirement until they're in their forties." He shook his head as if feeling sorry for those individuals. "You're doing just fine."

Ha! Take that *Money* magazine article.

"And the second thing?" Cole asked.

"I also wanted to talk to you about Trevor Baker," I said. "He was my neighbor, and I'm feeling so bad for his wife, Sandra. I'm trying to do whatever I can to help her out including, figuring out what happened to him." I didn't add the fact that if Sandra killed Trevor, then she knew exactly what had happened to him.

Cole's expression shuttered. "I'm happy to help you explore your retirement options, but I won't talk about Trevor. Now, you have a few options for retirement savings," he started.

"I don't want to poke my nose in where it doesn't belong," I said, cutting him off. Speaking of noses, if I were Pinocchio, mine would have grown six inches. I was exactly sticking my nose where it didn't belong. "I'm just trying to figure out where Trevor might have been the night he died."

"Why would I know that?" Cole said. "We worked together, but we didn't socialize." His tone had turned bitter.

"Had the two of you worked together for long?" I asked.

Cole looked down at the brochure he was holding about IRAs and said, "We opened the business together ten years ago. I'd been working for an investment firm in Abbottsville and wanted a job that would allow me to stay in Star Junction. The commute there and back every day was a lot for my family."

Abbottsville was forty-five minutes north on the highway. Many residents of Star Junction found work there that paid better than the jobs they could find in our small town. It was also where we went to go to the mall or to see movies if we didn't want to watch whatever the single-screen theater in Rose Lake was showing.

"You've worked together for a long time," I said.

Cole met my gaze. "Are you really here to talk about retirement planning?" He didn't sound angry, almost resigned instead.

"I am," I said sincerely. "*And* I want to talk about Trevor."

Cole nodded, looking thoughtful. "I saw your dad over the summer at the ren faire the next county over, and he mentioned that you'd helped the police solve a couple of murders in town. I couldn't believe it. I couldn't picture the Guinevere that

I knew from the circuit with blonde pigtails and a pink princess dress investigating a murder. I guess he was telling the truth."

"I don't try to get involved. It just kind of happens," I said with a shrug.

Cole rubbed his eyes with his hand. "I'm sorry for Sandra and her boys, but the business is better off without Trevor," he said.

"Better off how?" I asked.

"I can't go into details," he said. "All I can tell you is that I never knew where Trevor was when he wasn't at the office, and he wasn't here that often."

That caught my attention. "What do you mean, he wasn't at the office that often?" I asked.

"Trevor was the kind of guy who thought he was entitled to success and money without having to work hard for it. He relied on his good looks and charm, but there was nothing underneath it to back it up. After the first couple of years, the business was doing well and he just kind of checked out," Cole explained.

"Where was he when he wasn't here?" I asked.

Cole shrugged. "I have no idea. We fought about it, but nothing improved. I tried to buy him out of the business multiple times, but he was making residual income off of his clients' investments, even though I was often the one catching mistakes Trevor had made or filing necessary paperwork so that his clients didn't suffer."

He hadn't said anything about the embezzlement claims. I couldn't imagine why Sandra would make that up unless her goal was to give Cole a motive to murder Trevor to distract the investigation from the real killer. I had to find a way to check the validity of what Sandra had told me. Cole was being pretty forthcoming now that he'd started talking, but I sensed he might shut down with one wrong question.

"He was unreliable at work," I said as if I was processing the information. "Was that all there was to it?"

"What do you mean?" Cole asked with a hint of suspicion.

"I mean, someone who tries to skate through life on their good looks is someone who might resort to doing something illegal to get ahead," I said carefully.

Cole stared at me blankly. I stared back. It was like we were playing a game of information-chicken. Who was going to swerve first? It was me. I was definitely going to swerve first, and I knew no better way to swerve than to tell him the truth.

I deflated against the back of the chair. "Sandra told me that you'd accused Trevor of embezzling from the company."

Cole's expression remained impassive. "I think we should make another appointment to talk about your financial future when all this mess with Trevor is cleared up," he said tersely.

"So, it's not true?" I asked, still fishing.

Cole stood. "It was nice to officially meet you. I'll have my assistant contact you to reschedule."

I knew in that moment that I could pepper him with questions all I wanted. He wasn't going to give me more information. I stood too. "Thanks for meeting with me. I really would like to set up something for retirement."

He gave me a tight smile. "I look forward to that."

As he walked me to the front door and said goodbye, I wondered if he really did look forward to meeting again or if I'd need to find a different financial planner. I didn't like the idea of burning bridges, but I'd needed to know the truth.

I unlocked my car and got behind the wheel. My journal was in my purse. I pulled it out and added the fact that Cole had neither confirmed nor denied that Trevor was stealing from their company. As far as I was concerned, that was as good as a confirmation.

If Sandra had been lying, Cole would have been quick to deny it or at least have looked confused when I brought it up. He'd been stone-faced and ushered me right out of there. Something was definitely going on at Baker and Johnson Investments, something that gave Cole a reason to want Trevor dead.

I shot off a quick text to Penny, letting her know what I'd learned. She'd be out of school soon, so I had no doubt that I'd hear back from her before too long. I'd head to Camelot Flowers before going home. I'd left a few projects unfinished, and although my mom had said she would get to them tomorrow, I'd been spending too much time on my computer the last couple of days and not enough time with my hands on the flowers. I missed it.

My phone buzzed, but it wasn't a reply from Penny. It was from Chris. *Want to meet for dinner tonight?*

I missed the flowers, and the truth was, I missed Chris too. I texted back. *I'd love to. Tell me where and when.*

I'll pick you up, he texted back. *I don't have a lot of time because I'm meeting a potential donor for the center for a late drink tonight. How about five?*

Chris picking me up was a new thing in our friendship. Mostly because he was trying to show me that he was serious about wanting a relationship with me. What wasn't new was his commitment to opening a youth center in Star Junction to give teens a safe place to go after school.

We'd called it "the center" from long before Chris bought and started renovating the old building on Lincoln. He'd recently decided to name it The Hanger. He'd decorated it with a vintage airplane theme. The name combined his love of classic airplanes and played off the idea that teens would come there to hang out.

Dinner at five sounds great, I texted back. *I can meet you somewhere so that you can go right to your meeting after dinner. Bucky's?*

I chuckled as I sent the text, knowing that Chris thought Bucky's was a grease trap. It was a grease trap, but it was *our* grease-trap. I had a lot of happy memories at Bucky's over the years. Part dive bar, part family restaurant, the earlier you went in the day, the more restaurant vibe you got.

The little bubbles popped up, letting me know that Chris was writing back. They went away then came back multiple times before disappearing again. I put my car in Drive and started toward Camelot Flowers. It would only take me five minutes to get there. I'd known Chris long enough to know that he was agonizing over wanting the convenience of being able to head to his meeting without dropping me off first versus the way picking me up would turn our dinner into a real date. I'd give him time to work it out while I lost myself in putting together some beautiful bouquets.

CHAPTER ELEVEN

At four thirty, Chris finally texted me back, agreeing to meet at Bucky's. I was excited to hear about who this new investor was. I was also hoping to talk through what I'd learned about Trevor's murder, which to this point was sadly little.

I changed out of my Camelot Flowers sweatshirt into a cute blue sweater and touched up my makeup.

The parking lot was surprisingly full for a Wednesday night. Chris's white Dodge Charger was parked a few spots away from the door. I found a parking spot near the back and made my way inside.

Country music was playing on the jukebox. Chris was leaning against the bar, talking to the owner of Bucky's, Andy Fox. Andy's gray hair was a fraction of an inch longer than his usual military flat top, which meant he was probably due for a haircut. He was meticulous about maintaining that haircut. Chris had been watching the door. His eyes lit up as I entered, and my stomach gave a little flip.

Penny's campaign to help me get over Chris last year had started a week before he'd decided he *did* want to be more than friends. Unfortunately, by that point, I'd decided I might want to be more than friends with Finn. Chris's boyish grin still tugged at my heart, but it was nothing compared to the reaction I had to Finn.

"Gwen," Chris said as he approached, "you look beautiful." He leaned in and gave me a peck on my cheek.

"You don't look too bad yourself," I said sincerely. He was wearing a white button-down shirt and dark jeans, which meant he was more dressed up than many of the other men in Bucky's that night, especially the ones who'd come right from working their blue collar jobs.

"My meeting with the investor got pushed back to eight, so we have some extra time," Chris said.

"That's great," I said with a beaming smile.

Our roles may have flip flopped from me being hopelessly in love with a clueless Chris to him being the one pushing for a relationship, but Chris was still one of the most important people in my life. I loved him, and nothing was going to change that. Not even a police detective who had my whole body lighting up like a Jack o' Lantern.

"Do you want to order a drink first?" Chris asked. "I wasn't expecting it to be busy this early."

Most of the tables were full, even the booths toward the back.

"Andy says it'll clear out soon. Apparently, there's a band and choir concert happening at the middle school tonight, which caused this early rush," Chris explained.

"A drink would be great," I said as I followed Chris to the bar.

We grabbed two seats near the end, close to the jukebox that was now playing "Jailhouse Rock." A boy who looked to be about ten was walking back to his parents' table with a broad smile on his face. I'd always been so excited when my dad had slipped me money for the jukebox. It was heady power when you were a kid to be able to pick the song that a whole roomful of adults had to listen to.

Chris waved to Andy, who gave him a nod of acknowledgment but continued working on a large tray of drinks he was putting together.

"So, who's this new investor?" I asked.

Chris rested his arm on the backrest of my barstool. "First, I want to know how you're doing," he said. "I haven't seen you since you found Trevor Baker's body."

I pursed my lips in thought, wanting to give Chris an honest answer. "I'm doing okay. I haven't had any nightmares this time. I don't know if that's a good sign or a very bad one."

"How could a lack of nightmares be bad?" Chris asked.

"I don't want to get desensitized to this. What kind of person would that make me?" I asked, voicing the fear that had been floating around my subconscious the last couple of days.

"I think it makes you a normal person," Chris said. "Let me ask you this. What did you think when you found him?"

I didn't understand the purpose of Chris's question, but I answered anyway. "I was horrified. I'm pretty sure I babbled like an idiot. I seem to remember telling Finn, Tommy, and Debra from city hall that the scarecrow costume was filled with dead body instead of straw."

Chris chuckled softly. "See? A totally normal reaction from you. Remember that time we spent the day water skiing and tubing on Star Lake our senior year? You fell off the tube and lost your swimsuit bottoms. You babbled on and on about a fish wearing your hot pink bikini bottoms and how it wasn't fair because you'd just gotten them. You're not becoming desensitized. Be glad you're not having nightmares," he said.

I shot him a sideways glance as my cheeks flamed with heat at the memory. "I'd rather not remember that day at the lake, thank you very much. At least the lake water was dark enough that no one really saw anything and Sophia had an extra swimsuit bottom I could borrow."

"You were adorable that day. I love it when you babble. The most interesting things come out of your mouth," he teased.

"How come you can remember that horrible day, but you can't remember my birthday," I teased back.

Chris put his hand to his chest and pretended to be offended. Too bad his smile gave him away. "I forgot your birthday one time," he said insistently. "When we were twenty, by the way. I was going through my selfish stage."

I feigned an innocent look as I said, "Oh, I didn't know we'd finished that stage."

"That's it," Chris said. He tickled my ribs, which had been his go-to move anytime I'd gotten sassy with him since we were kids.

I giggled before I managed to grab his hand and twist it backward at the wrist.

"Ow," Chris complained. I released his wrist, and he rubbed it. "Where'd you learn a move like that?" he asked, playing up his role as the victim in this situation.

I faced the bar and imperiously said, "I have a right to defend myself." I couldn't hold the self-righteous expression for long before I broke into a smile. "I learned it watching the Jennifer Lopez movie *Enough*. My mom and dad watched it, and she used it as the reason she thinks Sandra killed Trevor. It put me in the mood to watch it. I hadn't seen in it forever. It's a good thing I did. I was able to defend myself against your attack."

Andy approached before Chris could respond, but his sly, sexy grin let me know this banter wasn't over. I'd forgotten how fun it was to flirt with Chris.

"What can I get you two?" Andy asked as he dried his hands on a white bar towel.

Chris gestured for me to go first. One of the joys of my life was to order ridiculous drinks from the bartender at the bowling alley, Ten Pins Down. I'd order something fancy that he considered too "big city" for Star Junction, and he'd bring me a beer. I didn't have that kind of game going with Andy. "I'll have a Coors Light," I said.

"Same for me," Chris said.

Andy poured the pints with a practiced hand. "I heard about Trevor Barker," he said as he set one full glass aside and started on the other.

"He was my neighbor," I responded.

Andy nodded as he slid the beers in front of us.

"Gwen is leaving out that she found his body," Chris said pointedly.

"Accidentally," I said, as if he didn't need to be making a big deal about it.

"Some of the officers were in here last night," Andy said as he leaned against the bar. "They mentioned you'd been the one to find the body *again*," he added. "Their emphasis, not mine."

I threw my hands up helplessly. "It's not like I'm *trying* to find dead bodies," I said.

Andy wiped up a wet spot on the bar. "Trevor was in here the night he died," he said casually.

I nearly choked on the sip of beer I'd taken. "He was?" I said through coughs as Chris patted my back. "His wife wouldn't tell me where he was that night."

Chris had stopped hitting my back, but his hand rubbed lazy circles that had my body tingling. "I'm okay now," I said quietly, not sure if I wanted him to stop.

"I know," he said lightly, his attention focused on Andy but his hand continuing to move along my back.

I tried to hide my smile but was failing miserably. Andy seemed oblivious to all of it.

"I remembered because I had to kick him out," Andy said.

I sat forward, causing Chris's hand to drop away. "You had to kick him out?" I asked in shock. "Why?"

Someone at the end of the bar called out to Andy. He glanced in that direction and held up a finger to indicate the man would have to wait a minute. "He started a fight with another customer. I'd have a talk with them, but every time I'd walk away, Trevor would start going at the guy again," Andy explained. "After the third time, I told both of them that they needed to leave."

"Trevor got into a fight that night?" Chris asked.

"Not a fistfight. Just jawing at the guy about his tattoos and then his biker jacket," Andy said. He shook his head. "It was like Trevor was asking to get beat up. The other guy must have had a good six inches on Trevor and another fifty pounds of muscle, but when Trevor gets drinking, he gets stupid. It's not the first time I've had to kick him out."

"Do the police know?" I asked. This was a good lead. The timing was too coincidental. Trevor picks on a guy bigger than him and then winds up dead that very night? Maybe everyone on my mini murder board was off the hook. Although, I wasn't sure a random biker would go through all the trouble of dressing Trevor up and posing him in front of city hall. And what about the note in his overalls?

"You guys talking about Trevor?" the man sitting next to Chris asked, interrupting my thoughts. The man had a bushy beard and a friendly smile. "Sorry, I didn't mean to eavesdrop, but I couldn't help overhearing."

"You know anything about it?" Chris asked.

Andy took the opportunity to walk to the other end of the bar to help the guy who'd hailed him down without answering my question about whether or not the police knew Trevor had been picking a fight the night he died.

The man extended his hand. "Greg Collins. I work at the foundry over in Rose Lake."

"Chris," Chris said as he shook the man's hand. "This is Gwen."

I reached past Chris and shook the man's hand, which was rough with callouses. "Nice to meet you," I said.

Greg leaned his elbow on the bar. "You work down at that flower shop on Main Street," he said to me.

I nodded. "Camelot Flowers. My family owns it."

"I've gotten birthday flowers for my wife from there. Nice place," he said.

"Thanks," I said warmly. "Did you know Trevor?"

"I was here that night he got into a fight and then got himself killed," the man said before taking a long pull off his beer. "I was coming in right when they were leaving."

"Do you think the guy he was fighting with killed him?" I asked with maybe a little too much excitement. I forced myself to calm down, when all I wanted to do was bounce in my seat. This felt like a break in the case.

Greg considered my question before saying, "I heard Andy say they weren't physically fighting in here, but that's not what happened in the parking lot. As soon as they were out the door, Trevor took a swing at the other guy."

"What happened?" I asked.

Greg snorted out a derisive laugh. "Trevor was so drunk, the other guy only had to lean out of the way and Trevor fell flat on his face," he said.

"That's it?" I asked in disappointment.

Greg scoffed. "The other guy started to walk away, but Trevor wouldn't let it go. He scrambled to his feet and tried to jump on the guy's back."

At this point, Andy was back, listening intently with the bar towel draped over his shoulder. A couple of other people at the bar were clearly listening as well.

"You're kidding me," Chris said.

"The guy shook Trevor off like he was an annoying mosquito," Greg said. As he'd amassed listeners, he'd grown more animated in his storytelling. "Then he said, 'Leave it, man. It's not worth it.'"

"Let me guess," the man sitting on the other side of Greg said. "He didn't leave it. I was here that night too, but I was inside when Trevor started throwing insults at the guy. That guy was just minding his own business drinking a beer."

"Nope," Greg said. "Trevor took one last swing. The guy blocked the punch and then hit Trevor hard enough in the stomach to knock the wind out of him."

"And what were you doing while all of this was going on?" Andy asked with a glint in his eye that told me he had a guess as to exactly what Greg had been doing.

"I was enjoying the show," Greg said with a mischievous grin.

The man next to Greg let out a booming laugh and slapped Greg on the shoulder. "That's what I would have done, man. Free entertainment."

Andy shook his head before walking away to help someone, but he was grinning like an indulgent parent who knows they shouldn't think their child's bad behavior is funny but can't help themselves.

"And that's it?" I asked. "The other guy drove away?"

"Not before issuing one more warning," Greg said animatedly. "He said, 'If you try that again, it'll be the last thing you do.'"

Chris let out a low whistle.

The guy on the other side of Greg said, "Trevor picked on the wrong guy."

Doubt niggled at me. I couldn't tell if Greg was telling the story as it happened or if he was embellishing for the sake of the crowd. Was he the kind of guy who came into Bucky's claiming to have caught a two-foot trout in Star Lake, when in reality it had only been a rather large guppy?

I had no doubt that the fight had happened. I just wasn't sure the mysterious biker guy had issued a final warning that sounded a lot like a death threat. "Anyone know who that other guy was?" I asked.

Greg shook his head.

The guy sitting next to him said, "I'd never seen him before."

Greg shouted down the length of the bar, "Fox," he called to Andy, using his last name, "you know who that biker guy was?"

"Not a clue," Andy replied. "I'd never seen him in here, and he paid in cash."

The mystery of where Trevor had been the night he died was solved, but now I had a new mystery: the identity of a man who sounded strong enough to kill Trevor and lug his body to city hall to set him up in the middle of the display. Once again, though, what would be his motive for that? Unless Trevor somehow knew the guy. Maybe Trevor picking at him was more personal than anyone knew. No one else in the bar had seen the guy before, but that didn't mean Trevor didn't know him.

I realized I'd never gotten one of my questions answered. "Andy?" I called out.

He turned and lifted one snow-white brow.

"Does Finn know about this fight?" I asked.

"I told the officers who were in here that night," Andy called back. "I assume they told him."

Shoot. I really wanted to have some new information to share with Finn. It felt good to be helpful. Let's face it. I was going to investigate this murder with or without Finn's blessing, but every time I was able to share something helpful, it decreased his concern—or at least his frustration.

"A table opened up in the back," Chris said. "Want to eat dinner at the bar or grab that table?"

I glanced in the direction Chris had indicated. "Let's move to the table," I said. We picked up our drinks. "Thanks for the information," I said to Greg.

Greg gave a curt nod, apparently back to his more reserved self. "Anytime," he said.

Chris and I settled at the table. Nancy, the waitress who'd been working at Bucky's as long as I could remember, blew by like a tornado, dropping menus at our table. "It's busy tonight," she said as she rushed by. "I'll be back in a jiff."

I set the menu aside. I always got the chicken fingers and fries. "Tell me about this investor," I said, moving the conversation away from Trevor's murder.

Chris glanced at the menu before closing it. "It's Trevor's business partner, actually," he said casually, as if it wasn't more than a coincidence.

"Really?" I asked in shock. "Cole Johnson?"

"You know him?" Chris asked.

"I met with him today," I said.

Chris looked confused. "Why were you meeting with Cole?"

I pulled my hair over my shoulder and started braiding it. "Officially, to see about opening a retirement savings account," I said.

"Unofficially?" he pressed.

"You caught that, huh?" I said sheepishly.

Chris tapped the side of his head. "Nothing gets past me where you're concerned," he said like he was making a joke, but I knew him well enough to know he was being serious.

"Except the fact that I had a crush on you since middle school," I teased, although my own joke stung just a little.

Chris took my hand, rubbing his thumb across my palm. "I'm going to spend the rest of my life making up for that," he said with a sincerity that stole my breath.

This is why flirting with Chris, although fun, was dangerous. My heart ached for it to be true. My heart also wanted Finn. Face it, my heart was as confused about its feelings as I was about who had killed Trevor.

CHAPTER TWELVE

Chris and I parted ways thirty minutes before his meeting, and I headed home. I was itching to call Finn and see if the officers who'd talked to Andy had told him about Trevor's fight. I was also interested in finding out what Finn had learned from Sandra's friends.

While the thought of stopping by and seeing if Finn was home was appealing, I was exhausted and wanted desperately to be in my pajamas. This time, cozy flannel won out over the thrill of seeing Finn.

As soon as I was dressed in my favorite pajamas, white flannel pants covered in pink hearts—a gift from my mom last Valentine's Day—and an oversize sweatshirt, I settled in front of the fireplace with a blanket across my lap and a cup of tea in my hand.

Delilah wandered in and gave me a sweet meow as a greeting. I'd called for her when I got home, but as always, unless it was mealtime, she showed up in her own time. I patted the couch next to me, and Delilah jumped up, settling down next to me.

"Let's call Finn and tell him what we learned," I said to her.

I'd left the lights off in the living room, allowing me to see out the large picture window that directly faced Chip and Rose's house. If I sat near the end of my couch, I could also see Trevor and Sandra's house. Watching Sandra's house wasn't going to get me anywhere, but it also didn't hurt anything.

Delilah purred next to me as I ran my hand along the white streak on her back that made her look like an adorable version of a skunk.

Finn answered with an exhausted-sounding, "Hey."

"Hey, yourself," I said. "Everything okay?"

"Yeah, sorry," he said, sounding more alert. "I've just been sorting through my interviews with Sandra's friends, and my head is spinning."

Choosing to go home and get into my pajamas had clearly been a mistake. I'd have loved to see those interview notes. Who was I kidding? How interesting would it have been to be able to watch those interviews live?

"Anything I can do to help?" I asked.

"Talking to you helps," he said, his voice low and sexy and delicious.

"You're sure that talking to me doesn't just distract you?" I teased.

"It's the best kind of distraction," he said.

I grinned, feeling warm from the flickering fire in my fireplace and the effects of Finn's words. "Are you home?" I asked.

"Why? Are you going to come over if I am?" he flirted.

"I can't," I said with overly dramatic regret. "I'm already all cozy in front of the fire. If I leave now, I'll probably die of hypothermia on my way there."

Finn chuckled. "It's forty degrees out."

"Exactly," I said. "Downright frosty."

"How have you survived living in Illinois all your life?" he teased.

"It's a wonder to us all," I said before switching gears. "I did have an ulterior motive to my call."

"Would that motive have anything to do with the investigation?" Finn asked. "And by the way, I'm still at the station."

"I went to Bucky's for dinner tonight and got to talking to Andy Fox about Trevor's murder. I didn't bring it up. Andy did," I hastened to add.

"Let me guess," Finn said. "He told you Trevor was there the night he died and got kicked out for getting into a fight with a biker."

I let out a deep sigh.

"What's that sigh for?" Finn asked, laughing.

"For once, I wanted to be able to tell you something you didn't already know." I sounded slightly whiny, but I didn't even care.

"As much as I have mixed feelings about your involvement in these investigations, you do help me," Finn said. "You've told me plenty of things I didn't know yet."

"*Yet*," I said. "Meaning you would have eventually discovered them without me."

"We could say it's a positive thing that I'm good at my job," Finn said, sounding amused by my complaints.

"I guess," I said dramatically. "Have you been out to Bucky's to talk to Andy about the fight?"

"It's on my list first thing tomorrow," Finn said. "It took me all morning to organize the things I'd learned from Sandra's friends so we can start tracking down their alibis, and then I spent the afternoon with the medical examiner trying to get a cause of death."

I wrinkled my nose in disgust. "I'm pretty sure the cause of death was I-could-see-his-brain."

"Yes," Finn agreed. "But I was looking for some parameters on a murder weapon."

That made sense. "And?" I asked, saying a silent prayer that this wouldn't be where he'd draw the line on sharing details of the investigation.

"The medical examiner said she needs another day, but her best guess is that he was hit in the head with a shovel."

"But everybody owns shovels," I complained. "I mean, I don't own a shovel, but I could get my hands on one if I needed to."

"Yes, it's always more complicated when the murder weapon is an everyday household object," he said.

I was already picturing every suspect on my mini murder board swinging a shovel at Trevor's head to see if seemed plausible. Cole stayed on the suspect list. I hadn't seen the biker guy from Bucky's, but from what I'd been told, he had the strength to kill someone with a shovel.

"I think you need to figure out who that biker is," I said, having a hard time picturing any of Sandra's friends swinging a shovel at Trevor's head. "It sounds like he'd be strong enough to kill someone like that, and after things got physical in the parking lot, he might have wanted to get revenge on Trevor."

"Wait a minute," Finn said. "What do you mean, things got physical in the parking lot?"

"You know, Andy kicked the guys out of Bucky's, and then Trevor went after the biker in the parking lot. The biker tried not to fight him, but Trevor just kept coming at him," I said, confused by Finn's confusion.

"I definitely didn't know that," Finn said, sounding distracted like he was writing something down.

I smiled wide and did a little shoulder shimmy. I'd managed to share something with Finn he didn't know. Just call me Guinevere Helpful Stevens. It would be better than my real middle name.

"You're celebrating right now, aren't you," Finn said, sounding amused.

I stopped my seated dance. "Not at all," I said in an overly innocent tone.

Finn chuckled. "I know you, Gwen. You're probably dancing around your living room in delight that you discovered something about this investigation that I didn't know."

"To be fair, it was just a little shoulder shimmy while sitting because I'm entirely too cozy to get out of the cocoon of blankets I have myself wrapped in, and I'm not celebrating because I beat you. I'm celebrating because I want to help you, and I just did," I explained. It briefly occurred to me that Finn would likely have learned that information tomorrow when he talked to Andy, but I brushed the thought aside.

"It was helpful," Finn said. "I'll be better prepared when I talk to Andy tomorrow. I'll also have to ask those officers why they didn't mention it to me."

It suddenly felt like I'd gotten someone into trouble, which was not my goal. "It's possible they didn't know," I said. "Andy wasn't the one who told Chris and me about the fight. A guy sitting next to us at the bar had been in the parking lot when Trevor and the biker were coming out. He saw it all happen. Maybe he wasn't at Bucky's when Andy told the officers."

"That makes sense," Finn said. "I didn't know you and Chris were hanging out tonight," he added after a suspiciously long pause. He tried to sound casual about it, but I knew Finn, and just like he'd been able to guess that I'd been celebrating giving him a scoop, I could hear the thread of tension in his voice.

I felt the urge to play off my dinner with Chris like it was no big deal. I felt the urge to get defensive. I wasn't sure which urge was going to win. I settled with a simple, "We had dinner."

The truth was, Finn and I weren't in a relationship, which meant I could hang out with whoever I wanted to. Besides, Chris was one of my oldest friends. I wasn't going to end that even if things became more official between Finn and me.

"I better get back to work," Finn said.

I bit back a groan of frustration. "Are you upset?" I asked.

Finn's tone softened. "I'm sorry. I'm really not. I'm buried in the details of this case. This is the hardest part of a murder investigation. I have a lot of information, but none of it is gelling yet."

"What can I do to help?" I asked.

"You've been helpful," Finn said. "I'll figure it out. I just have to keep moving forward. The truth has a way of floating to the surface."

"I'm sure it would help to find out where Trevor died," I said. "There wasn't any blood at the scene. There wasn't even any blood on his scarecrow costume." I shivered and pulled the blanket up around my neck.

"You're right," Finn said. "Top of my list is to find the murder scene."

"I can't even imagine how you'd do that. It could be anywhere. Someone's backyard, out in a random field, in someone's house," I said.

"Finding a primary suspect will go a long way to helping me find the murder scene," Finn explained.

"Seems like you have plenty of suspects," I said, thinking about Sandra's friends and my conversation with Cole earlier.

"Yeah," Finn said, sounding overwhelmed. "Sandra's friends have complicated the situation. I can't rule them out simply because the timing of their confessions seems suspicious. One of them could have done it."

"Or all of them," I said, thinking of how hard it would've been for any one of them to move Trevor's body alone.

"It better not be all of them," Finn said, sounding exasperated. "The last thing this town needs is five of its upstanding citizens banding together to commit first-degree murder."

"I was thinking maybe one of them killed Trevor and then the others came to the scene to help cover it up," I said.

Finn paused as if he were thinking it over. "The way the body was positioned in front of city hall with the note doesn't fit with a cover-up. Hiding or disposing of the body would be the smarter move if you wanted to increase your chances of getting away with it," he said.

"That's a good point. It's like whoever did it wanted to humiliate Trevor on top of killing him," I said. "Although, those women hated the way he treated Sandra. I could see them wanting to make sure the whole town knew what an awful person he was."

"And they did come in and confess, which doesn't indicate a desire to get away with it," Finn said. I could picture him sitting at his desk, his normally perfectly styled hair rumpled from running his hand through it in frustration. He let out a deep breath. "I'll just keep following the evidence. The truth will reveal itself. It always does."

I thought about all the cold cases that never got solved. Was this going to become one of those? Would Sandra ever get closure on who'd killed her husband? Or had she been the one to kill him with a hope that she'd never be discovered?

A light went out in the living room of Sandra's house. The witch next door cackled, although the sound was muted through my closed windows.

"I had a meeting with Trevor's business partner, Cole, earlier today to open a retirement account," I said. "Sandra mentioned Cole accused Trevor of stealing from the business, which she denied of course. When I asked Cole about it, he ended our meeting. Have you talked to him?" I asked.

"You had a meeting with Cole to talk retirement, or you used talking about retirement to ask Cole questions about the murder?" Finn asked with a hint of suspicion in his tone.

"Both?" I said tentatively.

"Did you learn anything helpful?" he asked.

"He got really upset when I started asking questions about Trevor," I admitted. "And he didn't deny that Trevor was stealing from the business when I told him about Sandra's claims."

"He's on my list to interview tomorrow," Finn said, not really confirming or denying if he'd already known about the supposed embezzlement.

It felt like Finn's attention was waning. He was certainly becoming less forthcoming with details the longer we spoke. "I'll let you get back to work," I said. "Let me know if you need anything."

"Margie's been on me all day about taking breaks these first few days of the investigation. What's your day look like tomorrow?" he asked.

"I'll be at work starting at ten, but this has been a slow week," I said. "I'm sure I can sneak away."

"Sneaking away sounds fun," Finn said. I couldn't see him, but I could hear the innuendo in his tone.

"Let me know how your day is going," I said. "I can be all yours."

There was a heated silence. A light turned on in a room on the second story of Sandra's house.

"I like the sound of that," Finn finally said.

My insides went all warm and squishy. I liked that too. A lot.

We ended the call, and I stared across the street at Sandra's house, willing the truth to reveal itself. I wasn't sure what revelation I was hoping to see. Maybe Sandra sneaking out of her house with a bloody shovel in hand.

Delilah stood from her nap on my lap and jumped down, sauntering out of the room without a backward glance.

"Well, goodbye to you too," I said to her retreating form. Cats were funny. Delilah was the kind of cat that people would say acted like a dog, but it was moments like this that I was reminded that she was fully feline.

My journal was all the way on the other side of the couch. I wanted to add what I'd learned from Finn about the possible murder weapon, but I didn't want to get up. I lunged to the side, just barely brushing against the pebbled leather cover. Two more lunges, and I'd managed to snag it. I dragged it over and opened to the right page.

Near the top where there was a gap between names of suspects and their motives, I wrote *Killed with a shovel?* I should have asked Finn what else it could've been. It sounded like the medical examiner wasn't sure.

I tapped the pen against my chin in thought. No one was asking where the killer had gotten the scarecrow costume. Was it something they'd just had lying around? Had the murder and subsequent posing of the body in the display at city hall been premeditated? If so, the killer would have needed to purchase the costume from somewhere.

Ordering a costume online was easy enough, and if that's what the killer had done, I'd never be able to track it. However, Henry had a seasonal display in the corner of Henry's Hardware downtown. At Christmas, you could find decorations and a small selection of toys and gifts. During the summer months, there were firecrackers, grills, and pool floats. This time of year, there were Halloween decorations and costumes.

The witch's cackle sounded faintly once again. If Henry was selling those witches in his shop, I was going to have a word with him. I made a note to stop over there tomorrow while I was at work to see if he had any scarecrow costumes for sale that matched what Trevor had been wearing. If so, he might know who'd purchased it.

I extricated myself from my blankets and stood, stretching my back and shooting a dirty look toward my neighbor's house, where the witch was making noise again. Was someone running back and forth in front of that thing? I had half a mind to take Penny's suggestion to make that particular decoration disappear.

With a sigh, I headed to the kitchen, deciding to refill the mug I'd been using for tea with creamy hot chocolate instead. I'd love nothing more than to get rid of that witch, but I wasn't the destroy-my-neighbor's-property type of person. Besides, things were going really well with Finn. The last thing I wanted to do was jeopardize that by doing something that would force him to arrest me.

CHAPTER THIRTEEN

Delilah's furry little face rubbed against my sleeping face way too early the next morning. "Why?" I moaned before turning over in an attempt to ignore her. She was not deterred. Her front paws pushed against my shoulder, followed by a pathetic meow.

"You act like no one feeds you," I said with a pout. I couldn't stay mad at Delilah for long though. Not when I turned and looked into her pale-blue eyes. She gently head butted me, which I took as her form of a hug. "I love you, too," I said as I climbed out of bed and pulled on the oversize cardigan sweater that I used as a makeshift robe in the winter.

Ten minutes later, I had turned the heat up, filled Delilah's water and food bowls, and was contemplating my day. My mom had texted me yesterday with some tweaks she wanted to make to the display in our front window after studying the other businesses' displays. She was determined to win the contest this year, including the prize of a small trophy and a fifty-dollar gift card to Bucky's.

I'd find time in there to stop by Henry's Hardware and see if he was selling the same costume Trevor had been dressed in. I also wanted to talk to Sandra's friends. Maybe they would tell me something they wouldn't tell Finn, even if by accident. Usually, I was trying to get someone to confess to murder. In this case, I was trying to get someone to confess to being innocent.

The coffeemaker beeped, and I went to work making breakfast with a fresh cup of coffee to help me finish waking up. I spent the next hour showering, doing a load of laundry, cleaning Delilah's litter box—my least favorite part of being a cat owner—and choosing the perfect outfit in case Finn really could sneak away for a break today.

I ended up wearing a pair of light-gray jeans with a slouchy oatmeal-colored sweater. Penny, who loved to wear the brightest colors the human eye could detect, would've called my sweater beige, but oatmeal sounded more attractive. I layered on a variety of gold bracelets and a gold necklace that fell just below the neckline of the sweater.

The weather had taken a turn overnight. No more sunny, warm days. At least for the rest of the week. I pulled on a black, waterproof jacket in recognition of the twenty percent chance of rain today. A bank of gray clouds hung low in the sky, and the wind whipped against my cheeks as I locked the deadbolt on my front door.

Rose was in her yard, bagging the leaves she'd been raking the day before. I decided to run over and say hi in case she'd seen anything suspicious at Sandra's house since I'd last talked to her. If Sandra and her friends had killed Trevor, they might have needed to return to the scene of the crime to clean it up. What better time to do that than in the middle of the night when no one would see them. Rose seemed pretty tuned in to what happened at Trevor and Sandra's house. If anyone would notice something suspicious, it would be her.

Halfway across the street, I opened my mouth to say good morning, when Kevin's witch decided to announce my presence with a loud cackle. Rose looked up from the pile she was raking into a large, black garbage bag.

"Gwen," she said with a nervous chuckle. "You scared me."

"Sorry," I said. "It's that stupid witch. I was going to say hi before I got too close, but it beat me to it."

"No," Rose said, waving away my concern. "It's not your fault. I've been jumpy since Trevor's death. I don't like to think of a murder happening on our quiet street."

Between the witch and all of Trevor's yelling at Sandra, I wasn't sure how quiet our street really was.

"I've got to leave for work in a minute, but let me help you," I said. "It's freezing today."

"It's the clouds," Rose said. "Without the sun, the wind feels like a knife. You don't have to help. I've got it."

"I don't mind," I said, taking the black lawn bag from her and holding it open. "I've been feeling nervous about Trevor's death too. Have you seen anything weird happening over there?"

In truth, I hadn't been feeling particularly nervous for my own safety following Trevor's murder, but my admission seemed like a good way to connect with Rose.

"What do you mean by weird?" Rose asked as she began raking the pile of leaves into the bag I was holding.

"I don't know," I said. I wasn't sure how much I should say about the fact that Sandra's friends had confessed, but this was Star Junction. It wasn't going to stay a secret forever. Still, I didn't want to be the reason it spread around town like wildfire. "Maybe people sneaking around the house?" I suggested vaguely.

Rose paused and looked over at Sandra's house. "I haven't seen anything especially weird." She looked thoughtful before saying, "I did hear a lot of yelling the night Trevor died."

She hadn't mentioned that the last time I'd talked to her, but I knew how easy it was to forget little details when dealing with something as traumatic as murder. "What kind of yelling?" I asked.

"Trevor was yelling at Sandra about something," Rose said, shaking her head in disappointment. "As usual, I couldn't hear Sandra at all. She never yelled back. I bet it wasn't safe to stand up to him. I always warned Chip that if he pushed Trevor too far, Trevor might do something worse than yell back about the property line. The fence was a risk."

"Do you remember what time this was?" I asked.

"I remember it was late. I couldn't sleep and got up to read for a little bit. We had our upstairs windows open because I like to be cold while I sleep," she said. "That's why I could hear Trevor yelling."

"I'm the same way," I said. "I like having my windows open on chilly nights." I threw a dirty look at the witch over my shoulder. "Kevin's new Halloween décor has gotten in the way of being able to enjoy it though."

Rose chuckled as she scooped the last little pile of leaves into the bag. "He's very proud of that witch."

I handed the ends of the bag to Rose so she could tie them together and then dug through my purse for my journal. If Rose heard Trevor yelling at Sandra late at night, then he'd made it home after the bar. Which meant he hadn't been run off the road by the biker and hit over the head in some field somewhere.

I found my mini murder board and made a note of this new information. When I had time to sit down with it, I needed to put together a timeline of Trevor's movements.

"What've you got there?" Rose asked.

Instinctively, I tilted the book away from her. People around town knew I'd helped Finn solve two murders, but there was knowing something in theory and actually seeing how seriously I took the task. I didn't want Rose to think I was weird.

"It's nothing," I said, sliding the journal back into my purse. "Just jotting down something I didn't want to forget."

"I saw Trevor's name on there," Rose said, pushing. "Is it about his murder?"

"Maybe?" I squeaked out, wishing a bird would fly by and set off that witch again. What I wouldn't give for a little distraction about now.

"So, do you officially help Detective Butler, or it's just more of a hobby?" Rose asked. She didn't sound upset or judgmental, just curious.

"I wouldn't really call it a hobby. I mean, who would call murder a hobby, right?" I said, giggling nervously.

I'd had to defend my decision to investigate murders to people who were worried about me and to suspects who thought it was none of my business. I'd never had to explain it to someone who was talking about it with the same level of nonchalance as if I'd taken up watercolor painting. It felt weird.

Rose's green eyes sparkled, and she leaned forward. "Have you figured out anything useful?" she asked with a great deal of interest.

The witch didn't save me with its cackle, but Rose and Chip's garage door went up, drawing our attention. The garage door opened to reveal Chip dressed in very short running shorts and a tank top, despite the chilly weather. He was jogging in place when he noticed Rose and me standing watching him.

"Hey, ladies," he said, approaching in a sort of jog-in-place move. "The yard looks great, hon," he said, giving Rose a peck on the cheek while still managing to keep those legs moving.

"Thanks, hon," she said. "Gwen was just talking about what she's learned about Trevor's murder so far."

"She is?" Chip asked, sounding just as interested as Rose. "Rose is convinced Sandra did it."

Rose nodded enthusiastically. "She snapped," she said with confidence. "It was only a matter of time."

Chip stopped jogging in place but switched to stretching side to side. Every time he leaned to the side, the edge of his shorts rode up dangerously high. I averted my eyes, and that's when I saw the shovel leaning against a work bench in the garage.

Sure, lots of people owned shovels, but what if that was the murder weapon? What if I could get my hands on it? What if Trevor had threatened Chip's fence one too many times and he'd snapped? Finn would find traces of Trevor's blood. Then the case would be solved, and Finn and I could go out. He'd been seconds away from kissing me in his office before all of Sandra's friends showed up to confess. Heck, at this point, I might just grab him and be the one doing the kissing. All this delaying was getting ridiculous.

"Gwen?" Chip asked.

He'd stopped stretching, and he and Rose were watching me with concern.

"Seems like we lost you," he said with a little chuckle.

Right. I needed to stop thinking about Finn's lips and start thinking about getting my hands on that shovel.

"You know," I said, putting one hand on my hip as I popped it out to the side in what I hoped looked like a very casual pose. "I'm planning a project in my backyard and realized that I don't have a shovel, but the project involves digging holes. Lots of holes, and so I was thinking I should get a shovel, but then I thought, what if I get a shovel that I don't like and I have to dig all those holes with a shovel I don't like, and then I saw your shovel, and it dawned on me that I could borrow someone's shovel to make sure I like that kind before I get one, you know?" I pulled in a deep breath, not having taken one the entire time I'd been talking.

Rose and Chip looked at me like I'd lost my mind.

Finally, Chip said, "You have a project with a lot of holes?"

"Yeah," I said, still working hard to play this scenario out as very normal. "You know how those projects go."

Chip looked over his shoulder at the shovel. "I mean, I would let you borrow it, but I'm in the middle of finishing this fence," he said. He cocked his head to the side. "You really don't own a shovel?"

I was feeling suddenly defensive. So what if I didn't own a shovel? I didn't criticize Chip for wearing ridiculous running shorts when summer was clearly over. Okay, maybe I did do that, but only in my mind, never to his face.

"I own a snow shovel," I said, not able to hide the defensiveness in my tone. "But that won't work for what I have going on."

"What are the holes for?" Chip asked, sounding suspicious.

"Come on, Chip," Rose chided. "Let her borrow your shovel."

Chip turned on Rose. "She can borrow it when I'm done with it," he said.

Now I'd started a marital spat. "It's not a big deal," I said, slowly backing away from them. "I'm sure I can borrow one from my parents."

"Or Kevin," Rose said, trying to be helpful.

"Yeah, or him," I agreed. "Have a great day."

"Thanks for helping with the leaves," Rose called after me as I booked it across the street.

"Anytime," I called over my shoulder with a wave. I made it to my car and unlocked the door.

"Honestly, Chip," I overheard Rose say. "Give the girl a break."

"I said she can borrow it when I'm done with it," he said as if he didn't understand what the big deal was.

I got in the car and closed the door, blocking out the sound of their continued conversation. Not wanting to loan me the shovel wasn't a big deal. That is, unless the real reason was because I'd just seen the murder weapon.

CHAPTER FOURTEEN

I stood with my hands on my hips in front of Camelot Flowers next to my mom, who was currently scrutinizing our Halloween window display. "I don't know, Mom. It looks perfect to me," I said after spending more time than I'd like to admit indulging my mom's idea that there was something missing. The knight looked great. The sword in the stone looked amazing. The flowers looked beautiful.

"But Burt at Cozy Cuts Pet Care has LED lights that come on at night. It really highlights his cat vampire and dog mummy," she said.

"So you want to get LED lights?" I asked.

"Exactly," she said definitively.

She could have just said that from the beginning. It was an easy enough task to accomplish. Easier than standing here in the cold trying to guess what she didn't like about our display.

"I think it'll give it that little something extra that we need to win this year," she said.

I rubbed my hands together. "Let's go inside. I'm freezing."

She followed me inside as she said, "We could wrap the sword or put some in the knight's helmet so that the little eye slits glow at night."

Glowing eyes could look sinister, but it was a Halloween display after all. At least the flowers would cut down on the creep factor.

"I'll run to Henry's and pick up some lights," I said, thankful for an excuse to head over there.

"Thanks, dear," my mom said. She took her phone from her pocket. "I'll let him know you're stopping by."

"Mom, I'm not going to his house unexpectedly. I'm going to his store to buy something. We don't need to let him know we're coming," I said with just a hint of exasperation.

"I suppose you're right," she said. Her phone made a little ding. "But I already sent the text."

Oh boy. Henry wouldn't mind. In his seventies, he'd probably text my mom back and thank her for letting him know.

"I'll be back," I said to my mom as I scooped up my purse and headed out the front door.

Based on the dreary weather, I'd rather have driven. Based on the fact that Henry's was one block away, that felt silly. I ducked my head against the chilly wind and made it to Hemry's in no time.

The ancient brass bell above the door gave out a cheery jingle as I walked in. The smell of wood was combined with the vanilla-scented wax Henry's wife, Rita, always had melting in a warmer plugged in behind the counter. It was a pivotal smell of my childhood, running to Henry's with my dad to pick up supplies for any number of projects he'd done around the house or the store.

No one was behind the register. While I'd grown up with either Henry or his wife Rita running the store, they'd hired a part-time worker last year to give them some much deserved time off, although Talia usually worked evenings and weekends, so Henry was probably here.

He'd not only gotten my mom's text but had likely heard the bell above the door. He'd appear at some point. Meanwhile, the display in the corner caught my eye. Two circular racks, the kind kids loved to hide from their moms in, held a variety of Halloween costumes. On the shelves nearest the racks were a mix of Halloween candy, decorations, and general fall décor.

I skipped the rack that held kid costumes, including superheroes, princesses, monsters, and professions deemed acceptable for costume-use, like doctors and police officers. I'd never seen a costume for a florist. We just weren't exciting enough.

The other rack held costumes in larger sizes. I'd expected to see some sexy costumes. Sexy nurses. Sexy police officers. Basically, the inappropriate versions of the kid costumes, but all the costumes on this rack were family friendly. I walked around to the other side of the rack and sucked in a breath. There was a costume with an attached straw hat wedged between a Superman costume and a white lab coat.

I hurried and spread the costumes apart, my heart sinking as I realized it wasn't the same as the one Trevor had been dressed in. Trevor had been in denim overalls and a red flannel shirt, but this costume was made up of a tan-colored jumpsuit with fake patches printed on the fabric. The only thing that was the same was the hats.

In looking at the scarecrow costume's cheap fabric, it occurred to me that Trevor's costume was really just normal clothes. Likely most men in town owned at least one flannel shirt, and overalls were common enough.

"Yoo-hoo," Henry's voice called out from somewhere in the store.

"Over here," I called back.

"Guinevere," he said kindly as he appeared from the end of aisle three and walked toward me. He cleaned his wire-rimmed glasses on the edge of his flannel shirt before settling them back on his nose. "Your mom mentioned you'd be heading over. Something about LED lights. Are you also looking for a costume?"

"No—well, sort of," I started out. "My mom wants LED lights for our window display. I already have my Halloween costume, but I was curious to see if you carried scarecrow costumes this year."

Henry rubbed his chin. "Scarecrow costumes," he said thoughtfully. "This wouldn't have anything to do with that body they found in front of city hall, would it?"

The way he said "*they* found" didn't escape me. Apparently, word hadn't gotten around that I'd been the one to find Trevor. I didn't see any reason to hide the origin of my question from Henry. "Trevor was my neighbor, and I'm just trying to help his wife out," I said. It was a partial truth. If she'd killed her husband, my poking around would help her go to prison where she belonged.

"The only costumes I have are on the racks," he said.

"Have you sold out of any costumes?" I asked. "Like maybe the killer bought the last one you had?"

"I'd have to check my original order against what I have left," he said. "Rita set up the display." He smiled proudly. "She did a right good job, didn't she?"

"It's perfect," I said sincerely. "A little bit of everything people might need for Halloween. It's nice to not have to leave town to get these kinds of supplies."

"You know, it's possible someone ordered that costume online," Henry said.

"I'd thought of that," I said glumly. "If that's the case, I'll never be able to figure it out."

"Or they've had that costume for a long time and pulled it out of storage to use," he added.

That hadn't occurred to me. I pursed my lips and put my hands on my hips, staring at the rack of costumes that hadn't been helpful in the least. "I guess I better get those LED lights and get back to the store," I said.

"I've got them waiting for you behind the counter," he said as he moved to the old Formica counter and took a bag from the shelves behind it.

That was one benefit of my mom contacting him ahead of my visit. "So, you didn't see Trevor's wife in here lately?" I asked.

"You're thinking the wife did it?" Henry asked.

"I don't know," I admitted. "Maybe. This guy was awful to his family."

Henry shook his head with a look of disdain. "It's a man's job to cherish his family. Not terrorize them," he said firmly.

I'd always loved Henry. He'd snuck me candy as a little kid. He always had a kind word to say about everyone. Now, I loved him just a little more.

"I don't know if I've seen her," he said. "I wasn't familiar with the name when I heard about the murder."

I got out my phone and opened Facebook. A moment later, I had Sandra's profile picture pulled up. "This is Trevor's wife."

Henry slid the glasses to the tip of his nose and peered at the picture. "Yes, she was in here last weekend," he said confidently.

"She was?" I asked in shock. "How could you possibly remember that?"

Henry made a tsking sound. "One of her boys got into the bags of candy corn while she was looking at the costumes," he said. "He'd opened fifteen bags, but only eaten one of them by the time she noticed. I didn't make her pay for the bags of candy. She was near tears when she realized what he'd done."

That didn't sound like a cold-blooded killer to me, but maybe Trevor wasn't killed in cold blood. If Sandra killed Trevor, she could have done it in self-defense. "Did she buy a costume?" I asked. "Was it a scarecrow? You know, the one that looks like the scarecrow from the *Wizard of Oz*?"

Henry looked off into the distance. "I can't right remember. I can look through our paperwork though," he said. "It might take me a while to find it."

"I probably shouldn't keep my mom waiting any longer," I said with regret. "She's worried we'll lose the costume contest to Burt at Cozy Cuts."

Henry chuckled and said, "He really outdid himself with that display this year, but yours is good too. It'll be a tough decision for the judges."

"Who is judging this year?" I asked. "I've been so busy, I haven't even thought about it."

"Last I heard, it was the mayor, the principal of the high school, and Detective Butler," Henry answered. He handed me the bag with the LED lights. "I'll call the shop later to let you know if Sandra bought a scarecrow costume."

"Can you call my cell?" I asked. "I might not be at the shop later. I seem to be all over the place these days."

Henry passed me a little notepad that looked like it was for writing the details of small purchases like nails and screws on it. "Write your number on the back of one of these," he said.

I did as instructed. Henry folded the paper and tucked it into the front chest pocket of his flannel shirt. "Say hello to your folks for me," he said.

"I will," I said. "And thanks for checking on this for me. I know it's a little weird."

"If it helps solve a murder, I'm happy to do it," he said.

Finn hadn't mentioned he was judging the Halloween display contest this year. It made sense he'd be chosen. The mayor's office liked to mix up who did the judging for city-wide events like this, and they always chose people they considered "pillars of the community." Finn definitely fit the bill.

What I couldn't decide was whether or not having Finn as a judge was going to help Camelot Flowers or hurt us. He had integrity, which I admired, but sometimes too much integrity had someone like Finn going overboard in the name of being fair. He might not vote for Camelot Flowers just to avoid any whiff of impropriety.

I heard a ding, followed by Henry saying, "Hold up, Guinevere."

I stopped at the door and turned.

"Your mom just texted," he explained. "She'd also like you to pick up a glue gun and a staple gun. I'll show you where they are so you can decide what sizes to get."

My mom could have just as easily texted me with the request, but this was par for the course in how she did business. I followed Henry to the back of the store, where a small crafting section was displayed next to a row of shiny shovels.

I sucked in a sharp breath and ran my finger along the edge of one of the shovels. It was sharp. Not sharp like a knife, but sharp enough to do the damage I'd seen to Trevor's head.

"Everything all right, hon?" Henry asked.

"Yeah, everything's great," I said.

I grabbed what my mom needed without much thought. A glue gun was a glue gun, right? After checking out, I headed back to Camelot Flowers.

If I could find the shovel that killed Trevor, Finn would have a prime suspect and be able to locate the crime scene. Heck, if I could find the shovel, I'd probably find the crime scene. I had no idea how to go about it, unless Chip's shovel was the one I was looking for. On the bright side, I'd had no idea how to find out where Trevor was the night he died and the information fell right in my lap. I needed to keep digging, no pun intended, and trust that the information would reveal itself.

My mom was delighted with the LED lights and was determined to get them set up that very minute in case one of the judges happened to walk by that evening. "First impressions are everything," she said as she pulled the LED lights from the box. "Even if they're not officially judging until tomorrow, they might dismiss us if we can't measure up to Burt's display."

"So, what's the plan?" I asked, rubbing my hands together to try to warm up after my walk back from Henry's.

My mom gazed at the lights. "I'm not sure yet," she said.

If she didn't know what she wanted, she'd pull me outside again to stare at the display from the sidewalk. I had no interest in going back outside. "I think putting some of them in the knight's helmet and some along the sword so that it looks like it's glowing is the right move," I said. "It'll be a striking image and will make the sword look like it's magical."

My mom gave me a beaming smile. "I love it. That's what we'll do."

Thankfully, we could do all of that from inside the store.

We went to work on the display, and ten minutes later, the knight looked alive and the sword looked like magic. Even in the daylight, it took the display to the next level. I couldn't wait to see it at night.

"How's Finn doing?" my mom asked as she fluffed the flowers coming out of the top of the knight's helmet.

"He's stressed," I said. "It's always like this at the beginning of an investigation. It's a combination of too much information with not enough information."

"Margie told me about Sandra Baker's friends all confessing," my mom said gravely. "I'm sure that's made it more difficult."

I leaned back against the front window as my mom continued to fuss with the display. "It would almost be easier if they would've come in together and confessed that they'd all had a hand in his death. Instead, all of them are insisting that the others are lying and they're the one telling the truth. It's confusing. I want to talk to them individually and see if I can get them to slip up and admit that they're just covering for someone. If I can take that mess off of Finn's plate, then he can search for the real killer."

"You don't think they're guilty?" she asked.

"I don't think they're all guilty," I said. "And maybe none of them are."

My mom let out a "huh" before saying, "Who are you going to talk to first?"

I'd been very concerned that my parents would freak out over the thought of me investigating a murder, but my mom had been surprisingly chill with it. "I was going to start with Michelle since I know where she works. Stopping into Lucille's Clip and

Curl will be easy enough. I don't know the other ladies though," I said.

"Margie mentioned Christine Thompson. She's the librarian at the high school if that helps," my mom said.

Christine had been the woman getting highlights the day I'd had my haircut and narrowly avoided a perm. "That's super helpful," I said. "I can go to the high school later today to visit Penny or Chris and find a way to talk to Christine."

I checked my watch. "Do you mind if I go try to catch Michelle?" I asked. "If I can get her to talk to me now, it will give me time to get over to the school right when it lets out. That way I can catch Christine before she heads home."

"Go, go," my mom said, shooing me out of the display. "I've got things covered here, and your dad will be back from Rose Lake any minute."

"Thanks, Mom," I said, giving her a quick hug.

"You be careful," she said.

"I always am," I replied.

She gave me a skeptical look.

"I *am* careful," I argued. "It's not my fault that whoever the killer ends up being is never careful around me."

My mom pursed her lips and narrowed her eyes doubtfully but didn't argue with me. Time to skedaddle before she changed her mind about me talking to people who'd just confessed to murder.

CHAPTER FIFTEEN

There were currently three cars in the small parking lot of Lucille's Clip and Curl. One I recognized as Lucille's 1960s baby-blue Chevy Camaro. It matched the aesthetic of her classic beehive hairdo. The other two were a red Honda Civic and an army-green pickup truck with a huge dent in the driver's-side door.

I hadn't been paying attention to the cars in the parking lot the last time I was here, so I had no idea if one of those cars was Michelle's. Hopefully she was working today.

I held back a sneeze as the smell of perming solution, hair dye, hairspray, and Lucille's *Giorgio For Women* perfume assaulted my nose. It wasn't that I was a perfume expert, able to distinguish the scents of any perfume. It was that I'd bumped into Lucille years ago near the perfume counter of Macy's at the mall in Abbottsville. She'd waxed poetic about her signature scent, which had been given to her by her first ex-husband in the seventies.

I might not have remembered that moment, but she'd excitedly dragged me by the elbow to the *Giorgio For Women* tester bottle and doused me with so much perfume, I'd considered showering in acid just to get the smell off of me. To say that that moment burned the name of her perfume into my memory would be an understatement.

A quick glance around the room let me know that Michelle was not only here today, but she wasn't busy at the moment.

Michelle sat in her salon chair with a copy of *People* magazine. Apparently, this was the year for celebrity divorces, at least based on the cover story that questioned why all of our favorite stars were splitting up.

A woman I didn't recognize was giving another woman a haircut across the aisle that separated the two rows of chairs.

Michelle glanced up from her magazine, did a double take, and then set the magazine on her lap. "Did you have a problem with your haircut?" she asked, looking around the salon. I wondered if she was looking for Lucille, since she'd been the one to cut my hair.

"No," I said, shooting a glance at the other two women who'd stopped their chatting and were clearly listening in on our exchange. "I was hoping to talk to you, actually."

"About?" she asked.

I didn't want to say too much in front of the other two women. "It's about our mutual friend," I said vaguely.

Michelle just looked at me, clearly confused, which made no sense to me. I was at the police station when she'd come in to confess. I'd been standing right next to Finn. She clearly remembered my haircut. She couldn't remember me witnessing her confession?

"Sandra?" I said in a fruitless whisper since the other hair stylist wasn't even pretending to work anymore. I had everyone's rapt attention.

Michelle sat up and dropped the magazine. "We can talk in the break room," she said, her words clipped, as if she wanted to make sure I didn't say anything more in front of the other ladies.

I followed her through a set of red curtains that led to a narrow room that ran the length of the salon. On one end was a washing machine and dryer, along with shelves of shampoos, conditioners, hair dye, capes, and towels. On the other end of the room was a little kitchenette with a table, microwave, and sink.

Leading the way, Michelle sat at the table and indicated I should do the same. "You wanted to talk about Sandra?" she asked, sounding defensive of her friend, even though I hadn't even said anything yet.

I'd never talked to a suspect who'd also confessed to murder, but I figured it gave me the benefit of being able to be blunt. "I'm actually here to talk about Trevor," I said.

"That snake?" she spat out. "What about him?"

"I know you confessed to killing him," I started.

Michelle looked down at her nails like I was boring her. "That's because I did."

"Your other friends also confessed to killing him," I said pointedly.

"They're lying to cover for me," she said. "I didn't ask them to do that."

"So, out of all five of you, you're the one telling the truth," I said, my tone skeptical.

Michelle nodded. "Yep," she said simply.

This wasn't getting me anywhere. Because I'd found the body, I knew things about the scene that the average citizen might not know. Because I was sort of dating Finn, I knew about the possible murder weapon. Time to find out how much Michelle knew.

"I was shocked by how Trevor was posed," I said, purposely keeping my description vague. "It seemed like it would have been hard to set him up that way."

Michelle studied me for a beat before saying, "It wasn't easy, but I had a lot of adrenaline from killing him. It gave me strength I don't normally have."

I nodded as if we were having a totally normal conversation. "That makes sense, but I mean *how* he was posed. It was so strange." The truth was, Trevor had been propped up next to the other scarecrow. Him being in the Halloween display was strange in and of itself, but there hadn't been anything particularly strange about his actual pose. Would Michelle challenge my description of it?

"I don't know what to tell you. I'm sure things shifted around during the night," she said.

Shoot. It was a plausible explanation without actually giving any details. "How did it even happen?" I asked. "I know you didn't like how Trevor treated Sandra, but it's a big leap from the gallows-humor of planning his murder to actually doing it."

"It was self-defense," Michelle said. There was no defensiveness in her tone, just a matter-of-factness that I found rather chilling.

"Self-defense?" I asked.

"I was sick over how Trevor treated Sandra," Michelle explained. "I confronted him about it. He was drunk and came at me. I had to do it."

Trevor being drunk matched what I knew about his activities that evening. Even the idea of him going after Michelle was plausible. If he was willing to take on a biker twice his size, he'd have no problem going after a petite woman like Michelle. Still, her details were vague.

"How did you do it?" I asked.

Michelle stood. "I'm done talking about this. I already explained everything to Detective Butler. I don't have to explain myself to you too."

I jumped up, blocking her exit. "I just have one more question. It's for Sandra. I really want to help her make sense of this. Give her closure, you know?" I was aware that my argument was weak. Michelle was closer to Sandra than I was. They didn't need me acting as a go between.

Just mentioning Sandra's name softened Michelle's expression. "What's your question?"

"You confessed to murder. Why do you think you aren't in jail right now?" I asked.

Michelle shifted her weight from side to side. "Detective Butler told me not to leave town. He has to sort through the details. My friends confessing didn't help anything. It just made it more confusing." The more she talked, the more anxious she sounded. "I'm sure he'll be ready to make an arrest in the next few days, and when he is, I'll be here."

Penny and Chris were my best friends. They both loved me in their own ways. I wasn't sure they'd be willing to go to jail for me. If Michelle was guilty, she'd have been able to share more details, maybe even mention the shovel she used. Even though my gut told me I couldn't trust her confession, I couldn't rule it out completely. She could be guilty and just not willing to talk to me about it in detail. What I wouldn't give to get my hands on Finn's interview notes.

"Thanks for talking to me," I said.

Michelle shrugged, but her expression was unreadable. I couldn't tell if she regretted giving me this time or didn't care at all.

"Gwen," Lucille's raspy voice said from behind me. "What are you doing back here?"

I shot Michelle a look, feeling like we were two kids caught doing something we shouldn't have been doing.

Michelle gave Lucille a smile. "We were just catching up on my break. Nice to see you again, Gwen." She shimmied past me in the tight space and pushed through the curtains back into the salon.

Lucille patted her beehive hairdo, which was a pale pink today. I'd never seen her stray away from platinum blonde. It was actually a good look on her.

"I love the hair," I said.

"Thanks, hon," she said, snapping her gum. "I was just about to move the towels to the dryer."

"Don't let me stop you," I said. "I was just heading out."

Lucille moved to the washer and dryer but then turned and said, "I didn't know you and Michelle were friends."

"Oh, um, yeah. It's, like, kind of a new friendship. You know how those things go. You see people around town your whole life, but you never really get to know them, and then one time you have a conversation and realize they're pretty cool and maybe you should have been friends with them sooner, but you just never did," I babbled.

People often looked confused when I got to rambling, but Lucille snapped her gum again and said, "I know exactly what you mean."

I didn't know if Lucille being able to understand my babbling was a good sign or a very bad one. I checked the time and realized I'd need to book it over to the school if I wanted to catch Christine before she left for the day. "See you later, Lucille," I said.

"See ya, hon," she said as she moved the black towels to the dryer.

Michelle was wiping down combs at her station when I walked by. She gave me a wary look. I hadn't wanted to make an enemy or upset her.

I got to my car and texted Penny. *I'm stopping by the school to talk to Christine about Trevor's murder. Am I going to have to sign in?*

I wasn't sure what the school rules were. School had gotten out ten minutes ago, but I knew campus security was a concern in a way it hadn't been when I'd been in high school almost twelve years ago.

I started the car, but my phone buzzed before I pulled out of the parking lot.

Penny had written, *You might have to sign in. Just say you're visiting me. I'll introduce you to Christine.*

I sent her a thumbs-up and drove to the school.

Star Junction High School was a two-story brick building with the gymnasium jutting off of one end to make kind of an L-shape. An indoor pool had been added in the eighties, much to the excitement of the parents of young children at the time, who finally had something to do with them in the long winters that didn't require wearing fifty-seven layers to keep warm.

I parked in one of the visitor parking spaces. The buses had already left, and the student parking lot was mostly empty. The remaining cars were likely from students staying late for tutoring, sports, or clubs.

The smell that greeted me when I walked through the doors transported me to another time. The woman behind the desk looked up from her computer. "Can I help you?" she asked.

"I'm here to visit Ms. Taylor," I said.

The woman pushed forward a clipboard. "Sign in and take a visitor's badge. Penny let me know you were on your way."

"Thanks," I said as I followed her directions.

"Do you know where her classroom is?" she asked.

"I do," I said. I'd helped Penny reorganize and redecorate over the summer. She'd said the nesting instinct of pregnancy had spilled over from her house to her classroom.

"Have a nice day," the woman said. She pushed a button, and the door to her right buzzed.

"Thanks. You too," I replied as I went through the door she'd just unlocked for me.

The route to Penny's classroom took me past the library, which was where I wanted to be, but hopefully having Penny with me when I talked to Christine would help her open up.

I walked into Penny's classroom to see her trying to reach something on the top shelf of one of the three bookcases that lined the back of her classroom. As an English teacher, Penny had a large collection of books, even with the school library right down the hall.

"Let me get that for you," I said as I rushed forward and got down the book her fingers had been pushing against uselessly.

"Thanks," Penny said, sounding sullen. "It's this bump. It keeps getting in the way of everything."

It took a lot to get Penny down. I tried to hug her, but her baby bump hit my stomach before my arms could wrap all the way around her.

"See?" she said, near tears.

"No, no 'see,'" I said as I shifted to her side and wrapped my arms around her shoulder. "Nothing's in the way."

"It is," Penny said, in despair. "I can't even get a book off my own shelf, and I'm not sleeping because everything's uncomfortable, and my shoes don't fit, and the baby will come, and then I'll never get to leave my house again. I won't be able to have any fun ever again."

The getting no sleep certainly explained at least part of Penny's mood.

"Do you know what would cheer you up?" I said in an overly enthusiastic tone.

Penny sniffed. "Taco Bell?" she asked hopefully.

"Okay," I said, adjusting to Penny's shocking answer. I wasn't sure I'd ever heard her crave Taco Bell. The closest one was in Rose Lake, but being only a fifteen-minute drive through the countryside, the distance wasn't a deterrent. "I was going to say talking to someone who confessed to murder, but we can also get Taco Bell if you want."

Penny swiped at a tear that had been dangling off the end of her chin and smiled. A smile was a good sign. "You'd go to Taco Bell with me?" she asked.

"Sure," I said. "Whatever you need. That's what best friends are for."

And just like that, the old Penny was back. She set the book I'd retrieved for her on her desk, grabbed her purse, and said, "Let's go catch Christine before she leaves for the day."

I followed Penny, who was moving surprisingly quickly through the halls. The promise of Taco Bell was obviously a powerful motivator. The doors to the library were closed, but we could see Christine sitting at her desk through the large windows on either side of the door.

"What's the plan here?" Penny asked in a hushed whisper.

"I just got done talking to Michelle," I said, matching Penny's low tone. "I want to be able to compare their stories. Someone isn't telling the truth, and if I can figure out who, it'll help Finn focus on the important parts of the investigation."

"Roger," Penny said as she reached for the door.

"Who's Roger?" I asked in confusion.

Penny paused with the door cracked open. "Roger's not a person," she said, sounding exasperated. "At least I don't think he's a person. I'm sure the term had to be inspired by someone." She dropped the door and cocked her head to the side. "Come to think of it, where did that term come from? Was there a guy named Roger who liked to use his own name when assuring people over the CB radio that he'd heard and understood what they were saying?"

Penny looked at me like she was waiting for an explanation.

"I have no idea what's happening here," I murmured.

Penny let out a long-suffering sigh. "Never mind," she said. "I understand the plan. Since I wasn't there when you talked to Michelle, I'll let you take the lead."

I hadn't been aware there was any doubt that I'd be taking the lead, but I simply said, "Thanks," as we walked into the library.

A grouping of round tables and chairs took up the first half of the room, with the circulation desk centered in front of the shelves of books behind it. At the table to my right was where Chris had asked me to prom senior year, "since neither of us had dates" as he'd put it. As you could imagine, it was incredibly romantic.

Christine looked up from her desk. "Hey, Penny," she said. "And it's Gwen, right?"

I nodded and decided it was best to cut right to the chase. I'd worried that Michelle would call Christine and tell her about our conversation, but her greeting was pleasant to the point of bland. I didn't think she knew why I was here. "Do you have a minute to talk about the whole Trevor mess?" I asked.

Christine's expression turned wary. "What about it?"

"It's just that it's confusing the way so many of you confessed to killing him," I said. "Unless you're all in agreement that you killed him together, some of you must be lying."

"Wow, really going for it," Penny said out of the side of her mouth.

Christine crossed her arms over her chest and said, "Everyone else is lying. I killed Trevor. He came at me. It was self-defense."

Now, that was interesting. It was the same thing Michelle had told me. "You explained all this to Finn, I mean Detective Butler? Is that why he didn't arrest you? Because it was self-defense?" I asked skeptically.

"He said not to leave town," she said. "I'm sure he'll charge me when he gets all the evidence he needs."

"Or he won't be able to charge anyone because you've all confessed and it's created too much reasonable doubt," I argued.

For just a moment, I saw a flash of triumph in Christine's eyes, and a new thought occurred to me. I'd always wondered if they could've killed Trevor together. It would certainly explain their ability to get him into that scarecrow costume and set him up in the Halloween display. Each of them had shown confusion or displeasure when another friend had shown up at the police station to confess. Their reactions had been enough to make me doubt the theory that they were in on it together.

The look of victory in Christine's eyes had me wondering if we were all underestimating these friends. What if they had all killed Trevor and hatched a plan to confess but to act upset when the others confessed too? If they'd all come in, even one on one, and confessed but seemed fine with their friends confessing, it could have strengthened the argument that they were actually guilty.

I rubbed my forehead. The mental gymnastics of this was making my head hurt.

"What about how Trevor was posed in front of city hall," I finally said.

"What about it?" Christine challenged.

"Why take that kind of risk?" I asked. "Why not just bury the body or dump it in Star Lake?"

Christine leaned forward. "Trevor did nothing but terrorize and humiliate Sandra. He deserved a little taste of his own medicine," she snapped.

I was about to argue that if he was dead, he didn't actually get to feel any of the humiliation, but Penny started humming the song 'Goodbye Earl,' referencing the way Michelle had used that Dixie Chicks song to talk about how they needed to kill Trevor for Sandra.

Maybe Penny was right. Maybe Michelle and Christine had followed through on their threats from the salon. Where did that leave their other three friends? Accomplices? Friends just trying to muddy the suspect pool?

I wasn't sure what else to ask. Christine's answers were very similar to Michelle's, which could mean they were telling the truth or that they'd rehearsed their answers in an attempt to hide the truth—someone else had killed Trevor and they were all covering for that person.

I planted my hands on Christine's desk and leaned forward. "Listen," I said. "I'm going to discover who's lying and who's telling the truth one way or another. If you're covering for someone, I'll figure it out."

Penny hooked my arm and pulled me toward the door. "And that's our cue to leave," she said in an overly sunny tone. "Thanks, Christine. I sent an email home to Johnny's mom about that missing library book. Hopefully, he'll bring it back tomorrow."

Before Christine could respond, Penny had me out the door.

"What was that for?" I asked as Penny dropped my arm.

"I have to work with Christine. Do you know how much power a school librarian has? Especially over an English teacher? We want to find the truth, but we don't need to make enemies in the process," she said, sounding like the rational one for once.

"But she's lying," I protested. "Or someone is." I clenched my fists. "Someone is lying, and it's making this whole thing more complicated than it needs to be. I need to talk to the other women who confessed."

"Was Lauren Becker one of them? She works part time teaching yoga at Titan Fitness, so she has time to volunteer for Christine a couple of afternoons a week. I know they're close," Penny said.

"Yeah, she was one of them," I said. "But I need to find some excuse to talk to her. I can't just show up at her house."

Penny looked thoughtful before she clapped her hands together. "Go take her yoga class."

"Her yoga class?" I asked. I'd never done yoga, although I wasn't opposed to the idea.

"I'd come with you, but I can't even see my toes, much less touch them," Penny said.

"Gwen?" Chris's voice came from behind me. I turned to see him walking toward us, a confused expression on his face. "What are you doing here?"

"Penny and I are heading over to Rose Lake," I said the same time Penny said, "Gwen is here asking Christine about Trevor's murder."

I shot her a look that said *traitor,* but she seemed unbothered.

"Learn anything useful?" Chris asked. "And what're you doing in Rose Lake?"

"Taco Bell," I said. "And I learned nothing."

"She didn't learn nothing," Penny said. "She's just frustrated that the murderer hasn't stepped forward with his or her hand in the air to say, 'Me, me, me. I did it.'"

"Does that ever happen?" Chris asked in confusion.

"No," I said sullenly. "And technically there are five people waving their hands in the air claiming to have done it. That's what's frustrating."

Chris looped one arm around my shoulder and the other around Penny's as we walked toward the door that would lead to the employee parking lot. We'd spent much of high school like this together, us against the world.

Walking through these halls, I felt sixteen again, when my biggest problem had been whether or not Chris liked me the way I liked him, not whether or not five women were working together to hide a murderer.

CHAPTER SIXTEEN

The trip to Taco Bell had been uneventful but exactly what Penny needed. We'd invited Chris, but he was meeting with Cole, Trevor's business partner, again to finalize the investment in Chris's youth center. Trevor embezzling should have hurt Cole's bottom line. How did he have enough extra money to invest in a nonprofit?

I'd dropped Penny off at her house with a bag of extra tacos that she'd claimed were for her husband, Jack, but could have just as easily been for her. I'd only been home for five minutes when there was a knock at the door.

I'd just added what I'd learned from Michelle and Christine, which was simply that they were sticking to their stories and those stories were suspiciously similar, to my journal. I set it on the couch and went to answer the door.

Finn stood on my front stoop with his back to the door and his attention focused on Trevor's house across the street. Several seconds passed before I cleared my throat.

Finn turned, his eyes bloodshot and his suit rumpled. Even his smile looked tired as he said, "I'm sorry to stop by without calling first, but I was on my way home and suddenly realized I'd rather see you. Is that okay?"

Was that okay? It was more than okay. "Of course," I said, moving to the side so he could come in.

He loosened his tie as he walked in the door, and I had a vision of what it would be like to have Finn come home to me every night. My stomach fluttered at the thought.

"Tough day?" I asked.

Finn moved my journal to the side and sat on the couch. "Tough week," he replied.

I picked up the journal and sat next to him, holding the journal on my lap. "Is it the case?" I asked. I was ninety percent sure it was the case, but Finn could be having a personal problem. His mom had to have surgery over the summer, and he'd spent a lot of time going back and forth. "Is it your mom?" I added before he could answer.

Finn had his head leaned back against the couch and his eyes closed. At my question, he turned his head to look at me. "My mom?" he asked, sounding confused. His expression cleared, and he took my hand. "No, sorry, my mom is fine. It's the case."

"Let me guess," I said. "You haven't been sleeping."

"I've been sleeping," he said with a sly grin.

"Fine, you haven't been sleeping enough," I said with a teasing smile.

"Bingo," Finn said. "Tell me some good news." He closed his eyes again.

"About the case?" I asked in surprise.

"No, just about your life," Finn said. "Although if you have good news about the case, I'll take it."

Delilah chose that moment to make her appearance. She weaved through Finn's legs, meowing pitifully.

I laughed. "Someone wants your attention."

Finn scooped Delilah up and set her on his chest. She snuggled in and purred as loudly as Chip's riding lawn mower. My heart melted right then and there. When I'd first met Finn, he was buttoned up to the point of seeming stuffy. He always wore a suit in a town full of men in jeans and flannel shirts. His truck was meticulously clean, while my Jetta was known to have at least a few food wrappers on the floor. He was a rule follower to a T.

He still wore those suits, but he'd relaxed in the months I'd known him. The old Finn wouldn't have wanted cat hair on his suit. This Finn loved Delilah because I loved Delilah. With sudden clarity, I realized I'd made my decision between Finn and Chris months ago. I'd just been too chicken to own it, much less communicate it to either of the men.

It was tempting to tell Finn the good news, that I wanted to date him and only him, but he was exhausted, and I didn't want to overwhelm him. Instead, I said, "We added LED lights to our window display at the shop today in an attempt to stay one step ahead of Burt at Cozy Cuts. Also, I heard a certain someone is a judge for the contest this year."

Finn ran his hand down Delilah's back, but at least his eyes were open now. "You heard correctly, but I took an oath to judge fairly. No personal feelings will sway my vote," he teased.

"*No* personal feelings?" I asked in an insinuating tone.

"I have to be an impartial judge," Finn said, his grin growing. He was clearly taking great pleasure in this.

I scooped Delilah off his chest. "Then no kitty snuggles for you," I said, pouting and enjoying teasing him about this as much as he was enjoying teasing me.

"What if it's not kitty snuggles I'm interested in?" Finn asked, all teasing dropping from his tone.

I swallowed hard and felt a tingle right down to my toes.

"It depends," I said, sounding breathless.

"On?" Finn asked, leaning forward until our lips were a breath away.

"On whether or not you're going to vote for Camelot Flowers in the contest," I said.

Delilah jumped from my arms and sort of bounced off Finn's chest before falling back on my lap and running away. In the chaos of her escape, she'd knocked my journal to the floor. Finn picked it up while I silently cursed Delilah for not sitting still for two more seconds.

"What's this?" Finn asked.

He held the journal open to my mini murder board. Back to business, I realized with a sigh.

"That's everything I know about Trevor's murder," I said, resigning myself to the reality that the moment had passed.

Finn tapped the page. "That's a good idea about the costume. Seems like a long shot, but I've seen long shots pay off too many times not to pursue them."

I internally preened under Finn's praise. "Henry said that Sandra was in there looking at costumes days before the murder. He's supposed to let me know if she bought anything that would fit Trevor."

"You're still thinking Sandra killed Trevor?" Finn asked.

"I'm keeping my options open," I said vaguely.

Finn nodded. I couldn't tell if it was a nod of acknowledgment or approval.

Pointing at another area on my chart, Finn said, "I tracked down the biker from Bucky's. Andy has a security camera near the front door, and it picked up the guy's license plate."

"And?" I asked impatiently when Finn didn't continue.

"The guy doesn't have an alibi for the rest of the night. He claims he went straight home after Bucky's and that he was home alone. I have an officer going over to Rose Lake to talk to the guy's neighbors, but it was pretty late when all this went down. It's possible they would've been in bed before this guy got home."

"So, another dead end?" I asked, feeling discouraged.

"Not a dead end. I have the guy's prints," Finn said. "I don't have anything to compare them to, but if I find the crime scene or the murder weapon…"

I snapped my fingers. "I almost forgot," I said excitedly. "I was talking to my neighbors, Chip and Rose, and their garage door was up. There was a shovel just leaning there. It looked sharp too. What if that's the murder weapon? What if Trevor threatened Chip's fence when he got home from the bar? What if Chip left the side door to his garage unlocked, and Sandra or her friends snuck in, took the shovel, killed Trevor, cleaned off the shovel, and put it back?"

The more I talked, the more I liked these ideas. "I saw on TV that you can't always get all the blood off something like that. You think you've cleaned it, but you really haven't. You should get that shovel. I bet it killed Trevor." I was practically bouncing in place by the time I'd finished.

Finn took my hand and gave me a bemused smile. "I would love nothing more than to test every shovel in Star Junction, but those theories aren't enough for a warrant. Almost every house in town is going to have a shovel."

"But not every house in town belongs to a person who was constantly fighting with the victim," I pointed out.

"Chip is a serious suspect for you?"

I hesitated. Was Chip a serious suspect, or was I just really wanting to solve this mystery? Maybe Finn was right. A shovel on its own wasn't a smoking gun, so to speak, but Chip did hate Trevor. "I don't know," I finally said with a sigh.

"I think it's unlikely that the killer would leave the murder weapon out where anyone could see it," Finn said.

"Unless Chip doesn't know it's the murder weapon because Sandra's the one who used it and put it back before Chip or Rose noticed it was missing," I said.

My phone buzzed, and I checked it to see a text from Henry. *Sandra bought two children's costumes last week. No scarecrows, and nothing that would fit an adult.*

"Well, shoot," I muttered. I showed Finn the text.

"Like I said, it was a long shot, but it doesn't mean it wasn't a good idea," Finn said kindly.

I blew out a breath. "For once, wouldn't it be nice to have the killer just stand up and confess?" I didn't even realize what I'd said until it was out of my mouth. "I guess that did happen. Too many people confessed."

Finn ran his hand over his short, dark-brown beard. "That's exactly right. Too many people confessed."

"I talked to two of them today," I said. "Michelle and Christine."

"Thoughts?" he asked.

He didn't ask me why I'd talked to them or question the wisdom of me talking to them. We were making incredible progress in working together to solve these murders. At least in my opinion. Totally possible it was more out of a sense of resignation on Finn's part.

"They both stuck to their stories that they'd been the one to kill Trevor, but both of their stories were vague and a little too match-y," I said.

"Match-y?" Finn asked.

"You know, it was almost the same story word for word, which could mean they were both there and they're lying about doing it alone or neither of them was there and they created the stories together," I said.

"I was thinking the same thing," Finn said.

"I'm going to go to Laura Becker's yoga class tomorrow morning," I said. "See if I can get anything out of her."

I thought Finn was going to argue that it wasn't necessary because he'd already interviewed all of them, but instead he said, "What are you hoping to learn?"

"I'm hoping that at least one of them will crack and admit that they're all covering for someone else," I said. "I'm really hoping that they'll say something to me, even if by accident, that they wouldn't say to you."

"And the person they're covering for would be...?" Finn asked, trailing off.

"Sandra," I said sheepishly. I felt bad that I kept thinking she was guilty, but it was the only thing that made sense in light of her friends' behavior. "Or they all did it together," I said.

Instead of commenting on my ongoing theory that Sandra killed her husband, Finn looked back at my journal and said, "Have you talked to Cole Johnson?"

I nodded. "He was upset that I was asking questions. Honestly, I think the only reason he was willing to say as much as he did is because he knows my dad from the Renaissance faire circuit and remembers me from when I was a little kid."

"I hope it goes without saying that anything I share with you stays between us," Finn said.

I sat up with interest. This sounded like it was about to get juicy. I held out my pinky finger. "I promise."

Finn looked at my finger in confusion. "What's that about?"

I let out a put-upon sigh, took his hand, and hooked his pinky with mine. "It's a pinky promise," I said. "Haven't you ever made a pinky promise before?"

"Not as an adult," he teased. He kept our pinkies hooked together, which I didn't mind one bit. "I confirmed that two hundred thousand dollars went missing from Baker and Johnson's investment portfolio. Cole swears Trevor has it, but it's not in any of the Bakers' bank accounts. At least not the ones obviously connected to Trevor. I have a forensic accountant looking into it."

"So, it's true," I said, looking across the street at Sandra's house. "Do you think that's why Trevor wanted to move? He's got the money stashed away in some offshore account and can't spend it anywhere near Star Junction."

"It's certainly a theory," Finn said. "I'll know more if we can track the money."

"What now?" I asked, even as my mind was spinning with questions about Cole. He'd just moved up my list of suspects. Maybe he had a shovel in his garage right now with Trevor's DNA on it.

"I'll keep chipping away at the evidence," Finn said. He rubbed his eyes and yawned. "Sorry, I'm running on fumes."

"I understand," I said. "Are you going back to the office after this?"

"Believe it or not, I'm going to go home and sleep," Finn said. "Margie finally got to me. That woman is persistent beyond belief."

"I think that's an excellent idea." I wanted to suggest he stay and hang out, but I could see how tired he was. Standing, I pulled him to his feet, which basically meant I tugged on his hand until he stood on his own. I was definitely not strong enough to lift him. Maybe if I went to Laura's yoga class consistently, I'd develop some sleek but strong muscles.

"I'll let you know if I learn anything at yoga tomorrow," I said. "I just wish it wasn't so early in the morning."

Finn shrugged into his coat. "I didn't know you had a membership to the gym."

"I don't," I said as I followed him to the door. "But I can buy a day pass. Who knows? Maybe I'll like it and get a membership. Then I'll get super strong." I put my arms up in the classic pose people used to show off their biceps. My bulky sweatshirt definitely made me look more buff than I was.

Finn's smile sent a riot of butterflies through my stomach. I loved making that man smile. "Go," I said as I herded him out the door. "No more working tonight."

He turned on the top step. "Yes, ma'am," he said with a sexy grin.

I bit my bottom lip and fought the urge to swoon as Finn walked to his big black truck and drove away. The witch next door let out a cackle. I jumped, slamming my hip into the wrought iron railing on my front stoop.

"Ow," I shouted toward my neighbor's house. Not that the witch cared that my hip stung and she'd totally killed the mood. "I hate you," I muttered as I went back inside and locked the door.

Tomorrow, I'd see if Laura's story matched Michelle's and Christine's. Finn had to work within pesky laws, including getting warrants, but I wasn't a police officer. I could do whatever I wanted. Okay, not *whatever* I wanted, but more than Finn could do.

How hard would it be to track down that biker? Finn said he had officers canvassing the guy's neighborhood, which is probably as much as I could do. Maybe Penny would be willing to do a drive-by of Cole's house with me tomorrow. We could see if he had a shovel hanging around. Maybe we'd even find the crime scene. Money was a powerful motivator, and Cole had two hundred thousand pieces of motivation to want Trevor dead.

CHAPTER SEVENTEEN

Delilah's incessant meowing woke me up.

"This yoga class is too early in the morning," I complained to no one. "I can't do it."

Delilah meowed again, this time right in my ear.

"Okay, okay," I said as I grabbed my phone.

Except it wasn't five thirty in the morning. It was two. "Delilah, go back to sleep," I said as I pulled the covers up around my neck. "It's the middle of the night."

She butted her head into my shoulder.

"I'm not feeding you at two in the morning," I said, annoyed.

She put her paws on my shoulder.

Downstairs, a floorboard let out a loud creak.

Bolting upright in bed, my heart raced. I scooped up Delilah and held her tight. "It was just the house settling," I murmured to her.

Creak.

I let out a tiny *eep* that roughly translated to—*Someone's in my house, and it's probably the murderer, and they've brought the shovel, and they're here to finish me off.*

My mind raced as my body sat frozen. I had to do something. Calling the police would take too long. The intruder was already in the house. A soft thud came from downstairs, and my stomach clenched with fear.

I had to do something *now*.

Whoever was down there needed to know I wasn't alone. I didn't have time for the police, but maybe I could make them think the police were already here.

"Did you hear that noise, Finn?" I said loudly. "It sounds like someone's in the house."

I was taking a huge gamble. Finn's truck was clearly not parked outside. If whoever was down there didn't believe my ruse, all it would do was alert them to the fact that I knew they were in my house. Was I just luring them up here faster?

"What's that?" I practically shouted. "Yes, I absolutely think you should get your gun and go check out what's down there."

There was a crash followed by the sound of the back door slamming shut.

I went into motion, scrambling from the bed and racing down the stairs. Maybe I could catch a glimpse of whoever it was. Just in case the door closing was a trick, I kept up my fake dialogue with Finn. "I don't think you need to arrest whoever is here. Just shoot them in the head. We can say it was self-defense," I shouted as I raced through the kitchen.

I tripped on a kitchen chair that had been knocked over and went sprawling on the floor. "Ouch," I shouted, but I didn't have time for self-pity.

The witch next door cackled loudly. I scrambled to my feet and ran to the front of the house, but no one was there. Standing on my front stoop in my blue pajama pants covered in palm trees, my arm aching from where I fell and my chest heaving with a combination of fear and adrenaline, I looked out over my quiet street.

A light went on at Sandra's house, despite the late hour. I sucked in a sharp breath. Could sweet Sandra have just broken into my house? Or was it her friends? Maybe they'd all done it. Had I almost been another victim of a best-friend-murder-pact?

I shivered and hugged my arms across my chest. I needed to call Finn. My phone was upstairs. I found it on my bedside table, right next to where Delilah was comfortably asleep in the warm blankets I'd abandoned to confront whoever had broken into my house. I went downstairs to the kitchen as the phone rang.

Finn's groggy voice said, "Detective Butler."

The guilt I felt at waking Finn up vied with my fear. "Finn?" I said tentatively. "It's Gwen."

"What's wrong?" he asked, sounding much more alert.

"I want to start by saying that I'm safe and everything's fine now," I said. I stepped over the chair I'd tripped on, feeling like I shouldn't touch anything until Finn could get over here in case the person had left behind evidence.

"I'm on my way," Finn said. There was a rustling in the background like he was getting dressed or pulling on a coat. "What happened?"

My back door was slightly ajar, the frame splintered where the intruder had jimmied the lock open.

"Someone broke in," I explained. My steady voice sounded impressive in light of the fact that my heart was trying to beat its way out of my chest.

There was a beat of heavy silence before Finn said, "Gwen, listen to me. I want you to lock yourself in the bathroom and wait for me to get there."

Catching the bottom of the door with my foot, I eased it open and peered into the backyard. The sound of my neighbor's witch seemed to indicate that the intruder had made it to the street and disappeared, but what if that wasn't the case? What if one of the hundred other things that had set off that infernal witch over the past few days was responsible for the sound?

No one jumped at me as I leaned out the door and looked around. Nothing moved in the shadows. "No one's here anymore. I scared them away," I explained.

"You what?" Finn asked, sounding upset. I heard something slam. Maybe his car door. "I'm leaving now."

"I'll see you soon," I said, pushing the door mostly closed with my hip, very proud of myself for not touching anything.

"No, don't hang up," Finn said urgently.

"Okay…" I replied slowly. "How was your day?" I added in a faux-sunny tone.

"Seriously, Gwen?" Finn sounded frustrated. "Someone broke into your house, we have no idea their intentions, and you want to talk about my day?"

"You're right. I'm sorry. I saw you right before you went to bed. I already know about your day," I said as I moved to the front of the house and looked out the window. All the lights were off at Sandra's house.

"You know that's not what I meant," Finn growled. "Why can't you have a healthy sense of self-preservation?"

My eyes flooded with tears. Not so much from Finn's tone, although I didn't appreciate being scolded. Blinking rapidly, I willed the tears back into my body, but one disobeyed me and escaped. I swiped at it. "This is how I cope, okay? I can't think about what could've happened. I can't even think about what did happen. Not while I'm here alone."

Silence.

"Finn?" I asked hesitantly.

"I'm sorry," he said, his tone softening. "I'm a block away. I'm going to hang up so I can call an officer to meet me at the house, but I'll be there in thirty seconds."

"That's fine with me," I said cheekily. "You're the one who wanted to stay on the phone." The good old coping strategies of denial and flirting were back. Hallelujah.

Finn chuckled before hanging up, but I had a feeling it was out of pity and only because he was pulling in front of my house right that very moment. He sat in his truck for a second on the phone before he cut the engine, got out, and looked around.

I watched all of this from the front window, not wanting to step back outside into the cold. I had a fleeting thought that I should change out of these pajamas, especially with other officers coming over, but before I could decide whether or not to change, Finn was on his way to the door.

I met him there, and he pulled me into the coldest yet warmest hug of my life. Cold from Finn's jacket seeped through my thin pajama top, but I'd never felt so safe. "Thank you for coming," I murmured into his chest.

"Always," Finn said. "I'll always come for you."

"You'd always come for anyone in trouble," I protested, although the warmth from the hug was quickly turning to heat at his words.

Finn took my shoulders and leaned me back enough to look into his eyes. "Especially for you," Finn said. "And not everyone in town has my personal number."

I adopted an innocent expression, batting my eyes for extra effect. "You mean not everyone in town has Detective Griffin Butler's private number?" I said, my voice growing breathy like Marilyn Monroe singing for the president.

"Brat," Finn said with a smile that ensured me that he liked it.

"It's be sassy or melt into a puddle of tears and anxiety," I said, still smiling.

"I'll take you either way," Finn said, sounding sincere enough that it threatened to break right through my perfectly good coping strategy.

"Do you want me to show you what happened?" I asked.

"Let's wait until Tommy gets here to go over the details," Finn said. "I want to clear the house."

"I'm telling you, no one is here," I said. "They ran off."

"And how exactly did you get an intruder to run off?" Finn asked.

"Um," I said, breaking eye contact. "I just yelled and stuff."

"Guinevere." Finn's tone was warning. "If you'd really just 'yelled and stuff,' you wouldn't be acting so suspicious."

He made a good point. If only I were a better liar. Although, then I'd be a liar, and that's not who I wanted to be either. There was no winning in this situation.

I put my hands on my hips, feeling a little embarrassed and defensive that this had been my go-to idea. "Fine. Delilah woke me up, and I thought it was morning and she wanted to be fed, but then I realized it wasn't morning, so I thought she was just being annoying, but then she wouldn't stop, and then I heard a creak coming from downstairs, and then a thud. Old houses creak, but they don't thud, so I knew someone was in here, and then I freaked out, and I didn't know what to do, so I pretended that you were here with me and started talking to fake-you really loudly and told you to get your gun and check out what was going on downstairs."

I'd delivered that whole speech in one breath, which left me sucking in a big breath before adding, "And then I heard the back door slam, so I knew they'd left."

"You pretended I was here?" Finn asked.

I couldn't tell if he was upset or not. "Yes?" I said tentatively.

His mouth moved in a motion I'd come to recognize as him trying to suppress a smile. I'd learned it because I'd seen it directed my way plenty of times since we'd met.

Headlights washed over the room, and we both turned to watch a police SUV pull up behind Finn's truck.

"We'll address the idea of me being here in the middle of the night another time," Finn said. His words sent delicious shivers through my body.

Finn met Tommy at the front door. "Got everything we need?"

Tommy held up a black duffel bag. "Yep." He turned to me and said, "We keep meeting like this."

Whether or not he was referencing the time he was the officer who'd responded to my 9-1-1 call when Justin was murdered, the time Justin's killer tried to kill me, or the time I just happened to be at the coffee shop when someone dropped dead, I couldn't be sure. Just the fact that I had to wonder threatened to give me a headache.

"Thanks for coming, Tommy," I said.

"Part of the job," he said simply. "Where are we setting up?" he asked Finn.

"I want to clear the house, although Gwen is sure no one is still here. Set up in the kitchen," Finn replied.

Tommy nodded and headed toward the kitchen.

I pointed after him and said, "I'm going to show him the broken lock on the back door."

"I'll be right behind you," Finn said as he headed upstairs.

He wasn't wrong about the fact that he'd be right back. My house was tiny. Two bedrooms and one bathroom at the top of the stairs. Just the living room, kitchen, and a tiny powder room downstairs. It wouldn't take him long to search the place.

As I made my way into the kitchen, I mentally sorted through what my room looked like, hoping I hadn't left anything embarrassing on the floor. Nothing I could do about it now.

Tommy had set the duffel bag on the kitchen table. He was staring at the overturned chair. "Did you knock this over?" he asked when he noticed me approaching.

I shook my head. "It was like this when I tried to get a glimpse of who'd been in my house. I tripped on it, but it was already knocked over. I think whoever was in here knocked it down when they were running out."

Tommy stood with his hands resting on his utility belt. "You chased after the intruder?"

I suddenly felt like I was in trouble. "I mean, chased after isn't the way I'd put it. I heard the door slam, so I knew they were already gone. I just wanted to see if I could figure out who it was."

"Still," Tommy said, sounding doubtful. "It's not a good idea to try to confront an intruder."

I opened my mouth to argue, once again, that I hadn't been trying to confront anyone, but Finn walked into the room, looking around before turning his attention to Tommy and me. "Gwen, why don't you go over what happened."

I grimaced, unsure if he meant that I should tell the *whole* story, including how I'd chased the intruder away. "Well, uh, first I was sleeping," I started slowly. Finn and Tommy waited for me to continue. "So, Delilah woke me up, and I heard a creak coming from downstairs. I thought maybe it was just the house, but then I heard a thud."

This is where I had a decision to make. Finn knew the whole truth, so I decided to be vague, and if he wanted more details in front of Tommy, he could ask for them. "I started yelling about checking out the noise. Then I heard a loud crash, which I think was this chair falling over, and the door slam. Then I ran down here and tripped on the chair in the dark and fell. A few seconds later, I heard my neighbor's mechanical witch cackle, so I assumed the intruder ran past it. I ran to the front door, but by the time I got there, the street was empty."

"So, you chased the intruder twice," Tommy said.

I didn't know where he got off being critical of my choices. I'd been in high school chemistry with Tommy. I was the only reason he'd passed that class. Maybe one thing didn't have to do with the other, but I thought it should earn me a little grace right now.

Before I could defend myself, Finn said, "I didn't know you'd fallen. Are you okay? Do you need to go to the hospital?" he asked.

I pulled up the sleeves of my pajama top and looked at my elbow. "No, I'm fine. Just some bruises that I'm sure will show up tomorrow." My hip was also hurting, but there was no way I was about to pull my pants down to check that out.

Finn turned to Tommy. "Let's dust the door and chair for fingerprints. We can't know what else the intruder might have touched, and I don't want to dust the whole downstairs."

"I don't know if this matters, but there was a light on at Sandra's house right after it happened," I said.

Finn looked at me appraisingly as Tommy said, "Why would that matter?"

"Gwen thinks Sandra might have murdered Trevor," Finn said. His tone held no emotion, as if he was simply stating a fact.

"Or her friends," I said. "Or all of them together."

"Her friends *did* confess," Tommy said as he pulled supplies from the bag. "At least we have their prints. Have any of them been in your house recently?"

"No," I said. "We're not close."

"Any theories as to why someone would've broken into your house?" Tommy asked.

I knew Finn had taken Tommy under his wing and was helping him prepare for the detective exam. Finn looked pleased with Tommy's line of questioning.

"I don't know," I said. "I was too freaked out when it happened to wonder about that."

"What about now?" Tommy pressed gently. "Any thoughts?"

I shrugged. "Could've been totally random."

Both Finn and Tommy looked at me like I was being absurd.

"What?" I said defensively. "It might have been random. You don't know."

Tommy went to work dusting both the doorknob and the frame of the door.

"It's best to work under the assumption that this is related to Trevor's murder," Finn said.

"Why's that?" I challenged.

"Because it's the most dangerous of the scenarios," he said.

Tommy nodded his agreement but kept working on collecting prints from the door.

"Most dangerous doesn't mean most likely," I said.

Finn didn't say anything, but I could see the frustration on his face, and I knew deep inside that it was really fear. I was scared too. I didn't like to think that the break-in had anything to do with Trevor's murder. I didn't like to think about the fact that someone had broken into my house for any reason.

"Gwen?" Chris's voice called from the front of the house.

I looked at Finn in confusion before heading toward the front door.

Chris stood in the open doorway in gray sweats and a white T-shirt. His hair was messy like he'd jumped out of bed and headed over without looking in a mirror.

"What are you doing here?" I asked.

Chris pulled me into a tight hug. "I'm so glad you're okay."

I was very aware that Finn had followed me into the room. I wiggled my way out of the hug. The front door was still open, letting cold air into the room. "You must be freezing. Where's your coat?"

I rushed to the couch and grabbed a blanket, wrapping it around Chris's shoulders. He gave me that charming smile that had had me wrapped around his finger since middle school. "I was worried about you. I didn't think of grabbing a coat," he said.

It was very sweet. And with Finn standing next to me, very awkward. I asked again, "What are you doing here?"

Chris ran his hand through his hair, which calmed it slightly. "You keep finding yourself in these dangerous situations, and I never hear about them until much later. Sometimes days later. I got a police scanner in case something really bad happened. I heard your address mentioned when Tommy was talking to dispatch."

I wasn't sure how I felt about Chris having a police scanner to keep track of me. The old me would have found it sweet.

Apparently, Finn knew exactly how he felt about it. "We'll talk about this later," he said to Chris.

"There's nothing to talk about," Chris said. "It's legal. I checked."

The two men eyed each other until Finn said, "We've got things covered here."

Chris had been dismissed.

"It's no problem, man," Chris said, his voice friendly but his expression firm. "I'm sure you guys have to log the evidence or something whenever you're done here. I'm staying to make sure Gwen is okay and the intruder doesn't come back." He turned to me. "I'll sleep on the couch."

"You don't have to—" I started.

Before I could finish, Finn interrupted with, "I'm staying too."

The men squared off like two silverback gorillas preparing to defend their territories. Actually, I knew way more about knights, thanks to my dad, than gorillas. They looked like two knights preparing to duel over my honor. I didn't hate it.

"I only have one couch," I said. Although I had two bedrooms, one was set up as an office with no bed. All my family and friends lived in Star Junction. What did I need a guest room for?

"I'll sleep on the floor," Finn said, not breaking his standoff with Chris.

I waited a beat for one of them to relent.

Instead, Chris said, "Gwen and I will be fine. No need to stay."

"As the person with a gun, I think I'm better equipped to protect Gwen," Finn countered.

"I can protect Gwen just fine," Chris said. "I've been doing it for years."

Now this was getting ridiculous. I wasn't sure what kind of protecting Chris thought he'd been doing in my relatively peaceful life, but I wasn't going to get sucked into their squabbles. I left them discussing who should stay while I went upstairs and pulled every extra blanket and set of sheets I owned from the narrow linen closet in the hallway next to the bathroom.

I carried it all downstairs and edged my way between Chris and Finn, who were still at it. They both stopped and watched me set the pile on the couch. I gave the blankets a little pat and said, "I have to be up early to go to a yoga class."

"I didn't know you—" Chris started.

I held up a hand to stop him. "I appreciate both of you wanting to make sure I'm safe. I'm going to bed. Work it out amongst yourselves. If no one stays, lock the door behind you when you leave."

"I'm staying," Chris said definitively.

"Me too," Finn said with just as much conviction.

The adrenaline of chasing someone out of my house was fading fast. If I didn't make it upstairs soon, I'd be the one crashing on the couch. Then the guys could share my bed. I barely suppressed a giggle at the thought.

"Great," I said. I passed between them and stopped long enough to give them each a kiss on the cheek. "Thanks for caring about me. I'll see you in the morning."

Without waiting for a reply or checking to see how each of them felt about the fact that I'd given the other one a very chaste kiss, I went upstairs and collapsed into bed. My alarm was going to go off much too soon after my exciting night, but I was determined to talk to Laura about her confession to Trevor's murder, an intruder keeping me up half the night or not.

CHAPTER EIGHTEEN

My alarm went off just a couple of hours later. Much too early. Why did people do yoga this early in the morning? Night yoga sounded doable to me. Even late afternoon. This morning stuff? Not so much. I groggily climbed out of bed, found the clothes I'd been smart enough to lay out the night before, and stumbled downstairs.

A pile of three neatly folded blankets on the chair and a sleeping Chris on the couch brought the events of the night roaring back. I groaned and detoured into the kitchen. I needed coffee, but I didn't have time.

I filled Delilah's food and water bowls. The lucky girl was still asleep, snuggled into my warm blankets. Checking my phone, I saw a text from Finn. *Left at five. I'm making running the evidence we collected from your house top priority. I'll be staying there until we catch whoever did this or I have enough evidence to convince me it's not connected to Trevor's murder.*

So, Finn had stayed. I'd wondered, because the blankets on the chair looked unused, but that actually tracked with what I knew of Finn. His house was clean. His truck was clean. The man was meticulous in everything he did.

I grinned as I texted back. *Thanks for rushing over here last night. You definitely didn't need to stay. I'm sure sleeping on the floor wasn't the most comfortable.*

I grabbed my coat and went back into the living room, where Chris continued to sleep away. I had a feeling he wasn't going to be willing to leave me alone with an unknown intruder on the loose, and the chances of him staying would quadruple if he knew Finn planned on staying.

Although I'd argued with Finn and Tommy the night before about whether or not the break-in was related to Trevor's murder, my argument had been more out of a mix of annoyance that they'd assumed the worst and fear that they were right. There was no way of knowing at this point. If I wanted my house back and for Finn and Chris to be able to sleep in their own beds, I was going to have to figure out who killed Trevor. And fast.

It was still dark as I got into my car. I sent a quick text to Chris thanking him for staying and telling him I'd be fine tonight, although I was sure he wouldn't agree with my assessment. I asked him to lock up when he left for work.

Titan Fitness was down the street from Camelot Flowers. I checked out our Halloween display on my way past. The knight looked amazing with the LED lights. There was no way we were losing this year.

I parked my car in the small lot next to the gym and hurried inside. A man stood behind a check-in desk wearing a name tag that read *Mike*.

"Good morning," Mike said entirely too cheerfully.

"Hi, I'd like to take the yoga class happening in a few minutes. Is it possible to buy a day pass?" I asked.

"Absolutely," Mike said. "Welcome to Titan Fitness. I'm the owner, Mike Petpski. You can buy a day pass for ten dollars, and here's a brochure of our member pricing if you decide you'd like to come back."

"Thanks," I said. I took the brochure, but I was pretty sure I wouldn't be back. I filled out the waiver saying I wouldn't sue the gym if I somehow died during yoga and handed over my debit card.

Mike walked me to a room in the back. The floors were hardwood, and the front of the room was lined with mirrors. Several women were setting up mats in the middle of the room. I didn't know Laura, the instructor, but I was guessing she was the one wearing the microphone talking to another woman in the front of the room.

"We offer yoga, Pilates, Zumba, and a variety of strength classes. I'll make sure you get a schedule on your way out," Mike said.

"Thank you," I said again.

"Gwen?" a voice said from behind me.

I internally groaned. I'd know that voice anywhere. Scratch that. I'd know that overwhelming stench of cologne anywhere.

I turned and gave Derek Thompson a tight smile.

"I didn't know you did yoga," Derek said, managing to make the simple statement drip with innuendo.

"I don't," I said. "In fact, I'm the least flexible person on the planet." I was sure that wasn't true, but I wanted to paint as unappealing a picture as possible where Derek was concerned.

"Derek, I wanted to ask you about something related to the event we're throwing next weekend," Mike said, pulling Derek away.

I'd never been so thankful in my life. I might join the gym simply out of gratitude for Mike's timing.

I used the distraction to walk into the workout room. I set my purse by the others in the back and grabbed a yoga mat. I wasn't sure if Derek was coming into the class or if he was simply passing by on his way to the heavy weights, but I didn't want to take any chances that he'd end up on a yoga mat behind me.

I set my mat up in the back, between two other women who gave me friendly smiles but otherwise didn't engage. That was fine with me. Six was too early to be making small talk.

I kept an eye on Laura as I mimicked the stretches the women around me were doing. Unfortunately, Laura's conversation with the woman she was talking to lasted right until the start of class.

The woman returned to her mat, and Laura clapped her hands together. "Welcome to sunrise yoga," she said in a soft, sweet voice. Her light-brown hair was sectioned into two braids that hung over her shoulders. Her face was makeup free, but somehow had a glow I'd need three different beauty products to get. It was probably all the yoga.

Between her soothing smile and calming voice, I liked the woman already. Even this early in the morning, which was saying a lot. I definitely couldn't picture her murdering anyone.

The first ten minutes of class involved a lot of breathing and stretching. I handled it like a pro. Most of the terms sounded familiar. It was hard to make it to almost thirty years old without hearing people talk about yoga, even if I'd never done it. What the terms actually meant was a different story altogether, but I was good at copying the poses Laura led us through and was starting to feel confident.

Derek hadn't come back into the room. I was keeping up with the class. Maybe I would join the gym. Sure, Derek practically lived here when he wasn't working or somehow bumping into me around town, but my schedule was flexible. I was sure I could find a time to work out when he wasn't here.

"Now we're going to move into crow," Laura said, her tone soothing. "This is an advanced pose, so I'll be showing several modifications."

Laura talked us through the pose as she squatted down with her feet together but her knees spread wide. She put her hands on the mat and leaned her hips up. Before I knew what was happening, her feet were off the floor as she balanced on just her hands with her knees pressed into her triceps.

There was no way. Except everyone else was getting into the pose just fine.

Laura dropped her feet back to the mat gracefully and said, "To modify, simply leave your feet on the floor. You'll still get the excellent stretch this pose provides as well as build strength in the arms."

I watched her skeptically. True, her feet were no longer off the floor, but it still looked impossible. I was currently the only one standing. Best to at least look like I was doing the pose.

Placing my hands flat on the floor with my knees bent, I leaned forward, resting my knees against my upper arms. I grinned excitedly. I was doing it. Sure, I was doing the modification, but I bet it still looked really cool. This wasn't even that hard. Maybe I could just kick my feet up a little bit. I'd always been good at the balance beam in elementary school the one month every year we'd done gymnastics.

With all the confidence that my seven-year-old self had used to jump and twirl on the balance beam, I kicked my feet up just enough to get them off the floor. With all the horror of my current twenty-nine-year-old self, I felt my body pitch to the right.

"Sorry!" I managed to yelp as I slammed into the woman next to me, who fell forward, knocking over her stainless-steel water bottle. It rolled, bumping into another woman, who didn't exactly fall but didn't exactly leave the pose gracefully.

My shoulder throbbed, my hip, which I'd injured the night before when tripping on the chair, screamed at me, and my face flamed with embarrassment.

"Are you alright?" Laura asked with concern as she hurried over.

I hadn't moved, which was probably a large part of her concern.

"Did you hit your head?" she asked as she knelt next to me.

"No," I said to my yoga mat, not wanting to meet her gaze. "I'm fine. Just dying of embarrassment and trying to figure out a way to crawl out of here with some of my dignity."

Laura chuckled and extended her hand to help me up. I took it, testing my muscles as I stood. The woman I'd knocked into was already up, and she didn't even look angry.

"It's happened to all of us. Right, Nicole?" the woman said to someone in the front row.

The woman in the front row laughed. "We promised to never talk about that again." She turned to me and added, "At least you fell out of something challenging. I was in warrior pose one minute and on my butt the next."

As the women shared their own stories, the flash of embarrassment faded to a warm, cozy feeling of belonging, growing my desire to join the gym.

"You're sure you're okay?" Laura asked.

"I'll be fine," I said as I took a step to grab my water bottle. I winced as I put pressure on my right leg.

Laura looked concerned. "Let me get you some ice. Nicole, can you finish the cooldown?"

Nicole nodded, and Laura said, "I'll be right back."

As I waited for her to return, I decided the best thing would be to sit in the back where I couldn't do any more damage. I limped over to a chair by the purses and gingerly sat. Laura was back a minute later with a disposable ice pack. She popped the seal inside and shook it out before handing it to me.

This wasn't how I'd planned to get some time alone with Laura, but I wasn't foolish enough to waste my opportunity. "Thanks for the ice pack," I said.

"Hopefully it's just a bruise," Laura said with concern.

"I'm sure it'll be fine. I tripped on a chair in my house last night and fell on this hip. I'll just have layers of bruises," I said with what I hoped was a disarming smile before adding, "I don't know if you remember me, but I was at the police station when you came in to confess to killing Trevor Baker."

Laura glanced over her shoulder at the other ladies in the room, but they were busy lying flat on their backs with their eyes closed. I couldn't believe I was missing out on what looked like the best yoga pose of them all. It was probably called something like *divine nap*.

"Now that you mention it, I remember," Laura said quietly. "I felt like you looked familiar. You're dating that detective."

"Sort of," I said, not knowing how to define my relationship with Finn for someone else when I didn't even know how to define it for myself. Getting back on track, I decided to take the same approach I had with Michelle and Christine. "I'm surprised Detective Butler didn't arrest you. Murder is a serious crime."

Laura fidgeted with the bottom of her tank top. "Well, he said not to go anywhere and that he'd be talking to me again," she said, sounding nervous.

"It's kind of confusing that you all confessed," I said. "Does that mean you all killed him together?"

Laura's eyes widened like I'd just suggested something horrific, although I didn't know how that was any different than her murdering him on her own. "No, my friends are just covering for me."

Laura seemed very kind and really anxious. I could use that to my advantage. While I'd tried to hint at details when talking to the other women, I went for a more direct approach, hoping to shock the truth out of her. "How'd you do it?" I asked. "I know that's a really personal question, but I figured that if you were willing to confess to killing Trevor, you probably don't mind sharing the details."

Now she looked like a deer caught in the headlights. "How'd I kill him?" she squeaked out.

Miraculously, the other women were still lying on the floor. *Divine nap* must be a pose you did for a really long time. I was jealous I was missing out.

"Yeah," I pressed. "How'd you do it?"

"Well, I just, um..." She licked her lips and wiped her hands on her yoga tights. "I just kind of, you know..." She made a sort of weak swooshing motion through the air with her hand.

Could it have been the motion of someone swinging a shovel into Trevor's head? Possibly. It could have just as easily been the motion of someone timid trying to hail a taxi in New York City.

"You just kind of..." I mimicked her movement.

"Yeah, like that," she said. "I had to do it. It was self-defense."

That tracked with what the other ladies had said. "He attacked you?"

She nodded.

"And so you had to—" I made the motion with my hand again.

She nodded again, as if she didn't even have the words.

While I'd left my conversations with Michelle and Christine considering that they were telling the truth in their confessions, I was fairly certain Laura had nothing to do with Trevor's death. She couldn't even describe it with any kind of conviction.

"*Namaste*," Nicole said from the front of the room. "Thank you all for coming."

"I better go," Laura said. "I hope you come back again. Maybe just ease into doing crow pose."

"I might come back," I said sincerely. "I liked it until I turned into a human domino."

"Don't say anything to anyone about the murder," Laura said quickly as the women started drifting around the room, putting their mats away and grabbing their purses or gym bags. "Nobody knows about it."

I wanted to point out that if Laura was willing to confess to murder, she must have realized that the news of her getting arrested, if it came to that, would make front-page news in Star Junction, not to mention the entire county. She must be covering for someone she really cared about to risk not just her reputation, but her freedom as well.

I thought back to the light that went on in Sandra's house right after someone had broken into my house. Coupled with how much her friends cared about her, the evidence, although circumstantial, was pointing more and more toward Sandra killing her husband.

"I won't say anything," I promised. I was determined to catch a killer, but I had no interest in spreading unnecessary gossip.

"Thanks," she said with a small smile before turning and talking to a woman in black joggers and a tight purple tank top.

I stood, testing the pain in my hip. It ached, but I'd survive. Gathering my things, I said goodbye to a few women on my way out. The rising sun was just tinging the sky a lighter shade of blue, and I wondered if Chris had managed to get up and make it to work on time.

The glowing *Open* sign in the window of Just Beans called to me like a beacon of hope. What I needed to get through the rest of the day was caffeine and sugar. Then I could decide what to do next in my efforts to find Trevor's killer, because one thing I knew for certain—someone was lying, and I was going to figure out who.

CHAPTER NINETEEN

The line was long at the counter of Just Beans, at least by Star Junction standards, but the tables were empty, which meant most people were grabbing coffee on their way to work. I lined up behind a woman who was carrying a purse, a diaper bag, and a backpack, despite the fact that she looked to be alone.

I tried to study the menu. Instead, all I could think about was how angry the bruise on my hip was going to look when I finally got a chance to check it out and how sure I was that Laura was lying.

If Laura was lying, it stood to reason that her friends were too. While I'd always leaned toward the idea that they were covering for someone, this was the first time I felt justified in my theory. The line moved quickly as Amanda, the owner of Just Beans, and another employee made drinks at lightning speed.

Before I could decide what I was going to treat myself to, I was next in line.

Amanda gave me a sunny smile and said, "You're here early. What can I get you?"

I splayed my hands on the counter and leaned forward like a cowboy finally making it to the saloon after a long day out on the range, except I wasn't about to order a whiskey. "The sugariest, most caffeinated drink you have."

Amanda quirked an eyebrow at my criteria but didn't comment. "That would be one of my new energy drinks. I'm calling them Hurricanes. You can order a Category One through Category Five. Five has enough caffeine to keep anyone up all night."

"Give me a five," I said with conviction.

She rang up the drink, and the guy behind the counter went to work making it. I didn't watch. I didn't want to know what went into something labeled Category Five.

"Rough night?" Amanda asked.

Thankfully, I seemed to have shown up at the end of the morning rush, as no one was in line behind me. "Rough night. Rough morning. Have you ever done yoga?" I asked.

Amanda's expression turned sympathetic as she took in my outfit. "Is that where you just came from?"

"A Cat Five Hurricane for Gwen," the man said, sliding a drink with a mound of whipped cream on the top across the counter.

Thankfully it was in a white cup, not a clear one. I could drink it without all the guilt of seeing exactly how many food dyes and other chemical components made up the drink. I'd just pretend it was the best-tasting green juice in history. I had a very good imagination. I'd honed it with my crush on Chris for over a decade.

"You got a minute, or do you need to get to work?" Amanda asked.

"I've definitely got a minute. The store doesn't open for hours," I said.

The truth was, I wasn't in a hurry to go back to my house. The break-in hung over the place like a creepy, dark cloud.

Amanda turned to the guy behind the counter and said, "I'm going to take a break."

"No problem," he said as he wiped down the espresso machine.

"Grab a seat. I'll be there in a minute," Amanda said to me.

I picked a seat near the gas fireplace and took my first sip of the Hurricane. I almost died and went to heaven right then and there. Who cared who murdered Trevor? Who cared who broke into my house? Who cared about when Finn would kiss me? That last one shook me back to reality. Actually, I cared. I cared about that a lot.

Amanda joined me with her own drink, probably healthier than mine. "Sore from yoga?" she asked sympathetically.

"Worse," I said dramatically. "Can someone actually die from embarrassment, because I might."

Amanda chuckled. "Oh no, what happened?"

I told her about falling and knocking over not one, but two other people in the class.

It was clear she was trying to suppress her natural reaction to my story, but her eyes danced with held in laughter, and I wasn't fooled.

"Go ahead and laugh," I said glumly.

It was like a dam breaking free. "I'm sorry," she said through gasping breaths. "It's just that I could picture every second of that."

"Great," I said. "Good to know I have a reputation for my clumsiness."

"No," Amanda said, still with a wide smile on her face, but at least she wasn't actively laughing anymore. "It's not that. You're a good storyteller. That's all it is."

"Right," I said, not buying it for a second. "To sum it all up, my hip is killing me, I'm going to have a nasty bruise, and I'm not sure I can show my face there again, although before I fell, I was actually enjoying the class."

"You can show your face there again," Amanda said with a scoff. "It sounded like everyone was super nice about it."

"That's true," I conceded.

I was tempted to tell her about the break-in at my house, but it felt weird to tell Amanda when Penny and my parents didn't know. It didn't mean I couldn't ask her about Trevor. As the only coffee shop in town, Amanda overheard all sorts of things.

"Do you know Sandra Baker?" I asked.

Amanda took a sip of her drink. "She came in with her friends sometimes on Saturday mornings. I got the impression that she didn't get a lot of time away from her kids."

Bingo. The friends were what I really cared about. I reached for my journal with my mini-murder board but realized that I'd left it at home. I scanned my memory for the names of the two friends I hadn't talked to yet.

"It's too bad about her husband, Trevor," Amanda continued. She shuddered. "And kind of creepy how he was posed like that. Seems like the kind of thing you'd hear about on one of those serial killer documentaries."

"Penny was saying the same thing," I said. "I told her we can't know if it was a random serial killer unless another body shows up."

"That's a cheery thought," Amanda said dryly.

I pictured the list I'd written in my journal. I'd already talked to Michelle, Christine, and Laura. That left Angie and Sarah.

"Sandra's friends," I said, steering the conversation away from the idea that a serial killer was living in Star Junction. "Do you know them well?"

Amanda shrugged. "A few of them come in for coffee pretty regularly. Her friend Angie is a firefighter in town. She comes in with some of the other firefighters during their shifts sometimes."

"Was she in this morning?" I asked. Penny's husband was a firefighter, so I knew their shifts were long and moved around during the week.

"I was running late this morning," Amanda said, looking sheepish. She called over to the guy behind the counter, "Did any firefighters come in this morning?"

He looked up from organizing packets of sweeteners. "A few of them," he said.

"Angie with them?" Amanda asked.

He nodded. "Yep, with Jack and Titus."

Amanda looked back at me. "There's your answer."

"Thanks," I said. "I better get home. As much as staying here by the fire sounds better, I need to get ready for work." *And stop by the fire station*, I added to myself.

"Yeah," Amanda said wistfully. "I should get back to work too. We get a second rush after school drop-off."

"Thanks for this." I raised my glass. "It was the perfect drink to wallow in my embarrassment."

We stood, and I followed her to the counter. "Why do you want to know about Sandra's friends, anyway?" Amanda asked. "It can't have anything to do with Trevor's murder."

I felt my smile slip. I was shocked that news of Sandra's friends confessing hadn't already gotten around town. Just Beans was a prime location for gossip. If something was working its way through the gossip mill, Amanda knew about it.

"Eh, it's more about wanting to make sure Sandra is okay. She lives across the street from me. I know her friend group is tight, so I'm checking to see if they know what she might need," I sort of lied.

"That's nice of you," Amanda said. "Let me know what you find out. I'm happy to pitch in to help that family."

"Will do," I said, feeling bad for bending the truth. I'd just have to remedy it by finding a way the people who wanted to help Sandra could get involved. Unless she was a murderer. That would definitely change how helpful I wanted to be.

I walked back across the street and got into my car. The sun that had tinged the sky when I was leaving yoga thirty minutes earlier had disappeared behind a bank of low, gray clouds. It was going to be another dreary, cold fall day. I said a little prayer that the day of the Halloween Festival would be sunny and unseasonably warm. The last thing I wanted to do was shiver all afternoon in my princess costume.

I came home to an empty house, as expected. Chris had slept on my couch on other occasions throughout our friendship and had always left a messy pile of blankets. This time, his blankets were sort of neatly folded on the couch next to Finn's pile of precisely folded blankets. Peer pressure had clearly gotten the better of him.

I said hello to Delilah, who was asleep on top of Finn's pile as if she were voting between the two men, and went upstairs. Bracing myself, I peeled off my yoga tights. As expected, a dark bruise in the rough shape of California covered my right hip. Against any sort of common sense, I poked at it, hissing at the pain.

Nothing I could do about it now. Although the more time that passed since the class, the more I was thinking about going back. Crow pose may have beaten me today, but I wasn't one to back down from a challenge.

A quick shower and breakfast later, I was ready to head over to the fire station to try to catch Angie. I made sure Delilah's bowls were full then went in search of my journal. I needed to add what I'd learned from Laura, which was that she was vague and nervous in her recounting of the event, and I would want to add whatever I learned from Angie.

The journal wasn't on the table next to the couch where I'd sworn I'd left it the day before. Finn, or more likely Chris, better not have read it. True, it held my notes about the investigation, but it also held plenty of my thoughts and feelings about Finn and Chris.

I groaned and began frantically looking for it, apologizing to Delilah as I moved the blankets to see if it had accidentally ended up under one of the piles. Delilah jumped down and trotted upstairs, likely to go back to sleep in my bed.

No journal. It wasn't in the cushions of the couch. It wasn't under the couch. It wasn't in the kitchen. It wasn't in the purse I'd been using yesterday. I stood in the middle of the living room with my hands on my hips.

"Christopher Crawford," I said to the empty room. "If you read my journal, I will kill you one thousand times and then kill you again." Out of the two men, he felt like the more likely candidate to willingly violate my privacy.

I was going to have to find a way to ask him without being a jerk, because it was possible it was lost somewhere in the house. I'd ask Finn, too, in case he'd seen it. "Nothing I can do about it now," I said to myself.

I found a piece of scrap paper in the kitchen and jotted down what I could remember. *Murder weapon likely a shovel. Abusive to his wife. Her friends hated him. Her friends were either too consistent or too vague with their confessions. They could have all done it together. Whoever killed him was angry enough to want his body found in a humiliating position with that note. His business partner thinks Trevor stole a lot of money from him. Trevor was always fighting with Chip over their property line.*

I stuck the paper and a pen in my purse. Until I found that journal, this would have to do.

I had an hour until I had to be at work, which gave me enough time to run by the fire station and maybe even say hi to Finn, who was likely at work at the police station next door.

I looked longingly at my couch with all the blankets piled on it. My hip was starting to remind me of my two falls with a consistent throbbing that had me wanting to call in sick from both Camelot Flowers and this murder investigation.

I let out a sigh filled with self-pity and left my house. I'd talk to Angie, go to Camelot Flowers, and then let my mom dote all over me.

CHAPTER TWENTY

The sight of Finn's black truck in the parking lot was like a magnet drawing me toward the door that would take me into the police station. With great restraint, I resisted the urge and went through the door just ten feet to the left into the fire station.

Two firetrucks were parked side by side, but no one was around. I heard voices coming from the back, so I skirted the ladder truck until I reached an open door that led to a large room housing a kitchen, dining table, and a few couches.

Titus, the firefighter who looked like a mountain man with his bushy beard and flannel shirt over his Star Junction Fire Department T-shirt, was stirring something on the stove, while Jack, Penny's husband, sat at the table filling out what looked like some kind of form.

I tapped on the open door and said, "Knock, knock."

Jack and Titus looked in my direction. Jack grinned but looked confused. "What are you doing here?" he asked.

I decided to have a little fun at their expense. "I have this cat stuck up in a tree…"

"Very funny," Titus said good-naturedly. He turned the heat down on the burner and set a lid on whatever was bubbling away in the pot.

"I'm actually wondering if Angie is here," I said.

"I didn't know you were friends with Angie," Jack replied.

"I'm not really," I said hesitantly, not wanting to get into why I was here. "So, is she here?"

"Does this have anything to do with that murder?" Jack asked.

He was too perceptive for his own good.

"It might," I said, wondering if Titus and Jack knew their coworker had confessed to murdering someone.

"I don't want you roping Penny into anything dangerous." Jack's smile was still in place, but it looked a little less friendly than it had before.

I gave him a you've-got-to-be-kidding-me look, refusing to defend myself.

"What?" he challenged.

"Between Penny and me, who's more likely to drag whom into dangerous situations?" I said.

Jack paused a beat before chuckling and saying, "That's fair."

"I haven't been able to control Penny since we were in kindergarten and she decided to walk around the baseball fields at the park on top of the eight-foot-high wall," I said. "Despite our mothers expressly forbidding us from doing it. I hope you know that I would never do anything to put her or your baby in danger," I added softly. "She's my family too."

Jack let out a deep sigh and rubbed his hand over his eyes. "I know," he said, sounding defeated. "I just didn't think I'd worry this much. Everything's changed with the baby, and it's not even here yet."

"That baby's going to be loved and protected by this whole town," I said encouragingly.

"I second that," Titus said, holding up a knife that looked like it could do some real damage. To be fair, he'd been using the knife when I'd made my grand statement.

"Angie?" I asked, getting us back on track.

"She's inspecting the hoses," Titus said. "It's just through that door." He nodded his head toward a door in the back of the room.

I headed in that direction, rehearsing the questions I wanted to ask. Asking each of the friends the same questions gave me a metric by which to measure their truthfulness. It didn't escape my attention that I was probably repeating what Finn had already done, but I clung to the belief that people might slip up and tell me something they wouldn't say to a detective.

I found Angie with a clipboard in hand and a neatly piled hose at her feet. I cleared my throat, not wanting to alarm her. Angie had muscles on her muscles. I wasn't sure if she'd ever competed in a bodybuilding competition, but she could win one. Easily.

She turned and gave me an assessing look. "I heard you might stop by," she said almost dismissively before returning to her checklist.

That wasn't good. I'd managed to catch the other three women before they'd had a chance to talk to one another about my questions. "I'm just trying to help Sandra," I said.

Angie looked over at me. "And you don't think that's what I was doing when I killed Trevor?"

Okay, so we were diving right into the confession. No need to beat around the bush with Angie. "I guess it doesn't make sense to me that you confessed to committing a murder, and here you are at work like nothing happened."

Angie finally turned to face me, tucking the clipboard to her side. "You'd need to ask your boyfriend about that one," she said with disdain.

Ouch.

"Can you tell me how you killed him?" I asked, hoping her story would stray from the other women's. With the attitude she was giving me, it was easy to believe she'd been the one to actually do it and that the others were covering for her. She definitely had the strength to hit someone over the head with a shovel and cause the wound I'd seen.

"I hit him," she said without emotion, as if she were describing how she'd stacked those hoses so neatly.

"And?" I asked.

"And what?" she said.

I swallowed a sigh. I had a feeling sighing wouldn't go over well with her. "You just hit him? Why? Was it self-defense? First-degree murder? Did you use a weapon? Are you the weapon?" I gulped, suddenly aware that I was alone in a room with someone who was not only strong enough to have killed Trevor, but someone strong enough to kill me. At least Jack and Titus knew I was back here.

"I don't see how that's any of your business," she said.

She had me there. Technically, none of this was any of my business.

"I'm just—"

"Trying to help Sandra," she finished for me in a mocking tone. "Where were you when Trevor was making Sandra think she was crazy? Where were you when he humiliated her in public? Where were you when she cried about how she could never leave him because he'd try to take the kids?"

Her questions brought the reality of Sandra's life before Trevor's death into stark focus. "Look," I said, my tone subdued. "If none of you killed Trevor and you're covering for someone…" Angie opened her mouth to say something, but I held up my hand to stop her and continued, "Or think that you need to cover for someone, then the real killer is out there and no one is looking for them."

"That's not my problem," Angie said. "Now, I've got to get back to work. I trust you know how to find your way out." Without giving me a chance to respond, she turned and walked away.

I stood next to the folded hose and wondered if I'd learned anything of value. She'd said she'd hit Trevor, which matched what had happened to him, but she didn't mention the shovel. So far, no one had mentioned the shovel.

My instinct to write a few lines about this encounter in my notebook reminded me that it was missing. I pulled my phone from my pocket and sent a text to Chris. *Hope you got some rest last night. Did you see a blue leather notebook on the table by the couch? I can't find it.*

Angie had left through the door that would take me back to the front of the fire station. I didn't want to run into her again, but I couldn't just stand back here all day, hoping a call came in that forced them to leave.

I waited another few seconds before feeling ridiculous enough to force myself to leave. I walked through the empty kitchen. Voices sounded from behind a closed door to my right. I kept going past the ladder truck I'd passed on my way in and made it outside without seeing anyone.

Chris was at work, which meant I might hear from him right away or not for hours, depending on how busy he was. I needed to head to Camelot Flowers. I'd told my mom I'd help her open the shop this morning, but I had enough time to pop into the police station and see if Finn knew anything about my missing notebook.

Margie was sitting at her desk when I walked in. She lit up at the sight of me, stood, and bustled around her desk before pulling me into a crushing hug. "I heard about what happened last night," she said. "Are you okay?"

I grimaced as she held me by the shoulders and looked me over. "Does this mean my mom already knows about what happened last night?"

"Guinevere," Margie scolded. "I know how to keep a secret."

I quirked a doubtful eyebrow at her.

"Fine, I'm not always good at keeping secrets, but I kept this one. You'll have to tell your mom what happened yourself."

In the chaos of the night before and the busyness of my morning, I hadn't considered that someone would have to tell my parents. It would get out eventually, even if it didn't come from Margie. Actually, it might be easier if it came from Margie. "Do you *want* to tell her?" I asked. "Then I wouldn't have to."

Margie chuckled and went back to her desk, not even bothering to answer my question. I took that as a no.

"Is Finn in?" I asked hopefully.

Margie shook her head. "He left about a half an hour ago to chase down a lead."

"What kind of lead?" I asked excitedly.

"He didn't say," Margie said as she folded her hands on the desk.

"*He* didn't say, or *you* can't say," I pushed.

Margie scoffed. "Believe me, I would tell you if I knew. You're as much a part of this investigation as Finn is."

"I don't know if he'd like that assessment," I said ruefully.

"Sometimes that boy doesn't know what's best for him," Margie said with conviction.

"And you do?" I teased.

"Without a doubt," she said sincerely.

"I better get going, then. I'm opening the shop this morning."

"I'll tell Finn you stopped by," Margie said.

"I'll text him and let him know," I said.

The phone on Margie's desk rang, and she waved at me as she answered it.

I sent a text to Finn as I walked to my car. *Stopped in to say hi, but you weren't at the station. I hope sleeping on the floor wasn't too bad. Did you happen to see a blue notebook at my house before you left this morning?*

My phone dinged by the time I'd buckled my seat belt with a reply from Finn. *I'm sorry I missed you. I didn't see a notebook this morning, but I wasn't looking for one. Is there a good time for me to come over and fix your back door so it will lock tonight?*

I hadn't even thought about my broken back door when I'd left this morning. Not that a locked door had stopped the intruder last night.

I wrote back, *You don't have to do that.* Although, I knew that nothing I said was going to change his mind about this, so I added, *I'll be home by four. Anytime after that works.*

Finn didn't respond right away so I started the car. My phone rang, and I answered it without checking to see who was calling, assuming it was Finn. "You really don't have to fix my door. I know you're busy. I'm sure I can get someone else to do it. Chris is probably free after school."

There was silence before Penny's voice said, "Is 'fixing your door' a euphemism for something?"

"I'm sorry," I said, laughing. "I thought you were Finn."

"Clearly," she said, her tone heavy with innuendo. "I'm serious. If 'fixing your door' is new code for what I think it is, it's very open-minded of you to not care if it's Finn or Chris."

"Stop," I said indulgently. "Someone broke into my house last night and broke the lock on the back door. Finn offered to come over and fix it." If I knew Penny, she was going to keep teasing me about this, so I added, "Why are you calling me now? I thought your prep period was after lunch."

Penny let out a long and very loud sigh.

Oh boy. "What's going on?" I asked.

"I woke up this morning, and my feet were so swollen and my favorite pair of maternity jeans didn't fit. My *maternity* jeans, Guinevere. The very jeans that are meant to go over a pregnant belly didn't fit me."

While my parents and many of their friends frequently called me Guinevere, it was rare for Penny to do so. I'd learned a lot over the past few weeks as Penny seemed to have reached a new level of despair over her growing size. The main lesson I'd learned was that trying to make her feel better just gave her something to argue about.

"So, what did you do?" I asked instead of trying to convince her that everything would be okay.

"What else could I do? I got a sub and took the day off."

Penny wasn't due for another six weeks. She definitely couldn't take the next six weeks off. She needed a distraction. "Do you want me to pick you up? We could help my mom open the store and then get lunch."

"I don't know," she hedged.

"I can't believe Jack didn't mention you stayed home today," I said.

"When did you see Jack?" She sounded much less despondent at the change in subject.

"I stopped by the fire station this morning to talk to Angie. She's one of Sandra's friends who confessed to killing Trevor," I explained.

"What did you learn?" she asked, sounding excited.

This was my in. "I'll pick you up and tell you all about it."

"I don't have anything to wear," she complained.

"I'm sure you'll figure it out," I said confidently. "I'll be there in ten." I hung up before she could try to talk me out of it.

Driving to Penny's would only take five minutes, but I wanted to give her an extra five to pull herself together. In lieu of my notebook missing, I added what I'd learned from Angie into the note I'd started on the scrap of paper.

Angie–defensive, strong enough to kill Trevor by hitting him, said she hit him, didn't mention the shovel, didn't try to claim self-defense like everyone else.

I looked at the notes. The information I'd learned wasn't really helpful at all. Maybe I should give up on the friends and focus my attention elsewhere, like trying to find the murder weapon.

I drove to Penny's house, trying to think of how I could find a shovel with Trevor's blood on it in a city full of homeowners who owned shovels. Not that I needed to search every house. There were a few suspects besides Sandra's friends. It was easy enough to start there. At least in theory.

I pulled up to Penny's house and gave a friendly honk with my horn. She came out a minute later wearing a cute maternity dress over black leggings. Her feet where in fluffy gray slippers, but the kind that had a hard sole on the bottom, which made it tempting to wear them outside as normal footwear.

She leveraged herself into my car with a grunt.

"Penny," I said in shock. "You look adorable. Why didn't you just wear that to school?" Not that I was going to complain about some extra time with my best friend.

Penny looked down at her outfit before looking at me and saying, "I wanted to wear the jeans," like it was the most rational thing in the world.

Another lesson I'd learned in this pregnancy—best not to argue with her when she was in a mood like this.

"Well, you look cute," I said as I backed out of her driveway.

"I look like a cow," she said, but the faint smile on her lips let me know she'd enjoyed my compliment.

"We'll get you settled at Camelot Flowers. My mom will love fussing over you," I said as we headed back across town.

"What did you learn from Angie?" Penny asked, getting right to it.

"Not much," I admitted. "She was the most defensive of the bunch. It was also clear that she'd expected me to show up. They've started talking to each other."

We approached the strip mall with Trevor and Cole's business and stopped at a red light.

"Angie can be a tough nut to crack," Penny said. "She's great once you get to know her, but that takes a while."

"That's Trevor's business there," I said, pointing at the sign that read *Baker and Johnson Investments*. "And that's his business partner, Cole," I added in surprise as I watched Cole lock up the office and head toward his car.

"Didn't you say he accused Trevor of stealing money from the business?" Penny asked.

"Yeah, and Finn confirmed that two hundred thousand dollars is missing, but it's not in any of Trevor's accounts," I said.

Penny let out a whistle. "I wouldn't mind getting my hands on two hundred thousand dollars. That's a strong motive for murder."

Cole pulled out of his parking space and turned left out of the parking lot.

"Follow him," Penny nearly shouted.

The light turned green. Camelot Flowers was straight ahead.

Cole drove past us in the other direction.

"Follow him," Penny said even more insistently.

Traffic was never an issue in Star Junction, and this moment was no exception. The one other car also waiting at the intersection had already turned right and driven away.

"We're going to lose him," Penny said. I had no doubt that if she could have, she would've reached her foot across the center console and stepped on the gas for me.

I whipped a U-turn that I wasn't sure was legal and followed Cole, now about two blocks ahead of us.

"Why exactly are we following him?" I asked.

Penny ticked off her reasons on her fingers. "He has a motive for killing Trevor. He's leaving work in the middle of the morning for no good reason. Maybe he's going back home to hide the murder weapon or something."

I could think of a lot of reasons someone might leave work mid-morning, but I was sticking with my goal to not argue with Penny during her rough mental health day. Worst-case scenario, we followed Cole and discovered he was heading to a dentist appointment. A little niggle of hope had me closing the gap between our cars to just one block. On the slim chance Penny was right, we might just crack this case wide open.

CHAPTER TWENTY-ONE

"What exactly are we going to do when Cole eventually stops somewhere?" I asked Penny as I took a right, making sure to stay a few car lengths behind Cole's car.

"We'll see what kind of shady business he's up to," she said with entirely too much enthusiasm.

"And what if he's not up to anything shady?" I asked.

Penny shrugged, seeming unbothered. "Then we'll have had an adventure."

I wasn't sure following Cole through the sleepy streets of Star Junction counted as an adventure, but it was the happiest I'd seen Penny all morning. Despite my theory that Cole could simply be running an errand, he wasn't heading toward any of the commercial parts of town.

A few minutes and a few more turns later, he pulled into the driveway of a one-story ranch and parked next to a blue minivan. I pulled to the side of the road several houses away. The garage door went up, but Cole didn't pull the car in. Instead, he left it in the driveway and disappeared into the garage.

"Let's go," Penny said, opening her door and struggling to her feet.

I scrambled out of the car after her. "What do you mean, let's go?" I hissed, despite the fact that we were alone on the street.

Penny started slinking toward Cole's house, which basically meant waddling from tree to tree, leaving me no choice but to follow her. "You said Trevor was hit with a shovel. Cole left his garage door wide open. The murder weapon could be sitting right there," she said.

This was a bad idea on so many levels. Jack's warning about not getting Penny into trouble made me feel guilty until I remembered my own argument that Penny was often the one pulling me into these situations. This case was a perfect example.

Penny had stopped at a tree across the street from Cole's garage. "See," she whispered as I caught up with her. "He went inside." She squinted. "Can you see anything?"

"I see two women who are going to get caught, and then I'm going to have to explain all of this to Finn," I said.

"Stop being such a baby," Penny said. "We need to get closer."

Before I could stop her—at this point, I wasn't sure *anything* could stop her—Penny was halfway across the street. For all her complaining that she couldn't reach things, and her jeans didn't fit, and her feet were swollen, she sure moved fast when properly motivated.

I had no choice but to follow her. If she got caught, I wasn't going to let her get caught alone.

Penny didn't stop at any number of trees she could have hidden behind on Cole's property, heading directly into the garage instead.

"This is a bad idea," I said, running to catch up to her. "We're going to get caught."

"Then help me look," Penny said.

Now that we were in the garage, it was clear to see why Cole hadn't pulled his car in. There was a large workbench that took up one side of the garage, with a table saw and a variety of tools. The other side of the garage was full of boxes.

"Was Cole planning on moving?" Penny whispered as she peeked into one of the boxes.

"Not that I know of," I answered with my gaze laser-locked on the door that led into the house.

A lawn mower sat at the back of the garage, with a weed whacker and rake leaning next to it.

"Bingo," Penny whisper-shouted.

I turned to see her standing next to a shovel with a deadly looking point on the end.

"It's even got something on it," she said excitedly.

I hurried around the boxes to her side and looked where she was pointing. "It looks like dirt," I said.

"We don't have red dirt here. It looks like blood and brains to me," Penny said.

"Gross."

Penny reached for it.

"Don't touch it," I said quickly but quietly.

Penny froze. "This could be the murder weapon."

Penny was impulsive on her best days, but even she should have realized the danger of contaminating evidence. Before I could argue my point, we heard voices coming from the house.

"What time are you and the kids heading to your parents?" Cole said to someone inside the house. After a short pause, he said, "And you'll be back Sunday?" I hadn't heard any other sounds coming from inside, which could only mean he was getting closer to the door.

I grabbed Penny and yanked her out of the garage, half sprinting, half waddling back to my car.

"I can't believe we're leaving behind crucial evidence," she said, panting as we reached the car. I pulled her around to the passenger side.

"If it's crucial evidence, then Finn needs to find it where we found it." I unlocked the car and gestured for her to get in. She gave me an epic pouty face but complied.

"Oh, here he comes," she said excitedly.

I dropped into a crouch next to Penny's open door. "What's he doing? Did he see me?"

"He's getting in his car," she reported. "Backing out of the driveway. Closing the garage door." She shot me a look. "Now we'll never get back in."

"We weren't going to go back in anyway," I said pointedly.

The sound of Cole's car grew quieter, and I risked standing. The coast was clear. I gave Cole's house one last glance before getting in the car and driving toward Camelot Flowers.

"Are you going to tell Finn about the shovel?" Penny asked.

I tapped my fingers against the steering wheel, the adrenaline of almost getting caught in Cole's garage making me jittery. "I don't know. I have to think about it. How would I explain knowing about it?"

"Just tell him what happened," Penny said. "Obviously."

"He wouldn't like us snooping around Cole's garage," I said. "What we just did was technically trespassing."

"Sometimes you have to break a few eggs to make a cake," Penny said, sounding unconcerned. "He likes *you*. That will go a long way toward smoothing over any other feelings he has about you snooping."

"Let's say for argument's sake that Cole's shovel is the murder weapon. Why would he keep it? Why not clean it off?" I asked, thinking out loud.

"Maybe he wanted to get rid of it and was interrupted," Penny said, which actually made sense. "It was shoved behind a bunch of boxes, like someone was trying to hide it quickly."

"But it's been days," I said. "He could have gotten rid of it some other time."

I pulled into the small parking lot behind Camelot Flowers.

"Telling Finn about it is the least we can do," Penny said as she got out of the car.

"The least we can do is nothing," I muttered as we walked through the back door of Camelot Flowers.

"What was that?" Penny asked.

I gave her a sunny smile. "Nothing."

She looked at me skeptically, but my mom called out from the front of the shop. "Gwen?"

We headed toward the sound of her voice. "And Penny," I said as we walked in to see my mom dusting the shelves of gifts we carried to go along with the flowers and live plants.

My mom set down the cloth she was using and held her arms out to Penny, who went in for a hug. "How's my favorite mom-to-be?" she asked.

"Huge," Penny said.

"Glowing," my mom gently corrected her. "Let's get you a snack."

She didn't bother asking why Penny wasn't at work, which was a good move on her part. Penny perked up at the mention of a snack, and I let them go back to the break room while I checked my phone.

I'd gotten a text from both Finn and Chris while Penny and I had been robbing Cole. Chris's said, *I slept great. I didn't see a notebook.*

Huh. I knew I'd left it on that table, but neither guy had seen it. Chris could be clueless when it came to my privacy, but he wouldn't lie to me.

The text from Finn said, *I have to run something over to the county lab at one. Are you free to come with me?*

His offer was intriguing on two fronts—spending time with Finn was always fun, and I'd get to learn what evidence he'd found that required a personal trip to the lab instead of sending one of the officers.

I went to the break room, where Penny and my mom were eating fresh-baked blueberry muffins. My mom must have made them this morning and brought them from home. She'd even left them in the muffin tin. There was an oven mitt nearby, like she hadn't wanted to wait for them to cool down before heading into work.

"Want one, sweetie?" my mom asked.

The smell was intoxicating. "I'd love one." I poured myself a cup of coffee as she put a muffin on a small white plate. "Do you mind if I go with Finn to take something to the county lab at one today?" I asked my mom.

"He's got new evidence?" Penny asked excitedly.

"He must, but I don't know any details. He sent a text asking me," I said.

"That's fine," my mom said. "Your dad will be in by noon. We've got it covered."

"Are you okay with me leaving later?" I asked Penny.

She waved away my concern. "I'll be ready for a nap by one."

As much as I'd felt all warm and fuzzy when both Finn and Chris had stayed to watch over me last night, I didn't want anyone to have to sleep on the floor again. "Did Jack just start his shift this morning?" I asked Penny.

"Yes," she said, sounding bummed. "He won't be off shift until tomorrow morning."

"Want to have a sleepover?" I asked.

Penny clapped her hands together. "Yes, absolutely."

"Perfect. I'll let you know when Finn and I are back, and you can come over." I sent Finn a quick text asking him to pick me up at Camelot Flowers.

My mom smiled, watching us hatch our plan for the evening.

"In the meantime," I said, purposefully not bringing up the fact that someone had broken into my house last night. I'd tell my mom. Eventually. Right now, the coffee and muffin were perfection, and I didn't want to ruin that. "Let's talk about where Trevor might have been killed. It's complicating everything that his body was moved."

I took a minute to fill in my mom on what I knew so far, which wasn't much. I ended with: "Knowing the timeline might help. The day before he died, Trevor yelled at Sandra in the Piggly Wiggly over something dumb, like getting the wrong apples."

"The next day, Christine and Michelle talked about how they wanted to kill Trevor when we were at Lucille's Clip and Curl," Penny added.

I nodded. "We found out that Trevor was at Bucky's Sunday night and got into a fight with a big biker guy, whose alibi is that he was home alone. Monday, I found Trevor in the garden club's fall display."

"So, Trevor died sometime between when he left the bar and the next day," Penny said thoughtfully.

My mom tsk-ed. "Getting into fights is never the answer, girls," she said.

Penny and I exchanged a glance. My mom had been giving us these mini lectures that had very little to do with our own behavior as long as we could remember.

"Okay, Mom," I said. "No fighting. We promise."

"Unless one more person tells me I must be due any day now," Penny muttered. "Then all bets are off."

While I didn't have any personal experience with what Penny was going through, I could imagine hearing that people thought she was big enough to be due any day while still having six weeks left until her due date would be annoying.

"You're perfect," my mom said to her. "Don't let anyone else make you feel otherwise. Why, when I was pregnant with Gwen, I was waddling like a duck months before I was due." She shook her head but smiled like it was a fond memory. "Worth every stretch mark."

Penny groaned. "Don't even get me started on stretch marks."

"About Trevor's murder," I said before Penny could get even more upset.

"Yes," Penny said. "We were going over the timeline."

"Here are the options," I said. "Trevor could have been killed at his house, at the killer's house, or somewhere totally random."

"That doesn't really narrow it down," Penny said skeptically.

"That's the problem," I agreed.

"Do you have proof he went home after being at Bucky's?" my mom asked.

"That's a good question," I said. I let out a deep sigh. "If only I had my journal. All my notes from talking to people were in it. I bet I have a note about if Trevor went home after Bucky's, but I can't remember off the top of my head."

"Where's the journal?" Penny asked. She eyed the plate of muffins. She'd already finished one and was clearly debating whether or not to have another.

"I don't know," I said dramatically. "Both Finn and Chris said they didn't see it last night, but I know I left it on the table by the couch."

My mom had gone to the sink to rinse out her coffee mug. "Why were Finn and Chris at your house last night?" she asked, turning to look at me with the soapy mug in her hands.

I shot Penny a *help me* look. She was too busy in a staring contest with the remaining muffins to even notice.

"Uh…" I started. "It's not like it's a big deal or anything, but Finn came over because there was someone sneaking around my house in the middle of the night and then Chris came over because he heard about it and wanted to make sure I was okay."

I'd conveniently left out that the person was *in* my house and that Chris had heard about it on the police scanner.

"You mean the person broke into your house," Penny corrected me as she finally gave in and picked up another muffin to put on her plate.

I shouted, "Penny!" the exact same time my mom said, "Guinevere Nimue Stevens! Someone broke into your house?"

Penny looked up from the new love of her life, the blueberry muffin, and said, "What?" She looked like she had no idea the trouble she'd caused with her correction to my story. She probably hadn't even realized what she'd been saying.

"It's no big deal, Mom," I said. "Finn is taking care of it. Something about running the prints being top priority."

"They took prints?" my mom practically shrieked.

I had no one to blame but myself for spilling that detail.

"Both Chris and Finn stayed to guard her last night," Penny said, trying to reassure my mom. "And I'm going to stay tonight." She patted my shoulder with one hand while she broke off a piece of the muffin with the other. "Gwen is totally safe."

My mom did not look appeased.

"Hey!" Penny said suddenly. "I bet that's where your journal went."

"What do you mean?" I asked, trying to figure out how to convince my mom, and my dad as soon as he learned what had happened, that I was going to be fine.

"What if whoever broke into your house took the journal?" Penny asked, sounding excited.

"Why would anyone take my journal?" I asked in confusion.

Penny looked at me like she couldn't believe it was taking me so long to catch up with her theory. "You have all the notes about the murder in it. Has anyone you interviewed seen you write in it? What if they wanted to get their hands on it to see what you know, like trying to figure out how close you are to solving it?" Penny beamed at my mom. "See, she wasn't in any danger. They just needed to get a look at her murder notes."

That probably didn't sound any better to my mom, but Penny might be onto something. "A lot of people saw me write in my notebook."

"Then that's who has your journal," Penny said confidently. "You find out who has it, you find your killer."

I watched Penny happily finish her muffin as I rolled her theory around in my mind, ignoring the look of concern on my mom's face. Penny might be right, but if the killer took my journal, I had just about as much chance of finding it as I did finding the location where Trevor had died.

CHAPTER TWENTY-TWO

Finn walked through the front door of Camelot Flowers a few minutes before one o'clock. In keeping my earlier promise to Penny, she and I had gone across the street to Just Beans for an early lunch. Now Penny was in the break room with my mom, showing her all the nursery ideas she'd pinned on Pinterest. Her mood had improved considerably since I picked her up. Meanwhile, my mood brightened at the sight of Finn, looking devastatingly handsome in one of his signature suits.

"Ready?" Finn asked.

I pulled my coat from under the counter where I'd stashed it earlier. "Mom," I called to the back. "I'm heading out."

"Wait one minute," she called back. She came rushing to the front, her smile beaming at Finn, but I recognized the look in her eyes. She was a woman on a mission. "So nice to see you," she said to Finn.

"Thanks for letting me steal Gwen away in the middle of the day," he said.

She waved away his statement. "Anytime," she said. "What I want to know is what you're doing about the break-in at her house."

"Mom," I said, mortified.

"What?" she said, sounding defensive. "There was a crime. I'm asking a police detective what he's doing to solve it."

"I'm so sorry," I muttered to Finn.

"No," Finn said. "That's a fair question. I'm driving the prints we collected over to the county lab myself right now. I'll fix her door when we're back in town, and I'll be staying at Gwen's, on the couch," he added, "until we find the person who broke in."

"You don't have to," I said. "Penny is going to stay with me tonight."

Penny had wandered out from the back during this exchange. "Yeah," she said a little too enthusiastically. "If someone tries to break in again, I'll take 'em out." She karate chopped the air.

Finn looked at her skeptically. "We can talk about this later," he said. "I want to get this evidence dropped off."

"Thanks for taking care of her," my mom said, looking slightly more relaxed. "I'm sorry if I came off a little strong. I'm just worried."

"I get it," Finn said. "I'm worried too."

"It was just a break-in," I said, ignoring how scared I'd been last night. "No one tried to hurt me. What are the chances they'd try to come back?"

"Better safe than sorry," Finn said.

"Exactly," my mom agreed.

Oh boy. Now they were ganging up on me.

"Do you need me to come back to the store to help you close up later?" I asked my mom.

"No," she said. "Get that door fixed, and don't worry about us here."

"Let me know when you're ready for me to come over," Penny said.

I promised I would and followed Finn outside to his big black truck, which was parked half a block away. We headed out of town toward Rose Lake, where the evidence lab was located next to the county courthouse.

"Do you think the fingerprints will help?" I asked as we drove past fields filled with dried corn stalks. The corn would be harvested and used as feed for cattle. The sweet corn, a staple in summer BBQs, had been harvested months ago.

"It's hard to say," Finn said. "The person could've been wearing gloves, or they might not be in the system."

I huffed out a breath. My life wasn't going to go back to normal until Finn, Chris, my mom, and probably Penny were sure I was safe from whoever had broken in. I decided to float Penny's theory past Finn. "Penny thinks that whoever broke in might have been after the journal I mentioned was missing."

Finn stopped at a stop sign in the middle of nowhere then took a left. In just a few minutes we'd hit the outskirts of Rose

Lake, the Pizza Hut the first sign we'd reached town. "What makes her think that?" he asked.

"It's just weird that it's missing. You and Chris said you didn't see it. I know I left it on the table by the couch. Plus, it's where I had all the notes about the murder. Penny asked if any of the suspects I'd talked to had seen the journal. Unfortunately, a few of them have. Do you think it's possible I already interviewed the killer and whoever it is broke in to see what clues I'd written in the journal?"

Finn was silent for a moment before saying, "We can't know for sure, but it makes sense. If Penny's theory is true, it makes what happened even more dangerous."

"I don't know about *more* dangerous," I said. "They got what they came for. The journal is missing."

"Until they read something in your notes that they don't like and decided to come back," he said ominously.

"Ugh. Let's change the subject," I said as we pulled into the parking lot for the county lab.

Finn grabbed a brown paper bag sealed with red evidence tape from the back seat. "This will just take a second. Then I have a surprise for you."

I perked up at that. "A surprise?"

"Be right back." Finn hopped out of the truck and disappeared into the building.

I tried to guess what his surprise could be but couldn't come up with anything. Obviously, his request that I come with him to drop off the evidence had concealed an ulterior motive. Not that I minded.

True to his word, he was back ten minutes later. He started the car and turned left out of the parking lot, instead of the right turn that would take us back to Star Junction.

"What's my surprise?" I asked.

"I asked them to put a rush on the prints," he said. "I should know something in the next few days."

"That doesn't answer my question," I said.

"It answers the important question," Finn teased.

He drove out of Rose Lake. Minutes later, he pulled into a gravel parking lot.

"Here we are," he said.

A low, cinderblock building sat at the edge of the small parking lot. A sign mounted above the door read *Rose Lake Gun Range*.

"A gun range?" I asked in confusion.

"You keep finding yourself in dangerous situations," he said with an intensity that revealed how much he cared. "I'd like you to know the basics of how to handle a gun."

I wrinkled my nose. "Then what? I'd carry one around with me all the time?"

"One thing at a time," Finn said vaguely.

I considered his words as I studied the dreary-looking building. I wasn't going to start *packing heat* as they said in the movies, but it didn't mean this couldn't be fun. "Let's do it."

Finn looked relieved that I'd agreed. "You sure? I know I kind of sprung this on you."

"Kind of?" I teased.

We walked through the door into the sparse entryway. White linoleum bounced the florescent light around the space, creating a sterile look. Along the back wall sat a row of black folding chairs. A copy of a Smith and Wesson catalog lay on the floor under the chair at the end of the row.

We crossed the room to a counter partitioned by a thick pane of Plexiglas with a small window cut into the center at the bottom. The acrid smell of spent gunpowder tickled my nostrils, causing me to sneeze.

A burly man with a crisp, military haircut looked up from his seat at the counter and smiled. "Bless you. You folks interested in doing some shooting today?"

Finn leaned against the counter. "That's why we're here."

"First time?" the man asked. According to his name tag, his name was Jason.

"First time at this range," Finn answered.

Jason turned and pulled a file out of a small rolling cart. He slid two sets of papers and two pens through the slot. "Fill these out, and then we can talk about what you're interested in shooting. Did you bring your own, or do you want to rent something?"

"We'll rent. This is her first time." Finn nodded in my direction. "I wanted her to have a few options."

Jason's already friendly face widened into an even bigger grin. "First time, huh?"

"Well—" I started to say, but Jason interrupted.

"We'll make sure your first time is a good one, right?" He wiggled his eyebrows at Finn.

To Finn's credit, he didn't rise to Jason's sexually charged bait. Instead, he said, "She's going to do great. I have no doubt."

Finn gathered the paperwork as well as two clipboards Jason managed to maneuver through the slot, and we headed toward the chairs. I took my copy of the paperwork and a pen and started signing my life away.

Did I acknowledge this was a dangerous activity? Check. Did I acknowledge Rose Lake Gun Range had no liability for anything? Check. It went on and on. Ten minutes later, I might have promised them my first-born child, but the paperwork was filled out.

We returned the clipboards to Jason. He scanned down the pages, tapping his pen at each small space for an initial or signature. He paused halfway down the top sheet on Finn's clipboard. "You a cop?"

"I am," Finn answered.

"Always happy to have an officer in the house," Jason said, a new level of respect in his voice.

"Thanks, man. That means a lot," Finn said.

Jason gave Finn a quick nod and held up the paperwork. "Everything looks good. I'll meet you guys on the other side of that door over there, and we'll get started."

A low buzz sounded from the door, and Finn opened it to reveal a long hallway. As promised, Jason met us on the other side. Now that he wasn't sitting behind his Plexiglas shield, I could appreciate the intimidation level he provided. If I owned a business housing hundreds of guns, I'd want Jason at the front door too. He was at least a few inches taller than Finn, who already towered over me.

Jason led us down the bare hallway to a gray, metal door on the left. He used a keycard attached to his belt and entered a code, causing another low buzz to echo through the hall.

We followed him into a room filled with black cages secured with electronic keypads tucked behind a long counter. Rows of handguns, shotguns, and even some military-grade weapons that seemed like they'd do more damage than I was interested in causing filled the cages.

Jason punched in another code and walked through a waist-high door built into the counter before turning to Finn. "What'll it be?"

Finn eyed something I'd swear I'd seen in a Jack Ryan movie, but he shifted his gaze to the handguns. "Do you have a Browning Buckmark Camper?"

Jason gave him a quick nod.

"It'll be a fairly gentle introduction to shooting a handgun," Finn said to me. He waited, as if asking for my consent. I shrugged and smiled. As far as I was concerned, this was his rodeo. I was just along for the ride.

He turned his attention back to Jason. "We'll start with that." Then without hesitation, he added, "I'll take a Beretta M9."

"Nice." Jason nodded his approval of Finn's choice.

As Jason walked to the back of the room to unlock the gun cages, Finn turned to me with a twinkle in his eye. "Thanks for being a good sport about this."

"Are you kidding?" I put my hand over his. "This is going to be fun."

Finn's face lit up, and he twisted his hand until it was holding mine.

Jason approached holding two cases. He set them on the counter. "Bullets are purchased by the box."

"We'll each take one box to start. Can we buy more later?" Finn asked.

"Yeah, of course." Jason reached under the counter and pulled out two boxes, handing them to Finn. He also handed both cases to him. "I'll show you to your bays."

I could've commented on how I was perfectly capable of handling my own case, but I could see the respect Jason had for Finn. I decided not to push the issue.

We walked farther down the hallway to another door labeled *Bays 1-5*.

"You'll be in here," Jason said, using his key card to let us in. "If you have any questions, I'll be up front. You picked a good time to come. We don't usually get busy until after five, so you should have the whole bay to yourselves."

Finn handed the cases to me and shook Jason's hand. "Thanks, man. We'll let you know if we need anything."

Jason headed back down the hall as we walked into a large room divided into narrow stalls. Hooks along the back held earmuffs in various shades of green. I set the cases down on the counter as Finn grabbed a pair of army green earmuffs.

I grabbed a pair for myself. "I don't know if giant plastic earmuffs are a good look on me."

"I don't know," Finn said as he took them from me and settled them gently on my head. "I think they're cute."

His last words disappeared into a muffled silence as the earmuffs settled on my ears. "What?" I tilted my head and looked up at Finn in confusion.

Finn pulled one of the muffs back and leaned in. His warm breath wound its way through my hair and tickled my ear. "I said, I think they look cute on you."

I leaned back and smiled slyly. "I heard you the first time. I just wanted to hear it again."

The look of shock on his face made me laugh. His eyes glinted, and a corner of his mouth turned up. He eased the earmuffs off my head, settling them around my neck. He reached up and brushed a lock of hair that had fallen across my face behind my ear.

We stood, frozen in the moment. Finn's gaze flicked to my lips, where they lingered for a moment before returning to meet mine. He blinked first, both literally and metaphorically as he took a step back and cleared his throat. "You ready to shoot your first gun?"

I focused on slowing my racing heart. It would do no good to accidentally shoot Finn because I couldn't stop imagining his lips on mine. "I'm ready whenever you are."

Finn stepped around me and opened the case holding the Browning. He pulled the small handgun from its black Styrofoam encasement and spent the next several minutes showing me how to load it. He was patient and thorough in his teaching. When he was finally done, he looked up. "You ready?"

"All set. Except, I'm kind of confused about how to hold it properly while shooting. I don't want it to kick back in my face," I said.

"Don't worry. I'll help in the beginning."

I nodded and gave him a thumbs-up. He clipped a target, a large circle surrounded by four smaller ones, onto the rack. Little red dots in the middle of the black circles marked the coveted bullseyes. Finn pressed a red button mounted on the wall of the bay, and the target slid away from us to the other end of the long aisle.

He picked up the gun from the ledge in front of us. "Let's work on proper stance and grip."

I lifted my hands in front of me. "I'm all yours."

A wicked grin spread across Finn's face, the dimple in his cheek making an appearance. "I like the sound of that." He came up behind me as I pulled my hair over my shoulder.

Finn reached around my body, placing the gun in my right hand. "You always want the gun pointed down range when the safety is off." He wrapped his other arm around me, grabbing my left hand and bringing it up to wrap about the hand holding the gun. His chest brushed against my back, and I leaned into him. I tried to stay focused as my body buzzed with the sensation of his touch.

"Point down range at the center target." His voice filled my head as he spoke the words into my ear. "Every gun's aim is a little different. Some you have to aim slightly higher than the target. Others slightly lower. When you're ready, take a deep breath, hold it, and pull the trigger."

I took a deep breath, acutely aware that all Finn would have to do is shift his head a fraction of an inch, and his lips would be on my neck.

"Good. Just like that. The gun will kick, but it won't be bad. If you're ready for it, you'll be fine. Any questions?" he asked.

"Hmm?" I said distractedly.

Finn's arms tightened around me. "Are you even listening to me?"

I gave my head a little shake, forcing back the images that flooded my mind with Finn's closeness. "Yeah, sorry. Point down range, aim for the middle. Small kick."

Finn took the gun from my hands and took a step back. I turned to see him watching me quizzically.

"It's not my fault that my shooting instructor is incredibly good-looking, and I can't focus when he's close to me," I said with what I hoped was a flirty smile.

Finn's gaze heated. "Is that so?"

"It is." I leaned in. "But don't tell him. I don't want him to get a big head."

Finn barked out a laugh. "Alright, Stevens. Let's see how you do with a little less distraction."

I looked back down the range. "Can I have a different target? I want the one that looks like a person."

"Do I need to be worried that you're in the mood to shoot the outline of a person?" Finn teased.

"Believe me," I muttered, looking down at the gun to make sure the safety was still on, "it's not you who needs to be worried." Images of Derek Thompson with his roving eyes and lewd innuendos flashed through my mind.

Finn turned back to me with one brow raised, a new target clutched in his hands. "Anything I need to know about?" All flirting had disappeared, replaced with what felt like genuine concern.

I pictured Finn hunting Derek down, and a small smile graced my lips. "Nothing you need to worry about," I reassured him. I'd been handling Derek for years. Although the thought of Finn putting Derek in his place brought me some level of satisfaction, I didn't need rescuing from Derek. If anything, Derek would need rescuing from me if he didn't back off.

Finn attached the new target, a black and white outline of a head attached to a large torso, and sent it down range. "Any questions?" he asked.

"Nope. I think I've got it." I pulled the earmuffs on, and Finn did the same. I picked up the small Browning, taking the time to become accustomed to the weight and feel of it in my hand.

I pointed it down range, taking a moment to size up the target. I turned my head back toward Finn, who was waiting expectantly behind the red line painted on the floor. He sent me a reassuring thumbs-up.

Without taking my eyes off Finn, I drilled five shots into the target; two through the head and three through center mass. I didn't need to look to know I'd hit my intended target. The expression on Finn's face told me everything I needed to know.

CHAPTER TWENTY-THREE

I comically blew on the end of the gun after setting the safety with a flick of my thumb. I set it on the ledge and removed my muffs.

"Wha—? How? I mean..." Finn ran a hand through his hair, his gaze darting between the target and me.

I closed the gap between us and quirked an eyebrow. "Did you really think that the only daughter of a father who secretly wanted a son and who grew up in hunting country has never fired a gun before? I've been shooting with my dad since I was ten years old. Mostly hunting rifles, but when I became a teenager, we started on handguns. It brought him some small comfort when I started dating."

Finn continued to stare at me in shock. "But I had to show you how to hold it, how to stand."

"It was cute the way you assumed I didn't know what I was doing. I decided to run with it. Besides, I don't know about you, but I found the lesson thoroughly enjoyable."

Finn looked at me with a level of newfound awe and respect. "You're just full of surprises, aren't you?"

"And don't you forget it," I said, pushing my finger into his hard chest. "Now can we get me a real gun?" I looked down at the Browning. "I haven't shot one of these since I was fourteen."

We traded in the browning for a Walther CCP, which had a little more kick and was a lot more fun. We spent the rest of our time at the range in a friendly competition. We couldn't shoot any of the larger guns indoors, but Jason suggested we come back sometime and try the outdoor range.

An hour later, I held up the target that had revealed my secret shooting skills to Finn as we walked across the parking lot. "Would you like me to autograph this for you?" I teased.

Finn looked at me out of the corner of his eye as he unlocked the truck door and pulled it open. "I think I'll pass, but thanks," he said dryly.

"I think it could be a nice souvenir."

Finn snatched it from my hands. "I guess it can be a reminder that I should never underestimate you again," he said playfully.

"That's right," I said with a laugh.

Finn offered me his hand, and I used it to leverage myself up into the truck. I settled into the seat, but Finn didn't let go. I quickly grew self-conscious under his gaze. "What?" I asked.

He tilted his head to the side. "That was fun."

My cheeks heated under his gaze.

He reached up and fingered one of my long curls, sending the smell of gunpowder wafting through the air between us.

I wrinkled my nose. "That's an attractive smell—gunpowder hair."

Finn leaned in, bringing our faces close. "I don't know. I kind of like it." Heat from his hand rippled up my arm, and nervous energy fluttered in my chest. Finn's dark-eyed gaze probed mine as if asking for permission to an unspoken request.

I leaned forward, which was all the invitation he needed. His lips brushed mine, and it was everything I'd dreamed it would be for all the months we'd been spending time together. I grabbed the front of his shirt and tugged him closer, deepening the kiss. My senses filled with him, his touch, the spicy smell of his cologne, the scratch of his beard, and the taste of his lips pressing into mine.

When he pulled away, we were both smiling like fools.

"That was a long time coming," I said.

"I didn't want to confuse you while you were making up your mind about Chris," he said, melting my heart with his thoughtfulness.

"What changed?" I asked.

His grin grew sheepish. "My weak willpower."

"I wouldn't say waiting months to kiss me was weak by any measure of the word," I said. I took a deep breath. "And I decided. I think I decided a long time ago, but I wasn't sure how to tell anyone."

Finn's expression grew uncertain. How he could be uncertain about anything after that kiss was a mystery to me. "And?" he asked.

"I want to be with you," I said, feeling suddenly shy. I almost never felt shy, and I knew how Finn felt about me, but saying it out loud felt like a monumental step.

Finn let out a whoop and pressed a hard but fast kiss to my lips. He jogged around the truck and got in.

"What's the rush?" I asked, laughing.

"I need to find whoever killed Trevor so I can stop worrying about you and take you on a proper first date," he said as he pulled out of the parking lot.

"I don't need a proper anything," I protested. "I like hanging out with you. It doesn't need to be special."

"I want it to be special," Finn said.

If he needed it to be special, then who was I to argue? "Then let's solve a murder," I said, feeling giddy from finally kissing Finn. My mood dropped. "Not that we haven't been trying. Have you had any luck locating the murder scene?"

The truck picked up speed as we left the town limits of Rose Lake and drove into the countryside. "No," Finn said, sounding dejected. "I was able to get warrants to search the friends' houses due to their confessions, but there was no signs of a struggle or blood residue at any of those locations. The medical examiner indicated Trevor lost a lot of blood before he was moved. It would be hard to completely clean a scene like that."

"Did you use one of those little black light thingies?" I asked while miming searching with a small flashlight. "You know they shine those on cement that looks clean on *CSI* all the time, and then—*bam!*—the area lights up like a Christmas tree."

Finn shot me a look somewhere between amused and indulgent as he said, "Yes, we used the black light thingies."

"Oh," I said, disappointed. "Did you check Sandra's house?"

Finn nodded. "We checked there too. She allowed us to search, so I didn't need a warrant."

"Hmm, maybe Sandra didn't do it." I snapped my fingers. "Unless she let you search because she knows she didn't kill him at the house. It would be an easy to way look innocent."

"Sandra is very low on my list of suspects," Finn said.

I knew he thought I was too focused on her as the killer, but it was the only way I could make sense of her friends confessing. Unless they'd all done it together, my other favorite theory.

Finn continued, "But it's possible, probable even, that the killer didn't do it at their own house, which would make finding the murder scene infinitely more complicated."

"You know, most people don't walk around with shovels just in case they need to dig a hole or bash someone over the head," I said, thinking out loud. "That means it happened somewhere a shovel was handy."

I described it as the scene played out in my head. "Trevor is alone with the killer. Or killers," I added. "They get into an argument about something, which sounds like a common occurrence for Trevor. The argument gets heated. Maybe Trevor comes at the person. They look around and grab the first thing they see. It's a shovel. They swing it at Trevor's head. Maybe they don't even mean to kill him. Maybe they're just trying to get him to stop, but the blow hits him just right, and he drops like a two-hundred-pound sack of potatoes."

This would've been the perfect time to tell Finn about the shovel at Cole's house, but I was still nervous that he was going to be upset. He'd finally kissed me. He was talking to me openly about the case. I didn't want to ruin the moment. I'd text him and let him know later. That way if he was mad, he could get over it before we saw each other again.

"All of this is why finding the crime scene is so important," Finn said. "The DA isn't going to file charges against any of Sandra's friends unless I can find solid evidence tying them to the murder. Their confessions would just muddy the waters with a jury." He sighed, shaking his head.

"I'm supposed to hear back from the forensic accountant later today," he continued. "If I can find Cole's missing money in an account that links to Trevor, I might be able to use that to get a warrant to search his house."

This would be the moment to tell him, but I couldn't bring myself to do it. I'd found myself in plenty of crazy situations in the months Finn had known me, but snooping around in someone else's garage while they were home in the middle of the day might have been the dumbest one.

"You'll figure it out," I said with confidence, avoiding the issue of Cole's shovel. "It's only been a few days."

"It's been five days," Finn said.

"Maybe we could set some kind of trap for the killer," I said, getting excited about the idea. "I could find a way to interact with everyone who knew about my journal and make it seem like I had some kind of evidence at my house that I'd found. I could tell them that I hadn't had time to get it to you yet. Then when they show up in the middle of the night to steal it, we nab 'em."

I beamed at Finn, waiting for his inevitable enthusiasm about the idea.

"No way," Finn said as he shook his head. "We're not using you as bait."

I wrinkled my nose with disappointment. "You're just saying that because you like me."

Finn chuckled and took my hand, pressing a kiss to my knuckles. "Is that a bad thing?"

"It is when it keeps us from solving this case," I said.

"I can solve the case without putting you in danger," Finn said with conviction. We passed the sign that read *Welcome to Star Junction. Population 5372.* "Do you want me to drop you off at home?" he asked.

"No, I want to check in at Camelot Flowers and get my car," I said.

Finn turned onto Main Street. There weren't any parking spots near the store, so he drove around back and parked by my car in the small parking lot. "I still want to come over and fix the door later. Let me check in on what's happening at the station, and I'll let you know some times that could work."

Then he leaned over and feathered a kiss to my lips.

"Is this what we do now?" I said, grinning like a fool. "Kiss all the time?"

"I'm going to kiss you every chance I get," Finn said.

I pretended to swoon, which made him laugh. Man, dating Finn was fun.

I opened the door and jumped down from the truck. "I'll be home in about an hour, so anytime after that should work for fixing the door."

Finn nodded.

"And don't forget that Penny will be there, so there won't be any kissing," I teased.

"In that case, who else did you say could fix your door?" he asked, giving it right back to me.

I stuck my tongue out at him. "See you soon." Closing the car door, I practically skipped into the store.

Penny and my mom looked up from where my mom was putting together a bouquet at the workbench near the row of coolers.

Penny shrieked, which made my mom jump and snip a flower much too close to the top.

I spun in a quick circle, looking for whatever had startled Penny, my heart racing. "What?" I asked. "What's wrong?"

"Your face," Penny said, moving toward me. "Something really good happened. I've seen this look before. The time you figured out how to ride your bike in kindergarten. The time you won the spelling bee in fourth grade. The time you made the swim team in high school. The time Chris asked you to prom." She gasped and put her hands over her mouth. "Finn kissed you."

My mom had been watching Penny, but her attention shifted to me. My cheeks flared with heat. "Maybe you should be the one solving this murder," I muttered. "How'd you figure it out?"

Penny looked confused as she said, "I just told you how." Then she squealed again and pulled me into hug. "It's about time." She pulled back and held me by the shoulders. "What are you going to do about Chris? Not that you need to do anything. This isn't the nineteen fifties. You can kiss whoever you want."

"I hadn't really thought about Chris," I admitted.

"Good girl," Penny said with a heavy dose of approval in her tone. "You've spent enough time thinking about Chris."

My mom scooted past Penny and gave me a hug. "Are you happy?"

"I am," I said, still smiling.

"Then I'm happy," she said.

"Me too," Penny said.

My mom laughed. "I think we all know how you feel," she said to Penny.

"Do you need me to do anything around here?" I asked. I turned to Penny. "I thought you were going to go home and take a nap."

"I was, but someone ran off with her boyfriend and stranded me here," Penny said, although it was clear she wasn't upset.

"You really think Finn is my boyfriend now?" I asked.

Penny and my mom exchanged a glance before Penny said, "You don't?"

"I guess we didn't talk about it in those terms," I admitted. I'd been so happy about the kiss, so happy about telling Finn I wanted to date him, I hadn't thought about whether or not we needed to have any further conversations.

"He's your boyfriend," Penny said with conviction. "Right?" she asked my mom.

My mom moved back to her flowers. "I'm not sure what you kids are calling things these days."

"Just introduce Finn to someone as your boyfriend and see how he responds," Penny said.

"Who am I going to introduce Finn to?" I asked skeptically. "He knows everyone in town. And if he doesn't know them, they know who he is."

"True, true." Penny tapped her chin in thought. She brightened up as she said, "You'll figure it out."

"Gee, thanks. I'm sorry I forgot about you going home to nap," I said. "Do you want me to run you home now?"

Penny leaned back against the counter. "If I'm going to make it to your house tonight for a sleepover, I'm going to need that nap."

"You're okay here by yourself?" I asked my mom.

"You just missed your dad," she said. "He should be back any minute."

"Let's get you home for that nap," I said to Penny.

She got her things from the back room and made me tell her every detail about the kiss on the way to her house. She laughed out loud about Finn's assumption that I didn't know how to handle a gun. Every time I tried to tell her something we'd discussed about the case, she waved her hand through the air and said, "I don't care about that. Get to the good stuff."

I dropped her off with a promise that I'd told her everything. I soaked in the wonderful feeling of certainty I felt now that I'd gotten off the fence and chosen Finn. I was going to enjoy this feeling. I'd worry about what to tell Chris later.

I turned onto my street and groaned. "You've got to be kidding me," I muttered to myself. Chris's white Dodge Charger was parked in front of my house. I guess I was going to worry about this now.

CHAPTER TWENTY-FOUR

Chris got out of his car as I pulled into the driveway. I racked my brain for a way to tell him about Finn. He gave me the charming smile that used to melt me into a useless puddle as I got out of my own car. In this moment, it just made me feel guilty. As Penny had said, I hadn't done anything wrong, but I knew telling Chris that I was choosing Finn was going to hurt him, and the last thing I'd ever wanted to do was hurt Chris.

"I wasn't expecting to see you. And how long have you been waiting?" I added.

Chris shoved his hands into the pockets of his jeans and said, "I haven't been waiting long. I wanted to check on you after everything last night. Make sure you're okay."

"That's sweet of you, but I'm totally fine, and before you ask, Penny is going to spend the night here and Finn is already coming over to fix the door, so you won't need to spend another night on my couch," I said.

Chris's smile dimmed slightly. "Guess you don't need me, then."

Ouch. I felt every bit of the double meaning in his statement. I needed to tell him. Rip the Band-Aid off.

The sun had finally broken through the clouds while Finn and I were in Rose Lake. The sunshine lay warm on my shoulders, and I felt the sudden urge to stay outside and soak up the warmth while it lasted.

"Let's sit," I said as I walked to the steps that led to the tiny landing in front of the door. I sat, and Chris sat next to me.

"Penny wasn't at school today," Chris said. "Is she okay?"

I moved my hand in a *so-so* motion. "Define okay. I think she's fine now. She had a rough morning emotionally. She's definitely ready to not be pregnant anymore."

"I'm glad nothing was physically wrong," he said. "When I saw she wasn't in, I thought maybe something had happened with the baby."

"No, she just needed a friend."

"So, you saw her today?" he asked.

I chuckled. "My plan was to take her to work with me and let my mom dote on her, but we had a little detour on the way that might have led to minor trespassing."

Chris leaned back against the top step. "How does someone minorly trespass? It's like being pregnant. You either are or you're not."

"We saw Trevor's former business partner Cole leaving work in the middle of the morning, and Penny insisted we follow him," I said.

"Okay…" Chris said slowly. "What did you think he was doing? Going off to hide evidence in the middle of a Friday almost a whole week after the murder?"

"I don't know," I said with exasperation. "You know how Penny gets. She shouted that I needed to follow him, and I complied without question."

Chris gave me a knowing look. "How did following Cole turn into trespassing?"

"We followed Cole to his house. He opened the garage door but didn't park in the garage because it's full of stuff. After he went into the house, Penny ran into the garage before I could stop her," I explained.

"You've got to be kidding me." He shook his head. "No, that actually tracks. What did she think she was going to find?"

"The murder weapon. The medical examiner believes Trevor was killed with a blow to the head by a shovel. The problem is Trevor wasn't killed in front of city hall. If we could find the shovel that killed Trevor, we'd know who did it," I explained.

"And?" Chris said.

"We found a shovel hidden behind some boxes. Penny wanted to take it. I barely stopped her before we heard Cole coming and had to run out of there."

"You're lucky you stopped Penny from taking that shovel," Chris said with conviction.

"I know" I said defensively.

"No," Chris said. "I'm serious, and you have to make sure she doesn't go back and try to get it."

"What's going on?" I asked, twisting to face him. "Since when are you into following the rules?"

"Think about it this way. Let's say that shovel is the murder weapon. Finn puts evidence together that reveals Cole is the killer. He searches his house, but there's no shovel because Penny took it. Then he finds out she has it, and he can't use it to make his case because it's been contaminated by Penny stealing it."

"I know," I said again, this time with a touch of attitude. "That's why I didn't let her take it."

"This time," Chris argued. "You need to convince her to leave it alone."

"She's going to stay with me tonight. I'll keep an eye on her," I said.

I hated how it felt like I was being scolded. Actually, it felt an awful lot like being lectured by Chris's dad, who just so happened to be a lawyer and spent every chance he had while we were growing up to practice his courtroom skills anytime he disapproved of Chris's behavior. I was usually just collateral damage.

"But you didn't come over here to lecture me over Penny's behavior," I said playfully, trying to steer the conversation away from Trevor's murder.

Chris glanced over his shoulder at my house. "You're right. I wanted to see how you were feeling after last night. We didn't get to talk this morning."

I bumped against his shoulder with mine. "That's because you were snoring away on my couch when I left for yoga."

"I needed my beauty sleep," Chris teased.

The familiarity of bantering with Chris hit my heart like an arrow of guilt. I loved Chris. I'd loved Chris since I was eleven years old. How I felt about Finn didn't change the fact that Chris was better than a brother to me. I could only hope that telling him how I felt about Finn wasn't going to shatter that, leaving us with nothing but broken pieces we could never hope to repair.

"You okay?" he asked gently.

I looked up to see his cornflower blue eyes filled with concern.

"What do you mean?" I asked.

"You were just teasing me, and then I lost you." He shrugged. "You looked sad."

It baffled me how much Chris had matured in the last year. Being accused of murder had been a real turning point for him. The old Chris would have never noticed how I was feeling.

"I have to tell you something," I said somberly.

Chris leaned in conspiratorially. "Is it that you killed Trevor?" he asked with a devilish grin on his face.

"No, I'm serious," I said.

"Because I'd help you get away with it," Chris continued, enjoying this joke a little too much.

"Chris—"

"Help you move to Mexico," he interrupted.

"I kissed Finn," I blurted out.

Everything about Chris froze, even the smile on his face. A car drove by, and my neighbor's witch let out an annoying cackle.

"Say something," I said quietly.

Chris dropped his gaze to his feet. "What are you telling me, Gwen?"

Tears stung my eyes. "I made my choice."

Chris sat with his head down long enough for my tears to track down my cheeks. How could I go from being so happy just an hour ago to feeling this devastated now? When he finally looked up at me, his smile was sad. "I'm going to need a little time to process this," he said, his voice thick with emotion.

"What does that mean?" I asked, swiping at the tears gathering on the tip of my chin.

"Don't cry," Chris said, looking horrified.

"I just feel really bad," I said.

Chris shrugged, but I could see the pain in his expression. There was no way he was going to convince me that he was fine, even if he was upset that I was crying. "I said I need some time. It doesn't mean I'm going anywhere. I get it." He put his arm around me. "I don't like it, but I get it. I waited too long. I missed my chance."

"You're making me feel worse," I wailed.

Chris pulled me into a hug. "Don't you dare feel bad for feeling happy, Guinevere Nimue Stevens."

"Using my middle name is a low blow," I said into his chest.

He chuckled and gave me one more squeeze before releasing me. Moments later, Chris stood and pulled his keys from his pocket. "I better get going."

"Can I text you later?" I asked hopefully.

"Give me the rest of the day," he said. My expression must have looked as anxious as I felt, because he added, "We're going to be fine. Trust me." He turned and walked to his car, driving away without looking back.

I let myself into the house. Delilah looked up from where she'd been napping on the chair closest to the fireplace. I walked across the room and scooped her up, holding her velvety fur up to my face. "Is anything ever going to be the same again?" I asked her.

She twisted around and licked my nose, causing me to giggle. She couldn't talk, but somehow, I knew she believed everything was going to work out. "You'll never guess what kind of mess Penny and I got ourselves in this time," I said to her as I headed to the kitchen.

I told her about the shovel as I refilled her water and food bowls and made myself a cup of tea. I hadn't heard from Finn yet about fixing my door. I wandered into the living room. The table where I'd last seen my journal caught my attention. Maybe Penny was right about one thing. If I could find out who'd taken my journal, I might just find the killer. Too bad I had no idea how to do either of those things.

CHAPTER TWENTY-FIVE

The next day, I sat at the front counter of Camelot Flowers, the lack of customers giving me too much time to think. Finn had come over after dinner to fix the door. It had taken him all of thirty minutes, and Penny had managed to tease him about kissing me for all thirty minutes of it. By the time he left, I'd considered sending Penny home and risking a home invasion alone. The only thing that had saved my sleepover with Penny was Finn ensuring me that he didn't mind being teased if it meant he could be with me. He'd followed it up with a kiss that had left me feeling in a forgiving mood.

Penny had slept at my house without incident, although I'd woken up three times during the night to check the doors. I still hadn't heard from Chris. The case was at a dead end. Overall, my mood didn't fit the cheery environment of beautiful flowers and charming gifts lining the shelves around me.

I watched someone walk into Fairy Tale Sweets across the street. What I needed was a chocolate pick-me-up. Before I could decide whether or not to ask my mom, who was in the back, to come watch the front, my dad walked through the front door and dropped a giant box on the counter in front of me.

"The supplies for our booth at the Halloween Festival finally arrived," he said. "April," he called to my mom at the back of the store, "I'm back."

My mom came around the corner, wiping her hands on a tea towel with, you guessed it, roses and lilies all over the fabric.

"It's about time," my mom replied. "I was worried we'd end up with an empty table. Is your costume ready?" she asked me.

"It's hanging in my closet, glowing like the pink monstrosity that it is," I said, teasing her just a little bit.

"It's a lovely color," she said. "Dennis, tell her it's a lovely color."

"That shade of pink didn't exist in the time of King Arthur, so we're not going to win any points on historical accuracy, but it's a good color," he said absently as he opened the box.

Only my dad would be worried about the historical accuracy of my princess costume. The Halloween Festival was not the Renaissance faire. No one would be judging whether or not Queen Guinevere's dress could've been that particular shade of pink. I had a feeling the kids would love it because of the Pepto-Bismol pink color.

My dad unloaded a sealed package of coupons we were going to hand out, followed by ten large bags of candy.

"Do you think that will be enough candy?" I teased.

He looked at the haul with concern. "Do you think I should get more?"

"I was joking," I said, glancing at my mom in case I was way off the mark. The Halloween Festival was a new event this year. Maybe this wasn't enough candy.

"We can always get more if we run low," my mom said with a reassuring pat to my dad's arm.

"I can't believe the festival is tomorrow and we're still no closer to figuring out who killed Trevor," I said. "I thought for sure the case would be wrapped up by now."

"Finn's hit a dead end?" my dad asked.

"I don't think he'd consider it a dead end. He seems to be more patient with the process than I am," I said glumly, still thinking about sneaking across the street for chocolate.

My dad nodded. "Finn knows you can only follow where the evidence leads."

"What if the evidence leads nowhere?" I asked.

Movement outside the windows caught my eye, and I looked over to see Finn walking toward the front door. My mood lifted instantly. My dad and mom both followed my shifted attention in time to see Finn walk through the door.

He paused, his hand on the doorknob. I tried to imagine the scene from his perspective. All three of us were looking at him expectantly. I probably looked a little swoony. The counter was covered in Costco-size bags of candy. It must have been an interesting sight.

"Is this a bad time?" he asked with uncertainty.

My mom rushed forward as if his question had broken some kind of spell. "It's never a bad time to see you, dear," she said, taking his arm and pulling him toward the counter.

"We were just talking about your newest case," my dad said as he starting loading the items back into the box.

Finn ran his hand over his dark beard. "That's actually why I'm here. Do you have a minute to talk?" he asked me.

"Did you find the crime scene? The murder weapon?" I asked excitedly.

"It's nothing like that," Finn said, interrupting my celebratory train of thought. "I was hoping to talk through what I have so far, see if you have any thoughts that could lead the investigation in a new direction."

"You should go for a walk," my mom encouraged. "Winter will be here before we know it, and we'll miss these sunny, warm days."

Finn looked at me expectantly. "Do you have time for a walk?"

I had time for a walk if we walked past Fairy Tale Sweets first. "Let me grab my purse and coat," I said before heading to the back room. It had been so nice out this morning that I'd walked to work, trusting my weather app that the beautiful weather was going to last all day.

I headed back up front, where my mom was talking to Finn about the storefront decoration contest. The winner would be announced at the Halloween Festival tomorrow. The judges had been by earlier this morning before we opened the shop, including Finn.

"Ready to go?" I asked, hoping I'd caught the conversation before my mom could do something foolish like try to bribe Finn to vote for Camelot Flowers.

"One moment," my mom said to me before turning back to Finn. "I think the addition of the lights really ups the excitement factor. I noticed that Burt's weren't on last night. Maybe they burned out. Maybe they'll stay burned out through the festival."

"Mom," I said in shock. "I'm so sorry, Finn. We should go." I took his arm and tugged him toward the door.

"A vote for Camelot Flowers is a vote for Gwen," my mom said slyly.

I shot her a look before successfully dragging Finn out the door. "I'm so sorry for that," I said. "You should vote for whoever you think did the best job."

"Especially because you're my girlfriend," he said with a grin.

I skidded to a stop, which left Finn two steps in front of me before he realized I wasn't next to him anymore. He turned and looked at me questioningly.

"I'm your girlfriend?" I asked.

Finn's expression turned stricken. "Is that not what happened yesterday?" he asked.

I smiled slowly, resisting the urge to jump up and down in excitement. "That's what happened yesterday. I just didn't know if you were thinking the same thing."

Finn stepped toward me. "I'm thinking the same thing."

"This calls for a celebration." I took his hand and tugged him across the street.

Five minutes later, I had a small, brown paper bag containing a peanut butter cup, a mint patty, and two dark-chocolate caramels. I sighed happily as I pulled the mint patty from the bag and popped it into my mouth. "What do you want?" I asked around a mouthful of chocolate.

Finn grinned at me like I was the cutest thing he'd ever seen. I didn't mind it. "I'm fine," he said. "You enjoy your chocolates."

"No, no, no," I said, turning and walking backward so I could look at him. "It's been scientifically proven that chocolate boosts brain power, so if we're going to talk about the case, you should really have a piece."

"Watch it," Finn said, swooping forward and wrapping his arm around my waist, pulling me against him.

I glanced behind me to see a tree that had somehow jumped right into my path.

"Walking backwards probably isn't the safest move," Finn said. His face was just inches from mine. As he held me in a classic romance-hero-pose, I willed him to kiss me. Instead, he released me and said, "I'll have one piece."

I handed him the bag, but my disappointment must have been evident on my face, because he said, "What's wrong?"

This was a critical moment in our new relationship. Was I going to be honest with him? Make him guess? Tell him it was nothing? As much as it felt embarrassing to admit why I was upset, I didn't want to start on a foundation of playing games with one another.

"I thought you were going to kiss me," I said with a shrug. I was going to be honest, but it didn't mean I couldn't also try to be cool about it.

Understanding dawned on Finn's face. "I wanted to," he admitted. "I just wasn't sure how much you were ready for the whole town to know we're dating. I want to be respectful of Chris's feelings. I know we've had our differences, but I can't help thinking about how I would feel in his situation."

"That's why you didn't kiss me? To protect Chris's feelings?" I asked in astonishment.

Finn took my hand as we continued down the road. Public hand holding was fine, but kissing wasn't? "Believe me, Guinevere Stevens. Once we figure all this out, I'm going to kiss you every chance I get."

"I already talked to Chris," I said as we passed Titan Fitness. My hip was feeling much better today, which I was supremely thankful for.

"You did?" Finn asked in surprise.

"He was waiting at my house after I got home from the shooting range," I explained.

"How did he take it?" Finn asked.

"He was surprisingly okay with it," I said. "He wasn't happy, but he said he was happy for me."

"Huh," Finn said cryptically.

"What's that supposed to mean?" I asked.

We turned off Main Street and continued down the tree-lined street.

"It just seems out of character for Chris to go quietly."

"I think he's maturing," I said, feeling strangely defensive of Chris.

"Maybe," Finn said, sounding doubtful.

This conversation wasn't going to end well. I squeezed his hand. "Do you want to talk about the case?"

"Yes," he said on a sigh.

I felt bad for him. I knew these murder cases weighed heavily on him. His desire to find justice for the victim and their loved ones was one of the things I admired about him. Hopefully, my nosiness was one of the things he admired about me. Or at least tolerated.

We turned onto my street. Somehow, we'd unintentionally headed to my house. Half a block away, I could see Rose and Chip working in their yard.

"Do you have any new leads?" I asked.

"We have no real evidence," he said. "We haven't found the crime scene. The area where you found Trevor's body had too much foot traffic to be able to find anything useful. Stan wants me to arrest the friends and see if it shakes them up. I don't think any of them did it, but I can't rule them out with their confessions on the record. If I can get them off the playing field, it frees up time and energy to run down other suspects."

"That sounds like a good idea to me," I said, thinking about Angie, who'd been borderline rude to me.

"It has it's cons," Finn replied. "It'll be news, maybe even farther reaching than local news, and if they are innocent, it won't shine a favorable light on the precinct."

The infernal witch cackled as we walked by my neighbor's house, and I jumped, grabbing Finn's arm.

Finn eyed the witch and said, "You okay?"

I tried to laugh it off. It was embarrassing to be so jumpy around a Halloween decoration. "I'm fine. I might murder that witch, but other than that, everything's good."

"Then I'd have another murder to solve," Finn teased.

"It wouldn't be hard. I'd gladly confess. And I believe it would only be destruction of property or something like that. I doubt that even comes with jailtime," I argued.

"Just what every detective wants to hear, his girlfriend plotting what crimes she can get away with." Finn tugged me to his side and put his arm around my shoulders.

I was never going to get tired of hearing him call me his girlfriend.

We reached my house. Rose and Chip had looked up when the witch signaled our arrival. Chip gave us a wave, leaned his rake against the white picket fence, and said something to

Rose. She took off her gardening gloves, and they headed in our direction.

I couldn't remember if Finn had ever met them so I whispered, "Chip and Rose."

He shot me a grateful smile.

Chip reached us first and held out his hand to Finn. "Detective Butler, nice to see you. I'm not sure if we've officially met. I'm Chip Mullins, and this is my wife, Rose."

Rose also shook Finn's hand.

"It's nice to meet you both," Finn said as he settled his arm around my shoulders again. "And please, call me Finn."

"Any update on the investigation into Trevor's murder?" Chip asked as he jerked his head in the direction of Trevor and Sandra's house. "Rose can't sleep at night thinking a murder happened right next door to us."

"This is such a safe neighborhood," Rose chimed in. "Isn't it, Gwen? We usually don't even have to worry about locking our doors, and now this?" Rose shivered, despite the unseasonably warm temperature.

Good thing she didn't know about the break-in at my house. I had a feeling it would push her right over the edge.

"We're following several leads," Finn said vaguely. "I want you to rest assured that it seems Trevor's murder was personal. There's no reason to feel unsafe in your own home."

"Personal?" Chip asked.

"He means it wasn't a random killing," Rose said, looking at Finn for confirmation that she was right.

Finn nodded.

Chip rubbed his chin. "If there's anything we can do to help, just let us know. We knew Trevor and Sandra as much as anyone knows their neighbors. There was always a lot of fighting coming from that house."

"What Chip means is that Trevor was always fighting with Sandra. We never heard her say anything back," Rose said, shaking her head as if the very thought made her feel sad.

"Do you think Sandra could have had something to do with his death?" I asked.

Finn stiffened next to me. I knew Sandra was low on his suspect list, but low on a suspect list didn't mean off the list completely.

Chip and Rose looked at each other. "That's what I've been wondering," Rose finally said.

"As I'm sure you've heard, Trevor was found in the fall display in front of city hall," Finn said. "I'm taking a team of officers back tomorrow morning to look at the area again before the Halloween Festival in case we missed anything. It would be nearly impossible for someone to move and pose a body like that without leaving behind some trace evidence. While we did a thorough search the day Trevor's body was discovered, it doesn't hurt to take a second look."

I suspected Finn wouldn't be going back to the scene of the crime, so to speak, if he didn't feel like he was at a dead end with the evidence and suspects he already had.

"I would imagine a lot of people walked through that display before and after Trevor's body was found," Chip said.

I thought about my own interaction with finding Trevor. I had no doubt I'd left behind evidence of my presence there.

"That's true," Finn said, "but we'll be able to rule out anyone who doesn't have a motive for the murder."

"Why not do it now?" I asked. "Why wait until tomorrow morning?"

"There are a number of factors that I'm not at liberty to discuss," Finn said.

It was quite the non-answer to my question.

"Well," Chip said. "Hopefully Rose can sleep easy tonight, knowing there's not a serial killer loose in Star Junction."

Rose put her hand over her chest. "Don't even say those words."

Finn's phone buzzed, and he pulled it from his pocket. His expression tightened. "I've got to run," he said to the group before turning to me and adding, "I'll call you later. Sorry to have to leave like this."

"Is everything okay?" I asked, worried.

"I'll fill you in when I can," he said. He looked around, and I got a sense he was regretting not having his car.

"Do you want to take my car?" I asked. "I wasn't planning on going anywhere."

"Are you sure?" he asked, sounding relieved.

"Absolutely," I said. Finn was lucky that I'd walked to work that morning.

"We'll see you later, Gwen," Rose said, and they headed back across the street.

I found my keys in my purse and removed the car key from the keyring. "What's going on?" I asked now that it was just the two of us.

"I'm not sure. Stan texted that he needs me at the station. He usually adds ASAP. This time it said *Now*."

Finn pressed a brief but scorching kiss to my lips. "I'll fill you in when I bring the car back," he said.

"Be safe," I replied, feeling suddenly aware that Finn's job could be incredibly dangerous.

"I always am," he said with a wink before running to my car and driving away.

I stood on the front stoop with my arms hugged across my chest as I watched him drive down the street and make the right-hand turn that would take him to the police station.

"Delilah," I called out as I went into the house. I needed some kitty cuddles. She didn't come running, so I went to look for her in her usual spots, which were basically any places she could be cozy and warm.

I found her on my bed, curled up on my pillow. Picking her up, I held her to my chest. She gave my chin a little lick before settling back to sleep.

Finn's idea to check the Halloween display again was a good one, but I worried that days of weather and people would've diluted any evidence left behind. What was he looking for? Blood they'd missed? Hair? Fibers from the killer's clothes? Fingerprints seemed impossible to find with all that hay, but maybe the killer had touched the other scarecrow when they were posing Trevor. And what was happening at the precinct?

"So many questions," I murmured to Delilah. "And not very many answers."

CHAPTER TWENTY-SIX

Two in the morning, and I was wide awake for no good reason. I'd tried everything, but after a mug of Sleepy Time tea, lying in bed for over an hour staring at the ceiling, and reading a chapter of a book that I wasn't even interested in, I'd given up. Delilah was currently curled up next to me on the couch because she never had any trouble sleeping.

I was wide awake, but at least I was alone. I hadn't heard from Finn. Tommy, one of the police officers and a former high school classmate of mine, had dropped my car off around seven with the message that Finn would call me when he could. I'd been worried, but Tommy had assured me that Finn wasn't doing anything dangerous. I was dying to know what was going on.

I also hadn't heard from Chris. So much for these men insisting that they weren't leaving me alone until they knew who'd broken into my house. Finn was distracted with work, and Chris was likely nursing whatever feelings he was having about my decision.

I'd switched to a book I enjoyed reading. If I was going to be awake, I might as well be having more fun. Actually, with a fire flickering in my gas fireplace, a cozy blanket on my lap, and a good book, it was an overall nice experience. Just not one I wanted to have in the middle of the night.

I'd taken a chance that the neighbor's witch wouldn't be activated by anything this late at night and opened the window across from me. Yes, it was counterproductive to have the window open and the fireplace on at the same time, but the combination was creating the perfect temperature for being cozy.

The sound of a car starting caused me to look up from my book. I stuck a receipt I was using as a bookmark into the book and got up to look out the window on the off chance that someone was stealing my car. Car theft was rare in Star Junction, but so were home invasions, and I'd just had one of those.

No one was near my car, but a car was pulling out of the driveway of Rose and Chip's house without its headlights on. Alarm bells went off in my gut. I shoved my feet into my shoes, grabbed my purse, and eased out the front door, leaving the porch light off. The car headed down the street. I raced to my car to follow.

I couldn't think of any reason Chip or Rose would be driving away in the middle of the night without their headlights on. Actually, I could think of a reason, and it wasn't an innocent one. Something told me whoever was driving that car was up to no good.

I also kept my headlights off, which felt very wrong, but it was the middle of the night and no other cars were on the roads. I stayed a block behind, and although the car's headlights stayed off, the brake lights flared to life every time the driver slowed to take a corner. It made following them easy.

I told my phone to call Finn. This might be nothing, but I'd learned from past experience to listen to my gut, and my gut told me something fishy was going on.

The call connected with a groggy-sounding Finn saying, "Hello?"

He'd obviously picked up without even looking at his caller ID.

"Don't worry," I started. "I'm totally safe."

"Is someone in your house again?" Finn shouted, sounding suddenly alert.

I felt bad. I hadn't really thought about how my words would sound to him. "No, no," I said quickly. "It's nothing like that."

Finn blew out a breath. "What's going on? I just got home an hour ago."

I wanted to ask why, including why he'd had to leave my house in such a hurry and couldn't bring my car back himself, but I needed to stay focused. Whoever was driving the car had just turned onto Moore Street and was approaching city hall.

"It might be nothing, but I couldn't sleep, and then I heard a car starting, and then I saw it was my neighbor, either Chip or Rose—I couldn't see because it was too dark—driving out of their driveway with their headlights off, which was super suspicious, so I followed them, and now we're getting really close to city hall, and I think maybe one of them killed Trevor," I said in a rush.

The driver had just pulled over and parked on the side of the road, close to the fall display where I'd found Trevor's body. I pumped my arm in the air. I knew it. No innocent person had a reason to go to that display in the middle of the night.

I pulled over, keeping my distance, and peered forward, trying to see who was getting out of the car.

"Gwen, stop following whoever it is. I'm going to call it in. I'll be there in ten minutes," Finn said firmly. "Do you understand?"

It was Chip. He looked both ways, and I slumped down in my seat, although it was so dark, I doubted he could see there was anyone in the car. Chip headed toward the fall display.

"It's Chip," I said excitedly. "He's heading right for where I found Trevor. He must have gotten spooked when you said you were going back in the morning to look for evidence. I can't believe he killed Trevor over a stupid property line and a fence. I'm going to try to get closer."

"Gwen, no," Finn said before I heard a loud crash. "Darn it," I heard him yell, but it sounded far away like he'd dropped the phone.

If there was a chance Chip was going to destroy evidence, I needed to be there to witness it so I could testify at his trial.

"Gwen," Finn said right into the phone. "Do not move."

"I'm going to stay far away," I said. "I'll stay on the line. Don't worry. I'll be perfectly safe."

Stepping out of the car, I eased the door shut, not even clicking it closed all the way. It was one of those cool nights when it felt like every sound carried. I didn't want to give away my presence by shutting the car door too hard.

"Get back in your car," Finn said. I heard a lot of rustling in the background, like he was trying to stay on the phone with me and get dressed at the same time.

"Stop talking," I whispered. "You'll give away my location. Oh, you should record this in case Chip says something incriminating."

"Why would he say something incriminating if he's alone?" Finn asked. "Don't try to talk to him," he added, as if he'd just realized that was an option.

"I'm not going to," I whispered back. "If you keep talking, I'm hanging up."

I stuck to the shadows, which wasn't hard to do. The few lights in the area were spaced far apart. Chip was looking around with his cell phone flashlight. The light of the flashlight disappeared, and I realized he was making a call.

True to my word, I'd stayed far away, which meant I couldn't tell what he was saying. I swallowed a groan of frustration and inched closer.

"I'll let you know," Chip said as I got close enough to hear. He ended the call and swung in my direction.

I ducked behind the haybales that made up the wall of the hay maze as the light from Chip's phone swung in my direction. Who had he been talking to? Was he in on this murder with someone else? Had he heard me? I held my breath, willing him to continue whatever he was doing without noticing me.

Chip stalked off toward the entrance of the hay maze and disappeared. He must have been worried there was some kind of evidence he'd left behind in the maze. Why would there be evidence in the maze? Was that where he'd killed Trevor?

I took off after him into the maze. Taking the first left, I clamped my hand over my mouth to muffle the scream that threatened to give away my location. I'd forgotten this was a haunted maze. Kid friendly for sure, but in the dark, even a kid friendly mummy would scare the pants off of an adult.

"Gwen, what's wrong? Did something happen?" Finn asked.

I definitely couldn't talk to him now. I was too close to Chip. I sent a quick text. *In the hay maze. I'm fine. Just forgot it was haunted.* Pressing my hand over my pounding heart, I continued, keeping an eye out for anything else that might scare me in the dark.

"I don't see anything," Chip said from somewhere in front of me.

I followed the sound of his voice, turning left past a white sheet ghost hanging from some kind of wire.

"I don't even know what I'm looking for," he continued.

I poked my head around the corner to see Chip's back to me. He was scuffing his feet in the straw that littered the grass right next to a life-sized witch. Ugh. Witches. Why did it always have to be witches?

Whoever was on the other end must have said something that angered him, because he snapped, "I'm aware. Look, this was a waste of time. I'm getting out of here."

While I couldn't make out any of the words, the person on the phone yelled back loudly enough for me to hear the sound of a voice. Chip pulled the phone away from his ear like it had hurt him. "Then you should have dealt with it," he shouted. He stiffened, like he'd just remembered he was in a public place in the middle of the night and he needed to keep quiet.

Chip hung up the phone. What would it mean for the case if Chip left? He hadn't said or done anything incriminating that would hold up in a court of law. It was weird to go to the hay maze in the middle of the night, but not illegal. I was now certain Chip had murdered Trevor, but a good attorney could argue that Chip had lost something in the maze and came back to look for it.

For once, I had a chance to be the one with the upper hand. I spotted a rake leaning against the haybales a few feet away from me but far enough around the corner that it would bring me into Chip's eyeline.

I peeked around the corner again. Chip was muttering to himself angrily as he continued to study the ground. The witch had a belt made of rope around its waist.

Setting my phone down with Finn still on the line, I flexed my hands and bounced on the balls of my feet. It was now or never. Let a murderer get away because I was a coward or be a hero. Besides, Finn would hear the whole thing. If anything went wrong, he could be here in minutes. He was probably already on his way.

Before I could change my mind, I lunged forward, grabbed the rake, and swung it at Chip's back. I didn't want to hurt him badly, although he'd done much worse to poor Trevor, but I needed him stunned.

The rake connected with a thud. Chip grunted and fell forward, hitting his head on a stack of haybales on the way down. Oops. He wasn't unconscious, but he seemed dazed. I leapt forward and ripped the rope from the witch. Seconds later, I had Chip's hands tied behind his back.

Racing back to my phone, I did a little dance of celebration and said, "I did it. I caught a murderer."

I raced back to Chip's side, but he wasn't trying to flee. He was kind of groaning, and I worried that the blow to his head on the way down had been worse than I'd thought. How hard was hay? I punched the bale next to me and winced. Pretty hard.

"That was incredibly, unnecessarily reckless," Finn said sharply. "Following him was a risk, but confronting someone who may have killed a man?"

He was upset. It was understandable, but I was riding high on adrenaline and couldn't feel anything but the rush of not only solving the case, but of taking down the bad guy.

The rush of victory popped like an overfilled balloon at the site of Rose coming around the corner with a gun in her hand. Finn continued to lecture me, but his words faded to meaningless noise.

"Hang up the phone," she said, waving the gun at me.

"You too?" I asked, my voice cracking with fear.

"Is someone else there?" Finn asked. "I'm on my way. Officers are on their way."

"I better get going, Mom," I said to Finn in an overly cheery voice. The last thing I wanted was for Rose to know I was talking to Finn. "Don't forget to set out those *roses* that need to be delivered tomorrow."

Rose jabbed the gun toward me.

"Okay, bye," I said in a rush. I hung up the phone before Rose could get trigger happy.

Hopefully Finn picked up on my clumsy clue that Rose was the one pointing a gun at me.

"Toss the phone to me," she said.

I thought about throwing it at her face and running, but with her being only a few feet away, I worried she'd get a shot off. It would be next to impossible to miss at this range. I tossed the phone at her feet.

"Untie him," Rose said, gesturing at Chip with the gun.

I inched toward Chip so it would look like I was complying with her request but tried to stall long enough for someone to get here to help me. "I think there's been a misunderstanding," I said. "I was checking over the display to make sure it was ready for tomorrow. That's why I was on the

Sunflowers, Scarecrows, and Scandal | 217

phone with my mom. We have a booth at the festival, and we donated..."

I looked around for something believable. "This witch here." I patted the witch on the arm like we were long lost friends. "I wanted to spring for the motion sensor version so it would cackle and move when the kids walked past like Kevin's, but my parents thought it was a waste of money. I found Chip like this."

"Shut up!" Rose shouted. The more upset she got, the more she was waving that gun around.

I shut up.

"I'm not an idiot," Rose sneered. "I know you didn't find Chip like this. Now untie him."

I grimaced. "I'll untie him, but I have one question first."

"What?" Rose snapped.

"Did you and Chip, like, kill Trevor together, or..." I trailed off, hoping she'd just fill in the blanks.

Rose's death stare was almost as scary as the gun she was holding. Chip and Rose had been the best neighbors. Always friendly. Always willing to give me an egg when I was in the middle of making emergency chocolate chip cookies. How had we ended up here?

"I know Trevor and Chip were fighting about the yard and the property line all the time," I continued when she said nothing. I gasped. "Oh my word, did Chip kill Trevor and you had to help him cover it up out of loyalty to him?" I leaned forward and stage whispered, "You don't have to go down for this. Testify against him. Save yourself."

I glanced at Chip, who had managed to flip himself into a sitting position. I could tell from the way he was moving around that he was trying to get free of the ropes. I'd spent a summer working at the boat dock at Star Lake. I knew how to tie a knot. He wasn't going to get out without help.

Rose barked out a very unfriendly sounding laugh. "The property line had nothing to do with Trevor's death. He stole from us, and he had to pay." She leaned forward with an evil grin. "And I made sure he did."

"You?" I squeaked out. I shouldn't have been surprised. She was holding me at gunpoint, after all, but I'd never considered that Rose had anything to do with Trevor's death.

"Yes, me," she shot back. "Trevor convinced us to invest our life savings with him. He promised us a huge return on investment. Big enough that we'd be able to retire early. Months after we invested everything we had, he told us there had been a blip in the market and all the money was gone. All of it!" She emphasized those last words by jabbing the gun at me.

I backed up but bumped against the wall of the hay maze. I needed her to calm down. "That's horrible," I said sympathetically as I said a desperate prayer that Finn would arrive before Rose could add another murder to her crimes.

"There was no blip in the market," she said with scorn. "I scoured reports about the market. I talked to Trevor's business partner. Trevor stole that money from us. I confronted him about it the night he died. I found him drunk and nearly passed out on our patio furniture in the backyard."

Rose scoffed. "He couldn't even find his own house. I told him to go home and find my money. He had the audacity to laugh in my face. He said the money was gone." Rose's other hand tightened into a fist. "I couldn't take it anymore. Trevor was a horrible human being who didn't deserve to keep on living. He didn't deserve to spend *our* hard-earned money."

"So, you grabbed a shovel and hit him," I said quietly as the pieces were falling into place.

Rose narrowed her eyes at me. "You know an awful lot about this case. I knew taking your notebook would pay off." She looked at me thoughtfully. "Although, we weren't serious suspects on your little chart. We should have gotten away with this."

"You broke into my house?" I said in shock. Once again, I didn't know why I was so surprised by these relatively minor things when she'd just confessed to murder, but I couldn't help myself.

Rose looked at Chip. "What's taking so long?" she snapped.

"I can't get the first knot undone," he said. He glared at me like all of this was somehow my fault.

"Why do I have to do everything myself?" Rose said with a frustrated sigh. She kept the gun trained on me as she knelt next to Chip and worked on the knot with one hand.

I risked inching backward. If I could get closer to the corner I'd come around when I hit Chip, I might be able to make a run for it.

"Don't move," Rose said. She abandoned Chip and stood, pointing the gun at my heart.

I put my hands up in surrender. "Please don't do this."

"It's too late. You know too much." Rose took a step toward me. "It's now or never," she said as if psyching herself up.

"I choose never," I said right before I put everything on the line and made a run for it.

A bullet slammed into the hay where I'd been standing, but I was already around the corner, running as fast as I could.

"Rose, get her," Chip yelled.

My heart slammed against my ribs as I raced toward the entrance of the maze. What if I took a wrong turn? What if I ran down a dead end and Rose trapped me? Thinking too much was going to get me killed. I tried to shut off my anxious brain and run on instinct, turning right then left. Rose screamed my name as she chased me.

I made another right. The entrance was just ahead. I put on a burst of speed.

"Oh no, you don't," Rose shouted.

I kept running, hunching my shoulders, waiting for the next bullet to hit me in the back. As I burst from the maze, hands grabbed me and yanked me to the side. I screamed, but Finn's arms wrapped around me as he said, "Shh. Shh. You're safe now."

Tommy and another officer filled the entrance to the maze with their guns drawn. "Don't move," Tommy said. "Drop the gun. Put your hands on your head."

I buried my face in Finn's chest, shaking at how close I'd come to being another causality tonight. While I probably deserved a million lectures for my reckless behavior, Finn simply rubbed his hands up and down my back and reminded me that I was safe until I stopped shaking.

There was a lot of commotion happening in the maze. Rose was screaming about how the officers didn't understand. Another voice called out that they'd found Chip. I didn't register any of it. All I saw was Finn's whiskey-brown eyes. All I felt were his strong arms around me.

"Thanks for saving me," I said. "Again."

"Thanks for solving my case," he said with a grin. "Again." He brushed a strand of hair off my face. "Are you sure you're okay? Did they hurt you?"

"I'm okay," I said. "No one hurt me, but I might have hurt Chip. Although he seemed fine when he told Rose to take me out." I grimaced. "Can we go home?"

Finn's smile was sad. "While I love the idea of going home with you, you know I have to stay here."

"And I probably have to give my statement," I said reluctantly.

"That too," he said.

"But after that?" I asked hopefully.

"After that," Finn said. "We can go home."

CHAPTER TWENTY-SEVEN

"Are you a princess too?" I asked the little girl wearing a Cinderella costume. She was only the second Cinderella I'd seen at the Halloween Festival, but the day was young, and I'd already seen a dozen other Disney princesses.

The girl did a spin and showed me a gap-toothed grin as she said, "I love princesses."

I leaned in and gave her a conspiratorial wink. "Me too."

"I'm Taylor Swift," the little girl next to her said enthusiastically. She was dressed in a pink sparkly dress and had a glittery pink heart painted around one eye, clearly from the *Lover* era.

"I love Taylor Swift," I said. "She's my favorite. I even convinced my best friend to listen to her, and he's a boy." I gave her a meaningful look as she giggled. "Let's get you both some candy."

I dropped a handful of candy into each of their bags before turning to their parents, who had been standing behind the girls. "And we can't forget your parents," I said. I handed each set of parents a coupon for twenty percent off one bouquet at Camelot Flowers.

"This is fun," one of the women said. She looked at her husband meaningfully. "I believe this is for you."

The man chuckled and gave her a kiss on the cheek.

I beamed at the happy scene. The sun was shining. The grounds of city hall were full of people enjoying the unseasonably warm weather. I didn't even mind the color of my dress today.

The families set off, and I straightened the coupons on the table. I'd successfully avoided looking at the maze in the hour I'd been here. If I pretended it didn't exist, I could pretend that the night before hadn't happened. At least that's what I told myself.

I heard a clinking sound coming from behind me and turned to see Finn approaching in what looked like a very authentic suit of armor. When he reached me, he gave me a bow and said, "Milady, I swear my fealty to protecting you. All I ask is one Reese's Peanut Butter Cup."

I giggled, but Finn didn't rise from his bow. He looked up at me expectantly.

"Oh," I said, realizing he was waiting for me to say my part of this little script that no one had warned me about. I gave him a curtsy. "My Lord." Finn gave me a sexy grin as he rose to his full height, and I fanned my face with my hand comically. "That's quite the outfit you've got there. Very nice."

"Your dad helped me put it together," he said. He held his arms out. "He said it was as authentic as I was going to get to the time period without having a blacksmith make me custom armor. I wasn't sure I was ready to take that step."

I snorted out a laugh. "Just you wait. You've set a dangerous precedent with my dad. He'll be dragging you to Renaissance faires before you know it. How do you think I got this dress?" I did a little spin like the girl dressed as Cinderella had done for me.

"Would you happen to be at these Renaissance faires?" he asked.

"Often enough," I said. "I am usually the one staying behind to watch Camelot Flowers, but if it's a big fair, my parents will close for the weekend. How did things go last night? Were you here all night?"

Despite Finn's promise, he wasn't able to go home with me. He'd dropped me at home making me say out loud that I would lock my doors, although I'd tried to tell him the danger was currently in handcuffs at the hay maze. I'd agreed just so he'd could go back to work without worrying about me. I would've locked the doors anyway, but I couldn't help giving him a little bit of a hard time.

"I got home around six this morning," he said.

"You poor thing," I said. "You should go home and rest."

"No," he said sincerely. "I want to work the booth with you. Besides, it's good for me to be at city events. People feel more comfortable dealing with a detective they feel like they know."

"And you have to announce the winner of the storefront decorating contest in a little bit," I said, wiggling my eyebrows. "Care to give me a hint on who won?"

"Actually, it looks like the mayor is getting ready to announce the winner," Finn said, dodging my question. "Let's get over there."

"Wait for us," Penny called out as she and Jack approached. She was dressed like an oven, with her belly, currently sporting a black T-shirt with a decal of a bun on it, sticking out of the oven door. Jack was dressed as a chef.

"Cute," I said as we reached the back of the crowd. "Bun in the oven."

"I've got to get over to the stage," Finn said. He kissed me on the cheek and headed toward the stage.

"Looks like your dad got ahold of him," Penny said with a laugh.

"That's exactly what happened," I confirmed.

Penny's smile dimmed. "I heard you had an exciting night." She pulled me into a hug. "I'm so glad you're okay, and I'm so sorry I wasn't there to protect you."

"I'm not," Jack muttered. "But I am glad you're okay," he added quickly.

"How did you hear about that already?" I asked. I'd purposefully not called anyone, wanting a morning of peace and quiet before coming to the festival.

"I saw Margie in the parking lot. She said you'd have to tell me the whole story but that your neighbors were the ones who killed Trevor and something about a ghost in the hay maze?" Penny said, sounding confused at Margie's description.

"Ugh," I said. "I'll tell you all about it, but not today. I need a break from murder."

The sound system from the stage crackled as the mayor said, "Good afternoon."

Penny grabbed my hand and pulled me forward.

"What's the rush?" I asked as we made our way through the crowd with Jack following. Penny's boxy costume kept bumping into people, but she didn't seem to care.

"I saw your parents at the front of the crowd," Penny explained.

My stomach fluttered with nerves. "My mom has her heart set on winning."

"That's why we need to be next to them, so we can celebrate with her when she wins," Penny said.

We moved through the last few rows of people with murmured apologies and stood next to my parents. My mom looked nervous as she gave me a quick hug.

A loud tapping sound filled the air, and everyone turned to face the stage that had been set up over the space where I'd found Trevor's body. Taking down that display had been the right thing to do.

The mayor tapped on the microphone again. Somewhere in his late sixties, he was tall and wiry with a fringe of gray hair around his head. "I want to thank everyone for coming to our first ever Star Junction Halloween Festival." He paused as the crowd applauded. "We'd like to thank our local businesses for hosting the booths today so everyone can have a grand time."

More applause.

"Now, the moment everyone's been waiting for. I'm going to announce the winner of the storefront decorating contest," the mayor said. "First, I'd like to introduce our other two judges."

My mom let out a groan of frustration. "Get to it already," she muttered.

Finn walked onto the stage with the principal of the high school, who was dressed like Doc from the *Back to the Future* movies. The mayor introduced them and then pulled an envelope from somewhere in his costume. "The winner will receive this beautiful trophy donated by Star Junction Print Supply and a fifty-dollar gift card to Bucky's."

My mom clapped wildly.

The mayor made a big show of opening the envelope. He leaned toward the microphone. "The winner is...Cozy Cut Pet Groomers with their pet cemetery."

Finn caught my eye and mouthed, *I'm sorry*. He looked truly worried that I'd be upset with him.

I gave him a reassuring smile, although I couldn't help wondering if his feelings for me had actually hurt our chances. Finn was ethical to a fault. He would've been very careful to be fair. Maybe too careful.

"I'm sorry, Mom," I said as Burt from the pet groomers walked onstage to receive his award. The mayor handed him an envelope that likely contained the gift card, as well as a golden trophy that his assistant had brought onto the stage.

"I can't believe there's a trophy, too," my mom said, sounding even more disappointed. Then she straightened up, sniffed, and pushed forward a smile. "I'll just need to make a better display next year."

"That's the spirit," my dad said heartily.

"I'm going to find Finn," I said. "I want to make sure he knows we're not upset."

My mom looked like she was about to argue with me.

"Because we're not upset with *him*," I said like a parent lecturing a child.

She blew out a breath. "No, of course we're not upset with him."

I left before she could change her mind.

I found Finn standing at the bottom of the steps to the stage. It was clear he'd been watching us.

"Am I public enemy number one?" he asked.

"Eh," I hedged. "My mom does have that ongoing feud with the owner of the garden center in Rose Lake, so maybe public enemy number two?"

"Is she really upset?" He looked truly worried.

"She'll be fine," I said. "Seriously. No one is upset with you."

"Because I really want your parents to like me," he said.

"Not voting for her display probably wasn't a good place to start," I said, enjoying teasing him about this entirely too much.

He looked stricken.

"I'm kidding," I reassured him. "Let's go back to the Camelot Flowers booth and hand out more candy. The kids are going to love your knight costume."

Finn agreed, and we worked our way through the crowd toward the booth.

"I can't believe I forgot to ask earlier," I said as we sidestepped a Chewbacca. "What was going on yesterday that had you rushing off so suddenly?"

"You're never going to believe it," Finn said. He leaned toward me as if he didn't want people to overhear. "I'm sure this will be in the paper soon enough, but someone broke into the canoe shed at Star Lake and managed to push all twenty-seven canoes out onto the lake."

"You're kidding," I said, trying to picture that many canoes just floating around.

"I'm not even done," he said. "Then they took the canoe paddles and arranged them to spell *Boogers* on the shore."

I snorted out a laugh. "I'm guessing your suspect pool is on the younger end of Star Junction's population."

"I was up late creating a suspect list with Tommy," Finn said.

"Was it basically the entire middle school?" I teased.

"Almost," Finn said.

Penny and my parents were already at the booth. My mom reassured Finn that she wasn't upset with him as Chris approached wearing a Hawaiian shirt over a pink T-shirt, and bright-blue swim trunks. He was holding a boogie board. "I just saw Margie in the parking lot," he said with concern.

I groaned. "Does she have a gossip stand set up out there or something?"

Thankfully my parents were distracted, talking with three families who had all descended on our booth at the same time.

"Are you okay?" Chris asked. He shot Finn a disapproving look, like he would have done a better job making sure I'd stayed out of danger.

Feeling defensive of Finn, who'd done everything in his power to convince me to leave Chip alone, I took Finn's hand and said, "I'm totally fine. Not a single scratch."

"So, everything's all wrapped up?" Jack asked Finn.

"Chip and Rose were remanded to county jail. The DA is filing charges on Monday. I don't see them being released before the trial," Finn replied.

"That's a relief," Penny said.

"Does Sandra know?" I asked.

"I stopped by to talk to her earlier this morning," Finn said. "She's glad to know her friends are off the hook. It wasn't her idea to have them confess."

"What's going to happen with the friends?" Jack asked. "Isn't it illegal to make a false confession?"

"I'll be having a talk with them sometime this week. Their confessions wasted a lot of time. I understand they were trying to protect their friends, and it seemed that each of them thought another one of the friends had done it, but it doesn't excuse what they did," Finn said.

"I know everyone probably has a million questions for Finn, but I have one for Chris," I said, trying to steer the conversation away from murder.

Chris looked at me expectantly.

"Who are you supposed to be?" I asked with a grin.

Chris glanced down at this costume and then gave me that charming, thousand-watt smile that used to have me melting into a puddle of goo right on the spot. Now it just gave me a warm feeling inside that felt a lot like the kind of platonic love I think we'd always been destined to have.

"You can't tell?" he asked, his blue eyes sparking mischievously.

"An out-of-work actor enjoying a day of boogie boarding?" Penny suggested.

"Nope," Chris said.

"A surfer guy," Jack tried.

"Too vague," Chris said.

"Just tell us," I said, laughing.

Chris held his boogie board in front of him. "I'm surfer-Ken. You know, like Ken and Barbie?"

We all laughed. It was the perfect costume for him. He did look a little like Ken, with his perpetually tanned skin and blond hair.

"Do you guys mind helping my parents with the booth for a second?" I asked the group. "I want to talk to Chris about something."

Finn looked at me questioningly. I gave his hand a reassuring squeeze.

"We don't mind," Penny said, looking at Jack for confirmation, who nodded his agreement.

"I'll be right back," I said to Finn.

"Take as long as you need," he said.

I gave him a grateful smile and turned to Chris. "Can we walk?"

Chris looked at me with uncertainty but said, "Lead the way."

I headed away from the crowds to a bench under a tree that still had some of its leaves. Sitting on the bench, I indicated

Chris should sit next to me. He leaned his boogie board against the tree and sat.

"What's up?" he asked, looking and sounding guarded.

I hated that he felt that way, but I had to trust that time would heal the hurt and disappointment he was feeling. "I wanted to see how you're doing," I said.

"I'm fine," he said, but his smile was a little too tight.

I laid my hand on his. "No, how you're really doing," I pressed.

Chris looked at my hand covering his before raising his gaze to mine. "Gwen, I'm going to be fine. I guess I'm getting a little taste of how you felt all those years, although in my defense I'd had no idea you wanted us to be more than friends."

"You were the only one," I said wryly.

"I know. I was too clueless for too long. I've got to work through this, but I'll be fine. Don't worry about me," he said, and he even sounded like he meant it.

"I think you should start dating again," I blurted out. It's what I'd really wanted to tell him, but I didn't know how to segue into the topic.

"I don't know," Chris hedged.

"Surfer-Ken needs to find his Barbie. Just think about it," I said. "It could be fun." We sat quietly for a moment, both of us watching the festivities happening across the lawn. "I don't want to lose you," I finally said quietly.

Chris put his arm around me and hugged me to his side. He pressed a kiss to my temple. "You won't lose me. Ever. It's me and you. That's my whole world."

I cocked my head to the side. "Did you just quote a Taylor Swift song to me?"

Chris's grin grew mischievous. "You caught that, huh?"

"Excuse me. You're only a Taylor Swift fan because I introduced you to her music," I said with faux indignation.

"No, I told you about the *Reputation* album, and that's why *you* like her," he countered. It was clear he was enjoying our spat a little too much.

"I started listening to her in middle school," I protested.

"Barely," he said with a scoff.

I stood, flouncing my skirt. "Penny will know I'm right," I said.

"Will she?" he countered as he gathered his boogie board.

I burst out laughing as I thought about how we must look standing next to one another in our costumes that were so different. "We're a ridiculous pair."

"We could both be in a Barbie movie. Just not the same one," Chris said.

He wasn't wrong.

Chris put his arm around my shoulders as we headed back to the table, still arguing about who was the bigger Taylor Swift fan. My heart swelled with happiness. My knight in shining armor was waiting for me across the lawn, and my surfer-Ken was cracking jokes like he'd done for all the years I'd known him. There might be a few bumps ahead, but in that moment, I knew we were going to be just fine.

ABOUT THE AUTHOR

Erica Wynters may have lived most of her life in the frigid Midwest, but now she spends her time in the warmth and sunshine of Arizona. She loves hiking, hunting down waterfalls in the desert, reading (of course), and napping. Can napping be considered a hobby? When not weaving tales of mystery with plenty of quirky characters, laughs, and a dash of romance, Erica works as a Marriage and Family Therapist helping others find their Happily Ever Afters.

To learn more about Erica, visit her online at:
www.ericawynters.com

Made in United States
Troutdale, OR
10/01/2024